CHEATIEBO, THE FOLKLORIST SERIES
2

EBONY, BEAUTY IN MOTION

GLENDA SIMPSON

innovo PUBLISHING

Published by Innovo Publishing, LLC
www.innovopublishing.com
1-888-546-2111

Providing Full-Service Publishing Services for Christian Authors, Artists &
Ministries: Books, eBooks, Audiobooks, Music, Screenplays, Film & Curricula

CHEATIEBO
THE FOLKLORIST SERIES

VOL 2

Ebony, Beauty in Motion

Unless otherwise noted, all scripture was taken from the American Standard
Version of the Bible. Public domain.

ISBN: 978-1-61314-804-4

Cover Design & Interior Layout: Innovo Publishing, LLC

Printed in the United States of America
U.S. Printing History
First Edition: 2022

Has God called you to create a Christian book, eBook, audiobook, music album,
screenplay, film, or curricula? If so, visit the ChristianPublishingPortal.com to
learn how to accomplish your calling with excellence. Learn to do everything
yourself, or hire trusted Christian Experts from our Marketplace to help.

Chapter 1

RETURN TO THE LION'S CAVE

Something awakened Puma. The light radiating from a mostly spent candle gave just enough illumination to see movement at the cave's entrance. The cooking fire had dwindled to a few pulsing coals. Instant fear shattered Puma's fog of sleep as her hand darted to the knife habitually prepositioned at her side. The klandagie's menacing posture signaled that the lioness was stalking prey, and there was no doubt that she herself was the prey. The cat's eyes were narrowed slits, and her ears laid close to her head. Her quivering, spring loaded muscles were ready to launch an attack. Puma knew that the lion had come to reclaim her lair.

Puma leapt from her resting place just as the lion launched its body the entire width of the cave. The impact slammed Puma back onto the mattress. The cat's momentum caused the hammock to swing backward and tilt vertically, spilling them onto the cave's floor. The jarring ferocity of the attack brought Puma to full alertness. The stuffed mattress followed the two of them to the floor. The superior strength of the feline overwhelmed the woman and, but for a fluke, would have been the end of Puma Woman. The swiping claws ruptured the mattress, releasing great puffs of cattail fuzz into the air. The near weightless floating particles disoriented the lion.

Puma was thinking, *kill or be killed with the outcome to be decided by the greater of brain or brawn.* According to the Cherokee People, pound for pound, the mountain lion is known as one of nature's most ferocious killers. The tawny attacker's slashing claws tore more openings into the mattress, further decreasing visibility. With each breath the combatants drew the floating fuzz into their mouths and nose. The suspended fibers adhered to any moist surface including the surface of the eyeball. The feline was forced to pause and rake the fuzz from her nose and eyes. Puma seized the moment to strike out with her dagger.

Under other circumstances the scene would have been humorous. The strangeness of the battle between the two lionesses, simultaneously struggling with asphyxia created a scenario that was too improbable for fiction. Since the woman's nostrils were smaller and sheltered by her facial architecture, the cattail fibers inhibited her respiration less that the lion's. Due to her superior intellect, she was able to stay focused as the battle raged. Her blade repeatedly found its target. The injured lion didn't run away as expected. Puma prepared herself for a fight to the death.

Oxygen starvation caused the lion to panic! The feline's movements became erratic as she struggled to inhale. Puma capitalized on the situation and managed to stab the beast in an eye as it lunged past her. The lion screamed out in pain and began shaking its head from side to side. Puma moved toward the crazed cat just as it leapt at her. The razor-sharp claws delivered a glancing blow to her upper arm. Puma whirled and sprang upon the lion's back, stabbing repeatedly with all her strength. She knew she had punctured a lung when the cat began spraying blood from its nostrils. A lull in the battle allowed time for the air to partly clear. The klandagie reversed its direction and pinned Puma to the floor of the cave. The lion bit down on Puma's neck and tore at her ear. Puma's reservoir of adrenaline blocked most of her pain and enabled her to continue defending the life of Patrick's unborn child.

The cat paused long enough to sneeze. This opened the nasal passages enough to inhale a breath of oxygen rich air. The lion's stood on hind legs and then sprang toward the adversary viciously biting and clawing. Puma's precise timing helped her stab the lion's remaining eye. Sightless, the screaming lion responded with frantic swiping at the air.

The panther began making the most surreal sound, part growl and part gurgle. Puma reached from behind its back and drove her knife to the hilt into the big cat's heart. Its scream was so loud it was painful to her ears. There was very little fight left by the time Puma slit the animal's jugular vein. She backed off to catch her breath while listening to the lion's weakening gasps and watched its crimson life force puddle and be absorbed by the sandy floor. The odor of warm blood nauseated Puma. She stepped to the cave's entrance for fresh air and expelled the fuzz from her nose and mouth. The lion's raspy breathing stopped. The only sound in the cavern was Puma's own breathing. The layer of cattail down that blanketed the cave's interior transformed it into a snowscape. The sight caused Puma to shiver from the perceived cold.

Puma Woman had narrowly prevailed in an epic clash with a sister lioness. She sank to her knees, weakened by the subsiding adrenaline overload. An eerie sensation caused the hair on Puma's arms to stand up. Some strange force had overshadowed her. The thought came to her that the disembodied spirit of the lioness was fusing with her own spirit. A Klandagi, lord of the forest, had challenged her right to join the elite society, a premier heritage of honor. The former Wathena had validated her right to wear the name Puma-Woman.

Puma felt compelled to honor the lifeless form and dropped to her knees to chant an ancient death song. She ran her hand along the sleek coat and caressed the silken ears. The tears that bathed Puma's face dripped onto the silken fur of the lioness, anointing her for her journey to the unseen world.

Puma's abstraction gave way to the throbbing pain radiating from her injuries. She feared for the welfare of her babe and removed her tunic. Her hands trembled as she ran them over her abdomen. She was relieved when a check found no vaginal bleeding. The most severe pain was coming from her left jaw and ear. After examining the wounds that she could see, she determined that no more than two of her wounds needed to be closed with stitches.

Puma set water to boil for brewing pain medicine. She opened Noisy Bird's satchel and removed a number of herb-filled leather pouches. She spread a blanket on the sandy floor and organized the items she would be using. She bound her wounds with temporary bandages to slow the bleeding. She put a second larger pot of water on the fire to boil. She grimaced as she traced her neck and jaw wounds with her hands. The bites to her neck were superficial, but her ear was dangerous ripped and punctured. It was mostly detached from her head. She hastily bound the ear to her head with a strip of blanket by tying it at the crown of her head.

She was thankful that Noisy Bird had insisted she bring the medicine bag. Puma selected a pouch marked with a charcoal symbol. It contained the crushed dried leaves of the yarrow plant. Puma stepped over the lion's body and built up the fire. She repositioned the lion's carcass to the cave's entrance. She softened a stack of singed and dried prickly pear pads in the hot water. A staple of the medical kit, they were ready for use as bandages.

One of the pouches contained a mixture of kava, chamomile, cannabis, passion-flower leaves, and powdered willow bark. She poured hot water over a bowl filled with the dried leaves and set it aside to steep. In another bowl, she poured just enough hot water to moisten crushed comfrey and sheep sorrel leaves forming the consistency of a poultice. Into the larger pot she dropped a handful of ground sassafras and left it to steep. The tea of sassafras is a time-honored medicine among the Cherokee. Though the medical professionals of the day lacked understanding of bacterial and viral infections, they were armed with the outcome of closely observed trial and error folk medicine. Puma had been told that the Cherokee were better healers than white doctors.

Once the sassafras tea had cooled, Puma irrigated her wounds, ridding them of infectious debris. She followed the sassafras tea by sprinkling yarrow leaf powder directly into the wounds. The stinging brought tears to her eyes. She drew a deep breath and continued by smearing the wounds with the comfrey and sheep sorrel poultice.

There wasn't much she could do to treat her ear. She blotted the blood away and poured sassafras tea over the left side of her head. Working blindly, she inclined her head and covered the wound with the poultice before positioning and bandaging her ear using a softened prickly pear pad held in place with a strip of blanket. She realized that she might lose the ear. It was out of her control. While she worked, she was consuming large gulps of the pain reliever. It was now time to stitch the most serious lacerations. She took out her largest needle, threaded it with animal sinew. With a deep breath she began the painful process. Puma fought off faintness as she forced the dull needle through each side of the torn skin and pulled it together and then used her mouth to help tie each knot. Over and over, she repeated the process until she had to stop and scream. She resumed the stitching. She was forced to stop several times. The task took more than two hours, but it seemed much longer. She was barely able to finish treating the wounds by smearing the cuts with the poultice and properly bandaging them with the prickly pear pads.

Faint and trembling from shock, Puma wrapped a blanket around her shoulders and sat in front of the fire gulping the willow bark tea that merely dulled the pain. Faintness caused her to collapse beside the fire for at least an hour. When she awoke, the cuts were throbbing, and she was experiencing chills while feeling hot. She knew she was running a fever. She consumed two full gourds of willow bark tea. The brew caused Puma to suffer from a strange vertigo, and she didn't dare attempt to stand. What mattered was that it helped relieve the pain.

After a period of sleep Puma changed from her blood-stained blanket to a fresh one. She cut a hole for her head and wore it poncho style. The pain was unrelenting. The slightest movement hurt and caused the forming scabs to crack and resume bleeding.

Puma's mental discipline helped her to function by compartmentalizing her pain. She prepared more willow bark pain reliever. While she waited for the tea to steep, she thought of the lion. It was important to preserve the animal's pelt as a sacred relic. And she wanted to consume a portion of the heart and liver, thereby assimilating its stealth and cunning. It occurred to Puma that she must hasten to prepare the lion's organs for cooking and the hide for tanning before her injuries incapacitated her.

After drinking more of the pain-relieving tea, Puma rose to remove the carcass from the cave to the top of the cliff where she could work on it. She became dizzy and almost fainted. She reconsidered and instead began eviscerating the lion at the cave's entrance? She opened the belly and the first thing she saw were two well developed kittens encapsulated in their uterine sacks. Puma felt heart sick over the sight. Maternal instinct explained the puma's persistence in reclaiming her den.

With tears running down her cheeks, Puma continued the gory task. She was taking an unthinkable short cut because of her injuries. She placed the heart and liver in a large cooking pot after eating a thin slice of each. She knelt to commune with the spirits and sprinkled tobacco on the fire.

Out of an otherwise still daybreak a strong whoosh of wind parted the vines and rushed into the cave. The sudden wind caused Puma to gasp, drawing a great breath of dust and cattail fuzz into her throat. She coughed and spat. How strange, she thought. The wind can only be attributed to a spiritual visitation.

She saved the skull, back, and breast portion of the hide and sent the rest over the edge to the stream below where it would be consumed by fish, otter, and other river creatures.

The pain from Puma's wounds was getting too intense to continue. She gathered the mattress and re-wrapped it tightly before it back in the hammock. Its bulk was half the former size. She was too ill to eat any of the stew and eased her body on to the hammock where she lapsed into a feverish slumber.

When Puma awoke, she was drenched in perspiration. Chills caused her to shutter. She noticed that her scalp contracted, and goosebumps covered her arms. Nausea made it hard to keep down the pain killer. The pain caused her to drink it in great gulps. She relieved herself by the cave's entrance and then splashed cool water on her face. She realized that both she and the baby were in jeopardy. She grasped the medicine bag hanging around her neck and earnestly petitioned the deities known for healing. Such dire times called for burning a pinch of tobacco on the coals of the fire. She added a few sticks to the few remaining coals and fixed her eyes on a puff of rising tobacco smoke. She felt a surge of resolve, tenacity prevailed. Her will to survive was too strong for the demons of darkness. She built up the fire and lighted a new candle before collapsing back on the hammock.

For three days Puma slept, except for brief periods when she applied medicine and took the last of the pain killer.

A week had passed when Puma awoke to a shocking sight. Her wounds were infested with maggots. During her delirium she had threshed about, kicked off her cover and loosened the bandages. Swarms of blow flies laid eggs into her wounds. The sight of the working mass of larvae caused her to swoon. When awareness returned, she recalled Falls-From-Heaven's lesson. He had insisted that maggots promote healing by eating away the dead tissue, and now she knew he had been right. A close inspection revealed that her wounds were much better. The swelling had subsided, and she only felt pain with movement.

After sponge bathing her entire body in sassafras tea to remove the puss and maggots, Puma dressed in a lightweight sleeveless tunic. Ridding her body of the stench of putrid flesh bolstered her mood. The pungent camphor scent of the medicinal herbs masked any remaining odor. The leftover stew was brought to a rolling boil by dropping red-hot stones into the covered cooking pot. After one taste, Puma realized that the stew was spoiled and disposed of it. Her pregnant body was craving fresh food. Recovering her strength for gathering food was an immediate challenge. Puma sang a chant and burned tobacco.

For a second week Puma stayed near the cave, spending most of her recovery resting upon the hammock. As she healed, she became restless and ventured from her sanctuary for a bath in the stream below. She gathered firewood and cut a new supply of cattail pods to replenish the mattress. She could feel her strength returning after a meal of catfish. By the end of the third week, she decided to hike to the canyon and check on Friend. She bathed in the creek and was presented with the opportunity to snatch a plump mallard duck paddling her way. She returned to the cave with the fowl and an armload of cattail pods and a nice mess of cattail shoots. The cattail rhizomes were tough and fibrous and would need to stew for hours. She was too hungry to wait and roasted thin strips of duck over the fire. The fatty duck meat was just what she needed.

Summer had passed midpoint, and the time was right for harvesting the wild food that she craved. The trip to check on Friend would double as a food foraging opportunity.

In preparation for the walk to Friend's box canyon, Puma coiled her braided leather rope and placed it across her upper torso. She slung her bow and quiver over the other shoulder and tied a leather pouch for collecting any fruit or nuts about her waist. She managed to walk the distance by stopping to rest several times.

Little Doe's favorite song came to mind, and Puma sang the words as if her daughter was walking beside her. The blue summer sky was decorated with lovely tuffs of clouds. Puma practiced her birdcalls. Several noisy jays showed curiosity. She spoke to the clamorous birds, "Ahhh, I fooled you!" It occurred to Puma that the pain of losing Patrick was less acute. For some reason this made her feel guilty. She was startled when she realized that she couldn't see his face in her mind or hear his voice. She questioned her sanity.

The barrier she had built at the canyon's entrance was still in place. She moved a small log enough to enter and hiked along the rocky streambed. She removed her moccasins and waded in the creek part of the way. It was second nature for Puma to be alert and aware of her surroundings. A death stench wafted to her nostrils. She hurried to the source of the sickening odor. She walked upon the remains of Friend lying on her side by the pool. Her bloated abdomen was partially torn away, and all the usual scavengers had been to the feast. Dear Friend! It would be lonely traveling without the animal. She recognized the foot prints of a grizzly. Upon approach, a gray fox was forced to end his meal of carrion. High above, three or four buzzards circled on wind currents. There was no way she could have known in advance that the box canyon lay within a grizzly bear's territory. The sobering knowledge demanded extreme caution. Puma hoped that Friend's death had been sudden.

On the walk back to the cave, Puma felt an intense loneliness. She stopped to gather some nuts under a partly dead black walnut tree. It had been struck by lightning in the past. Along a deep ravine Puma found a patch of raspberry vines. The vines had been trampled and crushed, indicating that a bear had napped after eating its fill. Puma took the precaution to locate a tree that she could quickly climb. She had been craving raspberries and ate almost as many as she gathered in the pouch. Puma decided to preserve some of the berries by drying them. There were so many uses for dried berries. If only she had the other ingredients for her favorite pemmican recipe.

Puma closely examined the bear's tracks and marked her tracking stick. From the measurements it was a monster of a bear. She had never hunted a grizzly all alone. Just thinking about such a dangerous task made her heart race. By the time Puma reached the shelter of the cave, she was exhausted and fell upon her bed. She noticed that the baby was unusually active, especially when she lay on her back. Her period of gestation was passing quickly, and without Friend, she would need to get back to the Otter Clan while she could still walk the distance. Ignorance of the future can be a blessing. The Puma-Woman was soon to be tested in ways she would have never imagined.

Puma's mental toughness sped along her recovery from the lion attack. She was regaining stamina and flexibility despite the pain. The thought of Oscar Jackson living a life of plenty consumed her. She was imaging the triumphant finish when justice would be meted out.

First, she would break into Jackson's store and take what she needed. The Jackson family lived in a log cabin a hundred yards from the main compound of buildings. She recalled that they kept hunting hounds. They were known to lounge on the porch of the trading post. They were not characteristically docile but had been trained to dislike people. They would snap at anyone that attempted to pet them. She must silence the dogs before approaching the store.

The trek led over rough country and required her to stop and rest. She allowed her thoughts free rein as she walked. She was recalling Tecumseh's master plan to cleanse the continent of Europeans. She questioned whether her people could revert to their primitive way of living. How welcome would be an existence that allowed The People to live free of European pox, firewater, and the intimacy sickness. Puma recalled Tecumseh's eloquence as he made his plea. Her village had listened intently and were recruited. The rift that developed split the clan in half. Puma's family, Stands-Alone, and most of the council of leaders sided with Tecumseh's grand scheme.

The distant baying of a hound awoke Puma's wondering mind. She had always deplored killing animals, but Jackson's hounds must be dispatched. Puma found a place on the river out of ear shot of the cabin for calling the dogs. She made a call from grass blades that mimicked the sound of an injured rabbit. After a few puffs on the grass, she heard the forlorn bawling. A chill came over her, and the hair on her arms stood as the baying grew louder. Puma braced her back against a small tree and held her bow at the ready. It was important to silence the animals before they raised suspicion. Her mind was flashing back over the evidence. There was no room for doubting Jackson's guilt.

Puma continued the short puffs of air to create a muffled squeal. Soon one of the blades tore, so she changed to a fresh one. Squeegee, squeegee, over and over, the sound floated across the bottomland. She varied the tempo and loudness. She surmised that there were only two hounds. She recalled that the hounds were large and aggressive. Puma decided to climb a small tree high enough to be out of reach. She locked her legs around a limb and continued her calls. Being well off the ground made her position safer, and that calmed her pounding heart. Darkness hid the dogs' approach. Suddenly they appeared and started to bay treed. The lead dog was a huge blue-tic. It reared on the trunk of Puma's tree just as the moon topped the trees. The hound was clawing at the tree-trunk and leaping. Puma's first arrow was perfectly placed, piercing its heart. It yipped and fell backward, dead when it hit the ground.

The other hound, a redbone, tucked his tail under and whimpered. He withdrew and concealed himself behind a dense bush for a few moments. Puma blew upon the call, and the redbone rushed forward and reared against the base of the tree. The animal moved just as Puma released an arrow, and it entered the dog's mouth. The hound flipped over backwards and started clawing at the shank. Puma dropped from the tree and quickly ended the dog's suffering. She listened for any indication that the dog's yelps had aroused Jackson enough to investigate. She covered both dogs with brush after removing her arrows. Some might be reused.

Puma decided to approach the Jackson property from behind the barn. The compound consisted of the store, a large barn, the black smith shed, a chicken house, pigsty, and two log cabins. The newest of the houses belonged to Oscar Jackson's grown son. It lay a hundred yards behind the larger cabin.

Standing in the corral outside the barn was a roan mare, possibly a filly. Puma's presence frightened her, and she snorted and stamped out a warning. Puma calmly walked to the corral fencing and offered the mare a hand full of grass. The suspicious filly tossed her head and trotted around the corral with her tail held high. Puma climbed the fence and walked to the center of the corral. Still holding the grass out to one side, Puma avoided facing the filly straight on. Puma spoke in soft tones, "Easy now, I come as a friend, what a pretty girl you are, you must be a fleet runner. Here now, let me touch your velvety nose, come closer lovely girl. There now, I am a friend. Do not be afraid."

Curiosity overcame the mare, and she slowly approached, still snorting and tossing her head. As she began to nibble at the grass, Puma rubbed her nose. Puma ran her hand along her neck and felt her musculature. The Tsalagii had been among the first of the eastern tribes to use horses for transportation and for bearing burdens. Small numbers of wild horses roamed Cherokee territory and were descended from the stock brought across the Atlantic by the Spanish Conquistadors. Most of the feral horses were easy to break and were powerfully built. The less desirable were hunted for food. Puma kept to the shadows as she walked to the barn and took a halter from a hook. The mare followed Puma into the barn. She accepted the halter but was a little frisky. Puma led her from the corral to a shadowy spot out of sight of the house. A carpet of succulent grass would keep her occupied.

Puma crept to the blacksmith shop. The door was unlocked but made a squeaking noise when it swung on its rusty hinges. She hid under a workbench in case the noise had attracted attention. Puma smelled cooking food. Next to her hiding place under the bench, was a wooden toolbox with a rope handle and a sturdy metal latch and hinges. She slowly opened the box and began removing the contents. Many of the items were things she needed, especially the box of nails. Ah ha, she had found the perfect rodent proof container. She noticed a currycomb hanging on a hook and added it to the box. She carried the toolbox to the door and left the lid ajar. The faint light that filtered into the shed was just enough to identify things she would take with her. She chose two grappling hooks, each with an eye in the handle. She selected a smaller single hook and a larger three-prong hook and placed them in the toolbox.

Puma needed a way to secure the wooden box to the back of the filly. She looked around for a saddle tree. She took a blanket and saddle from the tack room. The filly stood still while Puma tightened the cinch and adjusted the stirrups. She strapped on the saddle tree but did not load it up yet. She dumped the items upon the ground. She checked to make sure the mare was in a shadowy place to wait for a fast get-away.

Puma walked to the store, keeping to the shadows. She must hurry because she dared not leave the filly for long. She might become frightened and try to break free. There was a bushel of wormy apples by the barn, so she scooped up a dozen or so and dropped them on the ground before the filly. Because the house was nearby, any noise might be heard. The entrance to the store was locked, but a wooden shutter was left unlatched. Puma stood on a stool and crawled through the window. Inside, it was too dark to see. She used her sense of touch and managed to close the heavy curtains before lighting a candle from the shelf. She hurried to collect the items she needed starting with a bolt of red flannel. She gathered a linsey Woolsey shirt, and pair of men's trousers, large enough to fit her expanding girth. She tried on several pairs of leather boots before she found the right size. Next, she took two pairs of woolen socks and a black broad brimmed hat. Across the room, she spied a container of beeswax candles. To the pile of items, she added a card of needles and several spools of thread. The evening was unusually cool, so Puma slipped the shirt and trousers over her buckskins. She stuffed the goods she had assembled into a large leather bag found on a hook. On top of the boots, Puma placed the entire box of candles. She took three coils of hemp rope from a hook and stuffed them into the bag.

On the counter, Puma spotted a box of the music makers like the one the traveler had been playing. The harmonica would be a nice surprise for Little Doe. Salt, ah yes, and a bag of coffee. Several wrapped cured hams hung from a hook. Ham sounded good, so a small one went into the bag. Enough she thought, or the bag will be too heavy. On the way out she grabbed two sheathed hunting knives.

Puma chased the other horses from the barn and closed the gate behind them. When she approached the roan, the mare was nervous and pawed the ground. Puma loaded up the wooden box. She hung the handle of the leather bag over the saddle horn. Puma took the reins and led the filly into the thick canopy of cottonwoods at the creek bank. Just in case of pursuit she would leave tracks headed in the wrong direction for a convincing distance before entering the creek and reversing direction. After approximately two miles, Puma felt safe to leave the creek. The filly was glad to be back on dry land and pranced a little. She wanted to run but Puma held her back. "Easy, girl, you have a load. Let's take it easy."

Puma missed Friend the way one would miss a pet. As her mind drifted, she began to compare the nature of the mule to that of horses. Temperament wise, Friend had been affectionate and unusually docile, always perfectly willing to plod along at the desired pace. On the other hand, the roan was high-spirited. As the night hours stretched on the filly settled into a steady pace brought on by fatigue. The repetitive motion made Puma drowsy. Her padded hammock would be very welcome.

Phase one of her mission was accomplished successfully, and she considered the filly to be a bonus. After stashing her loot from the store in the cave, Puma rode the filly to the box canyon. She gave the roan a slack rein and the horse went from a cantor to a full gallop. The rushing wind was exhilarating and did them both good. Puma marveled at the smoothness of her gate and such swiftness, the kind that would leave pursuers far behind. Ah, the word breeze, yes, she liked the sound of the word. The young roan filly deserved a name, a fitting name like Breeze.

Puma hid the saddle and tact in dense foliage near the canyon opening. Before leaving the area, she took time to sweep away all sign of her presence. She walked back to the cave, feasting on the bounty of the forest. She took a short detour to visit a cluster of raspberry bushes. She took time to eat her fill and then gathered a gallon or so for later. In line with the path was a stately pecan tree. Its branches had been raining plump nuts on the ground below. She gathered at least ten pounds of nuts. Only a short distance from the cave she happened upon a prickly pear plant with a dozen or so ripe apples. She built a small fire and singed off the spines before placing them in with the berries. At the stream she removed her moccasins and waded a short distance to gather watercress. She shook the water from two large handfuls of the aquatic delicacy. That was when she spied a snapping turtle's nest and took only four of the eggs. She smiled and thanked the mother turtle. The wooden box would be perfect for securing her food from rodents, what a good find.

Ridding the box canyon of the grizzly could not wait. By sunrise the second morning Puma packed the needed gear for the hunt to the cliff top and hid it. She wanted to travel lightly, so she took only necessities. She lashed a spare bow and quiver behind the saddle. She brought two coils of hemp rope, one of which was attached to the grappling hook. She hiked toward the box canyon as fast as her healing body allowed. She stepped inside the barrier and right away saw the roan walking toward her. Was it possible that the mare had sensed her arrival? On the ride back to the cave Puma sang to her unborn infant and practiced bird calls. She loaded her gear and hurried back to the canyon for the hunt.

A male grizzly bear would have been a formidable adversary for even a heavily armed hunting party let alone a lone woman armed with nothing more than a bow and hunting knife. She summoned her most confident inner-self and shouted, "Brother Bear, wherever you are, prepare to do battle with the Puma-Woman!"

The plan she devised was simple. Bears always return to a kill for days afterwards. She would situate her tree stand somewhere along the animal's path and lie in wait, high off the ground. Throwing the grappling hook over a limb and climbing the attached rope was a good strategy and one she had used before. Tying knots in the rope would make it faster to climb. She decided to practice scaling the rope a dozen times, hoping to shorten the time needed for a quick escape.

She chose a tree with branches far from the ground. She grasped the rope about a foot from the hook and after four circles overhead, threw it at the branch. It fell short. The second try, it came closer to falling over the branch but missed. Next, she tried using a vertical windup before throwing the hook. This time it caught on a small branch and not the large one she was aiming for. She had a difficult time retrieving the hook, but it finally broke loose and fell to the ground. Puma decided to discard the windup technique and toss the base of the hook at the limb. The hook found its mark. She pulled to set the hook and tested it with her weight. Thanks to the barbs on the hook, it held steady as she climbed the rope. She successfully climbed up and down several times, improving on the time. There, she brushed her hands together and nodded her head in a decisive gesture. She was ready for the hunt.

The warm day intensified the sickening odor of decay. The remains of the mule would foul the stream. Puma tied on to a hoof and used the filly to pull the carcass well away from the stream. Daring to move a grizzly's kill was risky. It was a sure way to provoke an attack should the animal be hiding nearby.

Puma was thinking that grizzly bears are instinctive and predictable. Not far from the pond she spied an ancient oak tree, partly damaged by lightning. The trunk bore claw marks at least eight feet off the ground. The animal that made the marks was a giant, probably a male. She measured the width of the paws. They were the exact width of the track previously measured.

Puma investigated the scene of the kill. She marked her tracking stick. The well-worn stick was about three feet long. Using a tracking stick had been part of Puma's wilderness training under the tutelage of her beloved Uncle Falls-From-Heaven. The stick had once belonged to her father and was cherished as a keep-sake. The stick would be helpful for anticipating the general direction of movement and estimating where the next footprint should fall, even when the path was winding or the trail rocky. It would help identify specific animals. Interspersed with the grizzly paw prints were many other smaller tracks. Puma spent a few minutes reading the sign.

Interpreting animal sign was a skill Puma excelled in from early childhood. She never tired of reconstructing a scene. A bobcat had fed on the mule. They have four toes and walk with claws retracted. Unique to felines, Puma knew their hind feet fall directly into the print made by the front foot, leaving a single track. Next, Puma analyzed a canine track. There were four toes with visible claw imprints. Puma quickly concluded that the track was that of a fox. Fox are the only canine species that directly register when they walk by placing their hind foot into the front track.

Puma was grateful for Falls-From-Heaven's wilderness instruction. In her mind's eye she heard his voice saying, "Wathena, take notice, all other canine tracks indirectly register, that means the back footprint falls slightly behind and to one side of the front print." She recognized the tracks of raccoons, opossums and porcupines. She knew that porcupines as well as squirrels, and chipmunks have four toes on each front foot and five on the rear. The feet of raccoon and opossum are flat, almost humanlike with five toes on each one. The opossum track is set apart by a visible opposing thumb imprint.

Puma was facing the dangerous challenge head on. Her aim would have to be perfect. As Puma searched for the right tree to make her stand, she heard a sound behind her. It startled her, but it was made by Breeze. She called to her and spent a half hour giving her a good rubbing with dry pine needles. The mare grazed her way toward the far side of the pond where the grass was taller.

The upper end of the box canyon was a beautiful park. The sound of the trickling spring pleasantly musical. Puma drank deeply from the cold, clear spring water and refilled her gourd. She ate some berries from a vine growing next to the water fall. Puma kept an eye on the road, knowing she would be first to detect the approach of the bear.

Close to the bear's path that led to the pond grew an ancient oak with sprawling limbs. It would be a perfect stand. Puma threw the grappling hook, and after a second try, it caught on a medium sized branch. She tested its strength. It held her weight. Next Puma looked around for some fallen wood that could be used to construct a sleeping bench in the tree. High in a tree was the only safe place for Puma's bed. She tied the sticks into a bundle at the end of the rope and climbed up knot by knot, pulling the bundle of wood and her gear up behind her. Once her pallet was ready, she relaxed. It had been a long day and she needed rest. It was her favorite time of day for communing with nature. She faced the west and sat cross legged to watch the sun set.

Darkness brought on a primordial serenade. The musicians included birds, bullfrogs, crickets, and tree locusts. The fading light ignited stars, one at a time. The sad solo of a whippoorwill took Puma back to a cherished remembrance. Patrick, in one of his whimsical moods had moved the mattress from the bedroom to the front porch. Even with the bitter-sweet spell of melancholia Puma was grateful for the vivid memories. Puma visualized lying entwined in Patrick's arms. Beside them lay one-year-old Little Doe bundled in her night-clothes. The occasion muted Patrick's voice to a whisper, "The sounds we are hearing from the forest are nature's symphony. On holidays and special events, the orchestra of the local circus performed concerts on the town square. They played the classical music so popular across Europe. I wish you could hear music like that. Rory and I worked for the circus, and we were usually there to help with setting up for the crowds." Patrick's access to such music had been rare for a commoner. Puma realized that Patrick was homesick for his family and boyhood home. Patrick pronounced the names of the composers, very strange sounding names such as Wolfgang Mozart and Ludwig Van Beethoven. Puma loved listening to Patrick's voice whatever the topic. Little Doe had fallen asleep and was tucked into her crib inside the cabin. Before falling asleep Patrick and Wathena celebrated their unique adoration of each other, reserved for the truly devoted.

Puma placed her hands to her mouth and answered the whippoorwill. From the ridge above the spring came the call of an owl. Fatigue sped Puma into a dream state. She lay on her side with an arm surrounding her abdomen. Her other arm was folded under her head. Her waking recollections were responsible prompting a dream that was utterly realistic. She was rocking Little Doe in Patrick's handcrafted rocking chair, sitting on the porch when she heard Patrick callout from the tobacco field, "Wathena, bring the long rifle, hurry! There's a bear walking this way!" Puma awoke, frightened and perspiring. She heard grunts, sniffing, and heavy breathing. A bear was directly below fouling the air with its stench. It must be the one that killed Friend. Where was Breeze? Puma knew that the grizzly's sense of smell would have detected both she and the mare from miles away. The bear reacted to the sound of a stick snapping when she sat up on her pallet. He made a low, rumbling growl. In the darkness Puma could only see an outline of the creature. She must aim carefully and try to hit a lethal spot with her first arrow. What if she only wounded him?

The sniffling grizzly circled the tree. He left to drink from the pond. A raccoon scurried away from the bank as the bear approached. The lapping noise seemed loud and lasted for two or three minutes.

Earth's rotation sent a ray of moon light. It revealed the monster's bulk, causing Puma's palms to sweat. The scent of fear triggered the grizzly's aggressiveness. Trying to control her shakiness, she dried her hands on her tunic and readied an arrow. The bear reared and began clawing at the tree trunk. She gripped the limb that supported her with her legs until it hurt and inhaled. Her upper lip had gone numb. Perspiration ran from her hairline and dripped from her chin.

The bear continued to sharpen his claws on the tree. Vibrations traveled up the limb sending a sinister message. A nervous whinny and pawing hoofs caused the bear to snort and sniff the air. That is when the black hulk dropped to all-fours and loped toward the filly. Puma knew that Breeze would be attacked. She had to lure the bear's attention away from the horse. Puma quickly climbed down the rope, skipping the last two knots to land in a crouch. She shouted a challenge to the furry one. "Look at me, Great Beast, a lone woman. Prepare to die!"

Even faster than she expected, the bear turned and charged straight at her. Puma dove for the dangling rope. She dropped her arrow, but managed to place the bow over her arm as she scrambled up the first few rope knots. The beast closed the distance with unbelievable rapidity. While Puma dangled from the rope, the bear managed to grasp the rope's end in his mouth. Puma yanked the rope with one hand, and it slipped from the chomping snout. Puma ascended a couple of knots and brought the rope up with her. Her survival hung in the balance. It depended on the integrity of the rope and the anchoring of the grappling hook.

Seated upon her sleeping platform, Puma drew another arrow from her quiver. She ran her hand over the length of the projectile to check for imperfections. Slowly she fitted the arrow into the bow and began to pull the bowstring. Her aim for the throat missed, thrown off because the bear had suddenly lunged upward. The arrow pierced the giant's left shoulder instead. He halted the assault on the tree trunk and roared in pain. The explosion of sound was deafening. A second arrow hit him in the chest. It was hard to see the exact placement. From the sounds a third arrow must have entered the open mouth. The wounded bear clawed at the arrows and bucked with rage. He staggered away, making gurgling sounds. He rolled onto his back and threshed from side to side and then slowly shuffled toward some heavy brush. Puma sent one last arrow flying toward his fleeing bulk. Later Puma would learn that the arrow had lodged in his hindquarter. The giant paused in his retreat long enough to stand and emit a great tortured roar.

With the bear gone from the immediate area, the mare settled down to graze. Puma climbed into her blankets for some rest. It took an hour for her heart to slow to a normal beat. Gradually the night sounds returned, and restful sleep found the young mother. Bright sunlight awoke Puma. She reached her head over the edge of the sleeping platform to view the area around the base of the tree. She broadened the perimeter of her search, but the bear wasn't in view.

Puma sat up and stretched her arms. She yawned as her eyes searched the surrounding area a second time. She had hoped to see the dead carcass of the bear nearby. Her eyes were drawn to the pond where a pair of ducks were contentedly quacking as they navigated the glassy surface, leaving behind wakes.

Puma retied the leather throng about her forehead and laced her moccasins. She opened her satchel, removed a handful of nuts and berries, and ate the food without savoring it. She was focused on the hunt of her life. She spied Breeze grazing just across the pond. She quenched her thirst from her water gourd and began dismantling her sleeping platform.

Before descending from the tree Puma loosened the grappling hook and doubled the rope as she lowered herself to the ground. She coiled the rope and placed it over her shoulder. Puma followed the bear's blood trail far enough to feel confident that it had left the immediate vicinity. She decided it was safe to bathe in the pond.

It was a beautiful morning, and the brisk pool was invigorating. A perch nibbled at a little brown mole on her back, momentarily upsetting her repose. The swim helped to dissipate the stress of the bear encounter. Luxuriating in the moment, she was brought back to reality when a loud crashing sound came from the cliff. A little too relaxed, she looked around in time to see a boulder rolling from the ridge top, crashing into trees, dislodging other boulders on the way down. She recognized the crash as an aftershock connected to the powerful earthquakes that shook the Mississippi valley a few years before. Puma concluded that the gods were still angry.

A few feet away from where Puma lolled in the water grew a mat of water-lilies. The brilliant white blooms had a golden center and released a beautiful fragrance. She gathered a water lily blossom and placed it behind her left ear. Her right ear was still healing and would never look normal. She planned to grow her hair so that the deformity would be concealed. Puma stood on the bank and dried her body by running her hands over her skin. As she dressed, she sang a morning prayer. She opened her shoulder satchel and removed a chunk of jerky. Her appetite seemed to be keeping pace with her girth.

Without further delay, Puma took up the bloody trail of the grizzly. She would be using the tracking stick to determine the general direction the brute had taken. The trail curved back toward the entrance of the box canyon. He was dragging a front paw. Puma followed a few steps at a time. The hair on her head was prickling. No detail escaped her heightened senses. Each sound, smell, or disturbed plant was analyzed. Her muscles were primed for instantaneous action. Puma made sure to identify limbs capable of supporting her weight. A bloody patch of flattened grass indicated that the wounded bear had rested and then moved on. Puma found an arrow shaft without its point lying where the tortured beast had dislodged it and put it in her pouch.

After another hundred yards, Puma heard labored breathing coming from an opening in a rock wall. The bear had entered what she assumed to be his den. Puma decided to throw her grappling hook at a stout cedar branch only 20 or 30 feet from the den's opening. Just as she prepared to throw the hook, the ground shook. Boulders rolled down the embankment above the bear den. One odd shaped boulder bounced and took an erratic path directly toward Puma. She had to jump from its path. There were sounds coming from underneath the ground. Grinding noises, rock on rock. The earthquake lasted for about 3 to 5 seconds. Then a series of deep, rumbling growls came from the opening of the cave.

Puma hated killing of any kind. She prayed for the great grizzly, asking that his death be quick. The earth wasn't finished rumbling and expressed more anger. Though the temblor had rearranged many of the boulders around Puma's chosen cedar, it remained upright. Puma threw the hook at a substantial limb, and it caught. As before she tested to make sure it held her weight. The injured bear inched forward exposing his head and shoulders at the cave's opening where he met Puma's gaze. Puma was unsure if the bear was physically capable of charging her. Safe in the tree, Puma noticed that the bear had withdrawn back into the den. She searched her mind for a way to bring the bear out of the cave. She snapped off a branch and flung it at the opening. Again, the earth shook.

The aftershock reminded Puma of Patrick's heroism. He had been instrumental in saving many of the Thunder Clan the night of the first big earthquake. That first temblor had happened just as Tecumseh predicted. It took a moment for Puma to clear the memories and concentrate on the present.

Another aftershock caused the cedar to sway almost causing Puma to lose her grip. She locked her feet securely around the limb that supported her. The bear was not reacting to her provocations. She clapped her hands and sang out, "Brother Bear, come out to face your enemy." No response. Perhaps the bear was dying. After a few minutes, Puma came down from the tree, and started a fire near the dangling rope. There was plenty of dry material. She took a burning cedar branch and tossed it into the entrance of the den. The animal stirred and coughed. Puma tossed a second flaming branch farther into the cave and then withdrew to where the rope dangled. Some dried weeds at the entrance of the cave caught fire, making more smoke. Soon, the bear inched its way to the cave entrance. Seemingly unable to stand, he released a threatening growl. A foot-wide paw with six-inch claws struck at the air. Dried blood covered most of his mouth, breast, and front feet. It appeared that an arrow had pierced a lung and the bruin was dying from blood loss, sadly a slow death.

Puma honored the brother's bravery with a reverent bow. What a magnificent animal! Puma drew her bow. A series of arrows brought increasingly weakened cries until there was just silence. Puma waited and then cautiously approached. She tossed several stones at the motionless form. The small fire had burned out. Plenty of ground moisture from a recent shower prevented the fire from spreading. Puma, with knife drawn, carefully approached the massive head from behind. She grasped an ear and bent the massive head backward to expose the neck. Sawing through the fur, hide, and muscles with a mere hunting knife was no easy chore. Blood from the severed jugular formed a pool that gradually soaked into the ground. The pungent sweetish scent of warm blood was sickening to Puma's sensitive nose. The entire pregnancy she had been repulsed by certain smells. She detected a slight difference between the scent of bear and lion blood.

Because male grizzlies are solitary animals with a defined territory Puma was confident that the mare would be safe in the box canyon, at least from the threat of another male grizzly. Puma used every ounce of strength she could muster to open the bear's chest. The musculature of the animal forced Puma to sit astraddle the bear and stab at the breast bone with both hands. She stopped and found a stone to sharpen her knife. Back in position she was finally able to part the chest by pounding the knife handle with a stone. She removed the still warm, five-pound heart. It quivered when she touched it. Puma sang her ancient victory song as she held the heart above her head. Then she lowered the organ to her mouth and tore away a mouthful. A small amount of blood escaped her mouth and dripped onto her tunic. Puma wrapped the remainder of the heart and the liver in fresh leaves. Then she lined her satchel with a thick layer of dry leaves and grass to absorb blood.

Before returning to the cave, Puma located Breeze napping. As she approached, Breeze tossed her head and shied away. She was reacting to the scent of the bear and fresh blood. Puma bent to gather a handful of grass and walked toward the mare. After a time, Breeze settled down and allowed Puma to approach. She examined the horse to satisfy herself that she was uninjured. Then she sprang onto the bare back and coaxed her to lope around the pond, guiding her with her knees. She loved this horse. Fresh Breeze was the perfect name for the beauty. She left her near the pond in the peaceful box canyon and walked back to the cave.

Puma lit a fire and started a pot of water to boil. She sliced part of the massive heart into inch square cubes and threaded then onto sticks. She seared the meat before placing it into the boiling water. Arrowroot, salt, and dried onion from her food box seasoned and thickened the soup.

Puma was so glad to have her food and herbs protected in the new wooden box. It would save a lot of time collecting food. Puma relaxed by the fire and worked on a rope ladder. As she worked, she plotted the next phase of her revenge. The farm where she and Patrick had invested so much time and backbreaking labor would be her next target. As a crow flies, the farm was about five miles away. Puma steeled herself against the pain of returning to the farm. Momentarily disarmed, she acknowledged her ache of loss and homesickness. She could only hope the pain would become more bearable once Patrick was avenged. Puma shook her head to dispel a feeling of vulnerability.

Self-pity was at odds with her personality. She must stay focused and fully functional.

Puma packed the satchel with food, water gourd, and an extra knife. She would bundle her extra quiver of arrows and backup bow into a wool blanket to be lashed it behind the saddle. Over one shoulder she carried the grappling hook and rope. Her stride was brisk as she hiked to the box canyon to retrieve Breeze.

Puma found the filly near the entrance of the box canyon, seemingly waiting for her. The two of them had quickly bonded. The boulders from Puma's human-made rockslide had been somewhat rearranged by the latest temblor, but the monolith that limited passage remained essentially unchanged. Only a few smaller boulders needed to be rolled to the side.

Puma quickly cinched the saddle into place. Breeze pranced as Puma climbed into the saddle. She placed the rope with the hook over the saddle horn. She tied the extra bow and quiver and the empty leather bag behind the saddle. It was midday when she rode Breeze toward her farm. Puma hid her tracks by riding in the creek off and on and frequently stopping to sweep away any sign with a cedar branch. The afternoon was pleasantly cool. She came across a fully loaded berry vine, and she paused to satisfy her hunger and took a bag of berries with her for later. Where the forest allowed, she gave Breeze a slack rein.

At the familiar creek that bordered the farm, Puma hid Breeze after unloading the gear and taking her to drink. Puma removed her moccasins and wadded the stream. She was relieved that there were no barking dogs to alert her adversaries. The sun had set a half hour before, and she stayed in the shadows as she approached the farmhouse. Puma saw that lamps had been lit inside the cabin.

Suddenly, a large blue tic hound lunged at Puma from the brush. It caught her off guard. The dog knocked her on her back, and was biting at her neck. The hound was uncharacteristically vicious for the breed. Puma-Woman and the dog rolled upon the freshly ploughed field in a desperate struggle. Puma was able to push the dog's head to the side and then gouge an eye with her thumb. Puma grunted as she shoved the shrieking hound aside enough to slide her knife from its sheath. The dog let out one final yelp as the knife pierced its chest. Puma stood, and checked her body for injuries. The neck wounds were superficial. She ran back to her stash of gear and removed the gourd that held Bird Woman's special salve. Puma smeared a thin layer of the medicine over the bites and was ready to resume her mission.

Puma took a seat on a boulder and calmed herself. She was prepared to deal with a second dog, and as she grew closer to the house, she heard before she saw a second hound charging directly at her. This time she had time to draw down on the dog and dropped it mid-stride with an arrow in the chest. A single yelp sounded before the animal fell dead. A third dog, wasn't far behind. It was a small white terrier with brown and black spots. The little dog's wagging tail caused Puma to sit upon the ground and call to it, "Here boy, how friendly, yes, yes of course we can be friends." It was a relief not to kill this little cur dog; she supposed it to be a child's pet.

Once the sun had set, Puma advanced toward the cabin. Ever closer, Puma placed each step carefully. At first the spotted dog followed her, but Puma spied a duck on the creek and shot it. The little dog plunged into the water and retrieved the duck, laying it at Puma's feet. She praised him and then used her knife to slice open the duck before giving it back to the excited and obviously hungry dog. Puma made a quick get-away while the dog enjoyed his unexpected meal.

She could hear voices from inside the cabin. She crept to a partly open window. The cabin's interior was much as she had left it. A man, woman, and two children were sitting around the oak table, the very table that Patrick had worked so hard to craft. Anger welled up in Puma. Patrick's bear skin was still hanging over the fireplace. Beside it hung Patrick's souvenir buck antlers, harvested on their wedding day. The new occupants were voraciously feasting on plump ears of corn, red sliced tomatoes, and baked squash, all from her own garden plot.

The man's appearance was slovenly. His bare potbelly was visible beneath his shirt, his clothing was grimy and stained. His long sandy hair was greasy, and the teeth he had were badly decayed. Protruding upper teeth marred the fair skinned woman's appearance. She was dressed in a long calico dress and wore her hair in a single braid. When she stood to bring a pie to the table, Puma could see that she was in the latter stage of pregnancy.

Were these people really so ugly? Puma questioned her own perspective. Was her hostility justified? Their pasty pale skin made them look sickly and weak. Their blond hair lacked luster. Their overall appearance signaled mental dullness and the absence of vitality. Did the responsibility for her tragedy rest on these people or were they merely pawns under the influence of the Jackson clan? It dawned on Puma that the person she should be attacking was Oscar Jackson not these unsuspecting farmers.

Puma re-directed her seething hatred. She decided against burning the cabin for the present. She did not want to endanger the children or the unborn child. First off, Puma set the cornfield on fire using her flint and knife. That drew the people out of the house. They carried blankets and picked up buckets along the way. Puma could hear shouting above the crackle of the fire. The wind was out of the west, so the fire burned away from the house, and toward the creek. As the flames rapidly spread, Puma entered the house. She took down the bearskin, and antlers. She caressed the bearskin and placed the two items on the bed. She removed one of her handmade baskets and filled it with a poke of lead balls, a black-powder horn, and two handguns. Puma gathered the coverlet and knotted the corners as she fled the house. Patrick's keepsakes were back where they belonged.

Puma headed toward the barn, silently gliding from shadow to shadow. There stood Patrick's horses and two mules secure in their stalls. A separate pen with a milking stall held Brownie, the jersey cow. Puma went to Brownie and placed her arms around her neck. The cow obviously remembered her. The old spotted sow was bedded down in her pigsty. She was suckling a large number of piglets. The chickens were on the roost in the hen house. Puma had arrived with the intention of burning the barn to the ground, but she couldn't do it. An inner voice spoke to her, directing her to leave the farm as it was. She quietly withdrew to where Breeze waited. She securely bound the bundle to Breeze. The darkness forced a slow get-away. The stream was the only safe escape route since she was sure to be tracked as soon as the sun came up. As she rode, Puma planned the next phase, the pinnacle of her master plan. The Jackson Trading Post was next in her sights. Oscar Jackson would soon reap what he had sown.

After dropping the bundle at the cave, Puma took breeze to the box canyon and concealed the tracks. Back at the cave, she literally fell onto her bed, overcome with sad memories. In spite of her fatigue, it took several minutes to quiet her mind. It was early evening when the babe's movements roused her. She lighted a candle from a buried coal. She built up the fire and steeped some tea. Puma absently mindedly consumed a meal of jerky and dried berries.

Puma's pent-up passion for revenge energized her preparation to finally go after Oscar Jackson. She decided to wait for the following night. There would be no moon. Puma used the extra day to alter the men's clothing she had commandeered from the store. She hemmed both the sleeves and pant cuffs. Puma undressed and tested the new rope ladder. She descended to the stream below. She bathed in the brisk water, and lathered her hair and body with noisy Bird's yucca powder. Refreshed and rested, Puma spent the early evening painstakingly cleaning and loading the pistols. Patrick had wisely insisted that she become proficient with firearms. Puma sewed a double scabbard for the twin guns from a flap of rawhide. There were a few more items she would appropriate before burning the trading post. She needed more muslin and flannel cloth, thread and needles for sewing a layette and whatever caught her fancy. Little Doe and Trotter had offered to help prepare for the baby. Sewing a layette would be the first order of business once the three of them were together. When Puma thought back to the times she had shopped in the store, there had always been at least one bolt of red flannel on a shelf. The color red was Puma's favorite color and perfect for welcoming the babe.

Puma decided to carry a small clay pot of hot coals with her. That would speed up the fire making process. And she would be armed with the pistols, her bow, and knife. Sitting cross-legged in front of the fire pit, Puma closed her eyes and prayed to her medicine animal for wisdom and stealth. Then she removed the talisman bag from her neck. She felt the presence of Noisy Bird hovering nearby. Puma had never understood the medicine woman's reaction to the golden necklace during the naming ceremony. Puma fingered the sacred tokens, first a flake of turtle shell, a few turquoise beads, a turkey bone whistle, and the most powerful item, the claw of a puma. She chanted an ancient song. Viewing and handling the bag of talismanic objects calmed and gave Puma confidence in her ability to finish the task.

By noon the following day Puma arrived at the box canyon and found Breeze grazing near the entrance. As usual Breeze was expecting her. Breeze trotted to Puma with a bobbing head. She took a handful of grass from Puma. After a friendly rub down, she led the mare to the tree that held the saddle and tack. Puma tied the sawbuck saddle tree behind the saddle.

Puma disguised herself in the men's clothing. She approached the trading post from the east under the cover of heavy brush and willow trees. She didn't hear any barking dogs and assumed there were none. She watered Breeze and tied her in the willows a few hundred feet from the Jackson compound. She paused to surveil the site and waited for the darkness to deepen. Puma crept toward the buildings, keeping to the shadows. She regretted wearing the men's boots, her moccasins felt so much better.

A customer leaving the store as a woman, perhaps Lady Jackson, rang the dinner bell from the porch of the house. She looked very young, and her clothing was frilly. Puma recalled hearing rumors about the woman at the Moravian mission. There was even more gossip about the lecherous Oscar Jackson's perverted appetite for beautiful women. Puma watched as the elder Jackson and his adult son locked up the store and walked toward the log cabin lighting the path with a lantern. They were jovial and relaxed. The men stomped their boots to dislodge any dirt before entering the cabin. Puma could smell cooking food.

After a short wait, Puma tried to open the door to the store. This time she found the door and shutters securely locked. She used her knife to pick the locked door. The interior was totally dark. Once inside, she closed the curtains and lighted a candle. Puma began gathering the items on her list: fishhooks and line, cloth, needles, and thread. She added to her assembled items a jar of jerky and a bar of lye soap. She took a leather grip from a peg and filled it.

She tore pages out of a paper catalog and piled some wooden items over the paper. She sprinkled whale's oil over the paper. She used a horn of black powder to sprinkle a line of gun powder out the door. Next, she prepared the barn using the oil on a hay bundle and sprinkled gun powder in a line to the outside of the building and did the same with the other buildings. She made sure all of the animals were out of danger. The first building torched was the barn. Jacksons saw the glow from a living room window and ran shouting instructions from the house. Puma hid until they were out of sight. Then she ran to the store and placed a hot coal upon the line of black powder. The flames quickly became an inferno.

Puma glided from shadow to shadow back to the blacksmith shop. Once it was engulfed, she lifted the leather grip on to her back and ran toward where Breeze waited. Suddenly she was cut off by Oscar Jackson. The timing of the fire alerted him to her sabotage. Puma dropped the grip on the ground.

They stared at each other for a moment, and then he asked, "Who might you be?"

Puma said in perfect English and with her best imitation of a male voice, "Ah, I saw the fires and reckoned to lend a hand."

"So, then what ya got in that bag? Looks a lot like one from my store, here, let me see? Take off yer hat, I think I seen ya before."

Puma said, "Wait, let me explain," in a flash her right hand tilted the pistol slung low on her hip and fired through the open-ended scabbard. The bullet knocked Jackson on his back. The lead ball struck Jackson in the upper right arm shattering the bone. She glanced around and saw that the others were still fighting the fire. The fires were loud, and they didn't hear the gunshot. Puma drew her knife and held it in her teeth while she bound Jackson's hands behind his back with his own belt. He whimpered and begged, "Please, please, don't." She ripped a neck scarf from around his neck and a handkerchief from his pocket. At knife point she forced him to open his mouth and she stuffed the handkerchief into his mouth and tied it in place with the scarf. Puma bent low over Jackson's face and removed her hat. The light from the fires illuminated her face. "Remember me?" A shocked look flashed across Jackson's face when he recognized Larson's Squaw. He wondered just how much she knew!

Puma answered his question, "I know! You and Andrew Jackson made sure Patrick did not survive the battle at Horse Shoe Bend and dispatched your men to kill me and my child. My relative, Large Shadow saw Patrick shot in the back by your men and warned me to run and hide. Your greed has doomed you. You steal my land and kill my people. You only love gold. Your men chased us into the night with torches. Stop your begging! There will be no mercy for you. I crush you like a bug." Jackson was making cowardly noises. He begged for the very mercy that he was too hardened to extend to others. He was struggling against his restraint, but the belt held fast.

She placed her boot on Jackson's chest and made eye contact before spitting her words at him, "I think I will let you live, killing you is not enough. Puma removed her knife from its sheath and carved a circle around the crown of Jackson's head. He let out a muffled scream and fainted as his scalp was ripped from his head. She used the tip of her knife to blind both eyes. Lastly, she opened his trousers and grasped his scrotum. Oscar revived in time to realize that he was being castrated. When he kicked out at Puma, she walked a few feet away and picked up a splitting maul, shattering both of his knees.

Puma tucked the scalp inside her shirt. She wiped her hands on his clothing and said, "It is your turn to suffer. Alive or dead, you will never hurt anyone again!"

Puma hurried back to Breeze and loaded the loot onto the saddle tree. She knelt at the creek and washed the blood from her hands. Breeze smelled the blood and shied when Puma approached. The scene was hellish, permanently searing images into Puma's brain. She wondered if this was like the hell of Patrick's Bible? The sound of the flames consuming the buildings, the smell of the smoke, the shouting and screaming, and the wounded body of Oscar Jackson flailing upon the ground. She had planned to torch the houses, but the will to continue was gone. She needed to get away as far and fast as possible.

As Puma rode away her path was illuminated by light from the fires. She hoped to never again experience such mayhem. She was so overcome with emotion she wept for much of the journey back to the cave. Where was the relief and satisfaction she had expected to feel? Perhaps it was because the loathsome and arrogant Andrew Jackson still lived. It was premature to be celebrating. Puma forced her thoughts to visualize Patrick sitting with Large Shadow and the other martyrs, resting and enjoying eternity.

After two days of rest at the cave, Puma went back to the farm and took one of Patrick's horses to use as a pack animal. The time had come to return to the Otter Clan. Tracking Andrew Jackson would have to wait. She had been absent longer than planned, due to the lion attack. She knew that Trotter and Little Doe would be worried. The trip would be easier with the two horses. Patrick's beloved sorrel gelding would carry most of her gear held in place by the sawbuck saddle tree. The lion pelt had completely dried and was ready for the tanning process. Puma used it to protect Patrick's bear rug from rain and dust. Breeze would carry Puma and her weapons, unburdened and ready to run should a flight situation arise.

Chapter 2

TREACHERY

Puma was eager to return to Little Doe and Trotter. Along with the usual gear, she loaded her sleeping platform and the cattail down mattress. Puma was finished with sleeping on hard surfaces. Cattails were her friend. As was her habit, she planned to place a decoy bed on the ground by the camp fire, just a simple precaution that could save her life.

As a gesture of respect Puma swept out the cave and replaced the emergency flint and pottery on the shelf. Someday she hoped to revisit the cave with Little Doe and the babe. The Lion's Cave was a place of memories.

On the first day of travel, Puma camped early, due to a thunderstorm. She found some shelter under an overhanging rock ledge. She built a fire and spread her wet clothing over a limb to dry. Before climbing the rope ladder to the sleeping platform, she placed a duffle bag close to the fire and covered it with a blanket after shaping it like a sleeping person. But for the cattail mattress, she would have had a miserable night. As the night wore on, the storm clouds dissipated and a few stars managed to pierce the layer of fog. The fur lining of her bedding was dry and warm.

As the first light of morning appeared, Puma, with a hunger for two, climbed down the rope. She dug in the coals of the fire and unearthed some live ones. Piles of brush quickly caught, and the more substantial wood was soon burning. How thankful she was for the gift of fire. She rotated her body close to the fire. She consumed a quick breakfast of jerky and dried berries.

She went to the horses and rubbed their necks. The clouds had cleared out, but there was a chill in the air. Puma kept out a blanket for her shoulders before packing the horses. Lifting the food box produced an abdominal spasm. She set the box down and reminded herself to be more careful. Puma rubbed her belly to relax the contraction. After resting a few minutes, she removed some of the heavy items before hefting the box up to the saddle tree. She removed the scalp from the bag and hung it to dry on the pack animal.

Puma munched on a pocket full of nuts as she rode away from the camp. The first stream she crossed she stopped to water the horses. Puma was yearning for Little Doe and urged Breeze into a faster pace. The babe was restless and moved often. With her hand on her abdomen, she sang a traditional Cherokee lullaby.

> *Great Magical Hawk, Tanuwa, bless this babe I carry,*
> *God of the Sun, Selu, bring our child your gifts,*
> *Kana 'Ti of the Spirit world, provide us protection.*

Puma sang all of the verses of the ancient lullaby as she eagerly looked forward to the arrival of Patrick's second child.

By mid-afternoon, Puma came upon a heavily traveled wagon trail where it crossed a stream. She tied the horses and climbed to an overlook. A dust cloud was visible above the treetops. Then she heard the crunching of wagon wheels. While Puma watched the travelers stopped and set up camp near the creek bed. Puma decided to frighten them for the purpose of sending them back east and away from Tsalagii territory. Resentment welled up in her breast over the invasion of her People's sovereign land. Her mind went back to the evening Chief Tecumseh had visited the Thunder People and revealed his plan for purifying the homeland.

Puma painted her face with charcoal and red clay before creeping through dense brush and grass to spy on the campers. Puma would use the opportunity to support Tecumseh's mission.

From her hiding place Puma observed an odd sight. Suddenly she was questioning her own sanity. Had she gone mad? She lay back on the ground, and after a few slow deep breaths rose and looked toward the mirage thinking that it would have disappeared. No, he was still there. She was not having a vision, but rather witnessing the ultimate betrayal.

Puma had to be sure, was the man really Patrick? The way he carried himself and even the voice matched. The clothing was different, but when he removed his hat to dry his brow with his scarf, there was no doubt! There in front of her in plain sight was Patrick. Puma knew that this was not a case of mistaken identity. Patrick is not dead! Her first impulse was to run and jump into his arms, but what happened next stunned her. A child ran toward Patrick holding up her hands, yelling, "Poppa, Poppa, hold me, I sawed a rat and it skered me." The man was the right height, and yes, broad shouldered. Red curly hair spilled from under his broad-brimmed hat. He turned toward Puma as he shouted to the two children. The voice was so familiar. She was looking at Patrick Larson. She fell back into the grass in a swoon. After a moment, she rose to see if he was still there. He was unfastening the oxen from the wagon. She could smell the animals. A white woman collected wood for a cooking fire. The children were carrying water buckets to the creek.

What she saw was obviously not a vision! Had Large Shadow been mistaken? Did Patrick survive the Battle of Horseshoe Bend? Could Patrick have had a white family all along? Puma rejected the possibility. Perhaps Patrick was told that we are dead? There must be an explanation. "I will confront him." She went back to the horses and dressed in the men's clothing. She poured water upon her hands and removed the paint from her face. She pulled on the boots and tugged the black hat tightly over her head and then stuffed her hair up under the brim. She strapped the two pistols around her waist. It was a tight fit. She decided to surprise Patrick by riding Breeze into his camp. She would sense the truth when she saw his reaction.

Puma set her jaw and kicked Breeze into a trot. Then, almost as soon as the mare jumped into action, she pulled Breeze up hard. Just ahead, riding into view from a stand of timber was a column of approaching riders. It appeared to be Andrew Jackson on his white stallion leading the Tennesseans. Puma's mouth dropped open with shock. Her mind went back to that wretched day in February when she had bid farewell to Patrick. Yes, as the column drew closer, Puma recognized the golden headed Jackson. The sight of him made her skin crawl. He represented everything that is evil to Puma. She fought the urge to take a shot at him. He must be coming to meet Patrick. Puma decided to wait until dark and spy out the truth.

Following the regiment of mounted troops were two mule drawn wagons and several shabbily dressed women walking behind. From the looks of them, they must be cooks and laundry maids. Puma decided to blend in with the group of servants to gather information. The contingent stopped for the evening. They too chose the camp site because of the water source.

That evening Puma posed as a scout and lounged by a bonfire of the camp followers. A talkative maid in her early teens sidled up to Puma, supposing her to be a boy.

The girl said, "What's yer name?"

Puma followed with, "What's yours?"

"Jenny, Jenny Bunch, Ya want somethin' to eat?"

"Sure, thanks, and you can call me Dan, just Dan, okay?"

Jenny scurried away and came back with a wooden bowl of steaming stew and a cup of something hot, maybe sassafras or chicory. "Dan, that's a nice name, hey, slow down, how long since you et? I can get you more when that's gone."

Then Puma said between bites of stew, "My horse came up lame— a few days— ago, and I got left behind. What's the latest plan for the militia?"

Jenny answered, "Goin back to Nashville and then on to Louisiana. British are asking for trouble, and Andy Jackson is plannin' on oblige'n. Don't let on who told ya, sposed to be a secret, but everbody knows."

Then Puma faked a yawn, and said, "Time to get some sleep. I'll see ya around and thanks for the food."

Puma found her way through the darkness back to where Breeze and the packhorse stood, tied to a bush deep in the shadows. There, she armed herself with bow and quiver. Luckily, there was no moon. Puma replaced her uncomfortable boots with her well-worn moccasins. As she searched for Patrick's camping place, she saw, silhouetted by light from the many fires, what looked like Andrew Jackson walking along the trail? It was a very dark night. Puma jumped behind a tree and then followed Jackson at a distance. He led her directly to Patrick's camp. Patrick was standing by his campfire with a woman, who was holding a small child. Two older children sat on a log by the fire. Jackson walked directly to Patrick's campfire and shook hands with him.

Puma tried to edge her way close enough to hear the conversation between Jackson and Patrick, but before she got within earshot, a cur dog looked in her direction and came from under Patrick's wagon and barked. Puma, caught off guard, sprinted away through the dark, almost tripping over a tree root growing above ground. When she looked back, she saw the dog gaining on her. She ran even faster, putting as much distance as possible between her and the camp. Then she dropped to one knee and drew down on the dog with her bow. The arrow flew true and struck the animal in the chest. Only one yelp, and then it fell to the ground, lifeless. She retrieved her arrow. Sometimes the arrows could be reused. She hid the dog under some brush.

She started inching her way back toward the camp where Patrick was visiting with Jackson. By then, the woman and children had gone into the wagon. Jackson's erect posture and manner signaled arrogance. He monopolized the conversation. Puma cupped her hands behind her ears. "— Louisiana? Did you say your name is Larson? What brings you west?"

Patrick answered, "We heard about land for the taking, decided to visit my brother, and try to stake out a farm. Where do you figure the best land might be Col. Jackson?"

Jackson replied, "Depends if you want to put up with Indians. Not any land left around here, been some gold discovered and the rush is on. White folks are taking land that belongs to the Cherokee and they are a mad bunch of Indians, hitting the warpath. Of course, if you are willing to keep going, Tennessee might be a good choice for farming."

In a conversational tone Jackson said, "I'm lookin' for more recruits to help repel the redcoats. Seems they plan on occupying New Orleans. You want to come along? We can't allow the British to control the mouth of the Mississippi. Most important fight since The Treaty of Paris was signed back in '83. After the Cherokee fought with the Militia against the Red Stick Creeks at Horseshoe Bend, they got their backs up in the air. Got hoppin' mad when I refused to let them keep the African slaves, and the items they looted on the way back through Georgia. Believe I'll take a refill on the coffee, — thanks."

Then Patrick said a very strange thing. "Sorry, I cain't help, I need to find my brother, Patrick. He's supposed to have a farm not far from here. He doesn't know I'm coming."

Jackson abruptly stood interrupting the conversation. He drained his coffee and said, "You know, I think I met him a while back. Best I recall he looked a lot like you: married to a Cherokee woman. Good luck on finding your brother. Early day tomorrow, so I better get back to my tent. Thanks for the coffee."

Puma leaned against the tree she had been standing behind and slid to the ground. Were her ears failing her? Had she heard correctly? Then she heard footsteps. She stretched her neck to see around the tree. Patrick was headed straight at her. Only a few feet away, he stopped to whistle and called out, "Buster, here boy, come on, Buster" Puma was holding her breath. Again, he called out, "Buster, here Buster, where are you, boy?" Then he whistled for the dog one last time.

Puma slowly stood and started backing away, but tripped over a tree root, the same one that had caught her foot when she ran from the dog. She sat down hard. The man shouted, "Who goes there?" Puma decided to reveal her presence before she was discovered. She said "Just me, heading back to my camp, tripped over this root."

The man asked, "Seen a dog out here: a brown and white spotted dog, bout this tall?"

Puma in her deepest boy voice replied, "No sir, ain't seen no dog." Then the man was able to make out the bow and quiver, "You an Indian?"

"Half, Mom was a Seminole."

Then Rory walked over to Puma and said, "Here, let me help you up. What's yer name, boy?

"Dan, Dan River."

"Well, Dan, you need to be more careful coming up on folks in the dark. Good way to get shot."

"Sir, what is your name, ah, in case I find your dog?" The man reached out his hand and said, "I'm Rory, Rory Larson." Puma felt her right hand being gripped in his massive hand. "Picked up and moved west to find my brother."

"How do, Mr. Larson."

"Here, here, none of that Mr. Larson just call me Rory. Come on over and set a spell. I got a good fire go'in. Think I'll stay up a while longer and see if my dog comes back. Mighty fine hunt'n dog, rat terrier: must be on the trail of some critter." His voice, its tone, inflection was so like Patrick's it gave Puma chills.

Then Puma asked, "You got any coffee?"

Rory said, "Sure do. Come on and have a seat, it's still hot." Silently, the two of them walked back to the fire. Puma sat upon the log, and Rory handed her a cup of coffee. "Careful, it's hot." Puma drew a deep breath and cupped the tin cup with both hands. Her hands had turned to ice and the warmth helped to settle her nerves.

"What did you say is your brother's name?"

"Patrick Larson: we are twins, look just alike. Most folks cain't tell us apart."

Now Puma understood. She suddenly felt dizzy. The coffee slipped from her hands and spilled on her moccasins. Puma jumped up and kicked the moccasins from her feet. The coffee had burned her feet but not enough to cause blisters. Puma moaned and placed her face in her hands. Rory turned around, and said, "What's wrong, Boy?"

Puma removed her hat and allowed her hair to fall into place around her head. Her bobbed hair had grown, and she was looking more like a female. Then she removed the bulky shirt. Rory looked at her swollen breasts and belly. "You are a woman, why didn't you say so?"

Puma said, "Yes, a woman with child. Rory, I'm so sorry, but I killed your dog. He charged me while I spied on you and Andrew Jackson."

"Wait, you killed my dog, but why?" Then Puma said, "You better have a seat to hear the rest of what I have to tell you."

By this time Rory's wife was climbing out of the wagon. She said, "The kids are asleep, Rory who is this?" Puma stood, and said, I am Puma-Woman, formerly known as Wathena, — Larson. Then she looked at Rory and said, "I am your brother's wife."

The woman walked to Rory and put her arm around his waist. They both stood staring at Puma. Then Rory asked, "Where is Patrick?"

Puma, struggling to control her emotions, said in a very low voice, "Dead."

"What, did you say he's—Dead?"

Puma cleared her throat and made eye contact with Rory, "Andrew Jackson and the Tennessee Militia rode up to the farm and stopped to visit with Patrick. Patrick invited them to camp for the night. Jackson used his well-honed powers of persuasion and recruited

Patrick to join the Militia." Puma's words flowed staccato-like as she recounted the circumstances surrounding Patrick's death.

Rory sat down hard on the log with a look of utter shock on his face. "It's okay Puma, I have heard enough." Then he asked, "Where is his daughter? In his last letter he said he has a little girl."

Puma answered, "Yes, her name Little Doe. She is staying with my cousin. I am on the way back to her, before this baby." Puma had placed her hand on her abdomen.

Rory's wife stepped over to Puma's side and sat upon the log. "I am Elizabeth, but call me Beth." Then Beth put her arms around Puma and hugged her while she asked, "How long 'til time for the baby?"

Rory interrupted and asked, "Is that Patrick's baby?" Puma did not like the question. She stood from her seat and was about to leave when Rory immediately apologized. "Puma, I should not have asked, forgive me."

Then Puma sat back down and answered. "Patrick killed before he knew about this child." Her eyes filled with tears, as she said, "He would be happy—," Her voice trailed off, creating an awkward silence. Then Puma looked at Beth and said, "I think the baby is due in about six weeks, maybe sooner."

Rory and Beth sat down on each side of Puma. Beth placed an arm around Puma and took her hand in her own. Rory stepped to the wagon and brought back a blanket and placed it around Puma's shoulders.

Rory asked, "Where is your farm? Did you say it was stolen from you? What is this world coming to?"

After a short pause Puma said, "I will not try to tell you everything right now. The whites at Jackson's Trading Post were plotting to steal the farm from us while Patrick was gone to fight in Alabama. Thousands of White people have been pouring into the area, and they all want tillable land. The whites of the elite class conspired to pass laws against Indians owning land. Then they outlawed Indians bringing suit against white people. Add to that finding gold on the property and Patrick admitting to educating the two black children of slaves, our fate was sealed." Puma pulled the lion shaped gold nougat necklace from under her tunic.

"Another thing, Patrick made the mistake of showing Oscar Jackson the nougat. Patrick thought nothing of answering Jackson's questions. He always assumed the best of people. He purchased this gold chain from him. There had been a few other discoveries of gold in the area. That's about the time the whites all went crazy with *gold fever*. When word arrived that Patrick was dead, they came to our farm to kill Little Doe and I. We were gone into the forest to grieve, so they killed our two black families and scalped bed-ridden Large Shadow, who had been wounded in battle in Alabama. The Jackson family that owns the trading post is related to Andrew Jackson. Before Large Shadow died, he managed to drag himself to the trail to intercept me. Large Shadow warned, 'There is a team of men lying in wait for you at the farm. Run and hide, save yourselves.' Little Doe and I had to flea in the dead of night. They trailed us for hours, but we were able to hide in a cave. Later, when I went to spy on the farm, there was a white family living in our house, using our belongings and eating our food."

Then Beth said, "Enough for tonight, you need to rest. Can I get you something to eat? Rory, why don't you go and get Puma's gear. We will fix you a bed here under the wagon." Then Puma stood and said, "No, I will go alone. But I will come back here and sleep beneath your wagon." Puma squeezed Rory's hand and hugged Beth, "I'm so glad we crossed paths." Puma donned the hat and large shirt she had placed on the log. Characteristic for one of the people, she walked into the darkness without another word.

While Puma was gone, Rory cleared the area under the wagon of rocks and smoothed the dirt. Then he spread a piece of canvas to protect Puma's bedroll from the damp ground and collapsed onto the log. His face was distorted, and his breathing was shallow and quick. When Beth placed her arm around his slumped form and touched his hand, it was ice cold. With tears cascading down her cheeks, she whispered, "Dear, dear Rory, I am so sorry. I know how you loved Patrick. She caressed his bent back as she murmured, I loved him too." Rory wiped his face on his sleeve and said with a husky voice, "I don't know how I can go on without him. Part of me is dead. Beth, it's gonna take some time to get my mind around this."

Just then one of the children called out, "Mommy, where are you?"

Beth walked to the back of the wagon and said, "I'm coming soon, go on back to sleep."

Rory said, "Beth, I would never get through this without you and the children. Go on to bed, I want to wait up for – ah,— Puma. I need to think."

There was a struggle going on inside of Rory. His mind was rebelling, refusing to believe that Patrick was really dead. Half of Rory's identity was ripped from him. Since before they were born, he and Patrick had always been like two parts of the same person. Being separated for the past nine years had become intolerable for Rory. From the letters he had received from Patrick, he had felt the same. *If only I had come sooner, maybe he would be alive. Life, going forward, — how—?* Rory was suddenly racked with sobs, great heaving explosions of grief. Beth joined him.

Puma was in a quandary about what to do about Andrew Jackson. Should she wait or take advantage of the opportunity to avenge Patrick? *I have vowed to take revenge, and I must keep that vow. Another opportunity may never come. I, the Puma-Woman must seize the opportunity and strike tonight.*

Darkness provided cover as Puma slipped among the officer's tents until she found the largest one. It must be the one, since it was the only tent with a guard standing in front. The uniformed soldier stood at the doorway with a musket over his shoulder. Puma was not expecting a guard to be present. She decided to create a distraction that would pull the sentry away long enough to gain entry by slitting the backside of the canvas from the bottom. She would wait for things to settle down before slipping under the back of the tent. Puma listened outside and could hear Jackson snoring. *How easily he sleeps, a man without regard for others.* Puma suddenly realized that she had hit upon the reason he could rest. He was suffering from a heart turned to stone.

It was a sickness of the soul, a hardened heart according to the Bible, and in medical terminology such a person is called a sociopath.

She silently removed two tent stakes from the soft ground. Then she used her knife to slit the canvas, an inch at a time, waiting after each cut, to see if the sleeping man would be awakened. The soft snoring continued.

Puma withdrew from the tent and went to create a diversion. She located an unoccupied tent apart from the others and set it on fire and hurried back to Jackson's tent. The guard heard the crackle of the fire first and ran to help with the bucket brigade. Puma lay on her back to squirm under the split canvas, feet first. Her pregnancy was too advanced to crawl on her stomach. Jackson was asleep on a cot facing toward the side wall. Puma slowly removed her knife from its scabbard.

Raising the knife, Puma drew a deep breath, and tensed her muscles. Jackson suddenly snorted and shifted his position. Puma drew back behind a line of hanging clothes. She searched for something to hold over the man's face while she cut his jugular. There was an extra blanket under his cot. The blanket would smother any sound he might make. Then, there was a stir outside the tent, as a group of soldiers rushed to fight the fire. Suddenly wide-awake, Jackson threw back the covers and groaned as he prepared to rise from the cot. Puma's heart pounded as she hid behind the clothing. He grunted as he pulled on his boots. Puma slowly dropped to her knees and prepared to exit the tent. Jackson stood and walked to the door of the tent. Light from lanterns backlit his profile. He looked heavier and shorter. There was some excited mumbling, and then she heard him swear and say, "I can't help you there, you need to see Andy Jackson. Here, I will take you to him." The man reached back into the tent and removed a long coat from a chair and left. Puma released a sigh and was grateful that she had not killed the wrong person. As soon as it was quiet outside, she scooted, feet first thru the slit. Puma's connection to the spirit world led her to conclude that perhaps the Great Spirit had intervened in her quest for justice. For now, Puma decided that it would be unwise to pursue Andrew Jackson further.

Trail weary, and emotionally spent, Puma led the two horses to the Larson camp and prepared to unload them before staking them out. The baby in Puma's belly was moving more than usual. She tried to calm herself by taking some deep breaths. Suddenly Rory was standing beside her and insisted on unloading the heavy box and bags. He pushed them under the wagon.

Then he asked, "Is there anything you need?"

Puma whispered, "No, just rest. Thank you for the help." After settling down in her blankets under the wagon, her mind was uneasy. She was thankful that the identity of the man in the tent was discovered in time. Too confused and at the point of exhaustion, Puma knew that she must find a time to commune with the Great Spirit and burn some of her sacred tobacco perhaps on the morrow. Then her thoughts went to Little Doe, how she needed to see her. She could feel her spirit calling. And seeing Rory only made Puma yearn for Patrick the more. Then she wondered why Patrick had never mentioned that he was a twin. She thought, he was saving it for a surprise.

In her lifetime, Puma had only seen one or two sets of identical twins, and none were as similar as Patrick and Rory. In spite of her fatigue, Puma couldn't find a comfortable position. The cattail mattress was rolled up and bundled in with her other gear. As quietly as possible, she untied the bundle and removed the mattress. When she almost had the bed ready to crawl back into, she realized that Rory was out of the Wagon with a gun in his hand. She looked at him and signaled that she was fine but was trying to get more comfortable. He nodded and silently slipped back into the wagon. The mattress made a big difference, and she was soon sleeping.

Little Doe's laughter woke Puma. She abruptly sat up and bumped her head on the wagon axel. She lay back down and rubbed the knot on her forehead. It took a moment to recall exactly where she was. She realized that the laughter belonged to Rory and Beth's children. Puma crawled from under the wagon and began rolling her bedding. The three children gathered around her, full of curiosity. Puma smiled and said, "Hello and good morning." Beth walked over to where Puma knelt on the ground. "Good morning, Puma. I am sorry that the children woke you. I hope you rested enough. Breakfast is almost ready." Puma smiled and said, "Um, sure smells good." Puma walked back to the fire with Beth. Then Beth, flashing a proud smile introduced Puma to the three children. Beth retrieved her spatula and stirred the skillet of eggs and said, "This is our eldest, Heath, he is ten. And this is Rosemary, she is seven, next month, and the baby is our little Annie, three years old this month." Puma reached over and tickled Annie's chubby chin. The child exploded with giggles, showing her baby teeth and beautiful blue eyes. Puma took note that all three of the children had Patrick and Rory's curly red hair and blue eyes. The middle child, Rosemary was just about the size of Little Doe. Puma, with a sigh, visualized the two of them playing together.

When Rory dropped an armload of firewood upon the pile, Puma walked up to him and said, "Rory, how are you doing?"

Rory nodded his head back and forth and said, "Puma, I am struggling to keep from falling apart. What about you, were you able to sleep?"

Puma answered, "It took a while to settle my mind, yesterday was a day I'll never forget. You do understand that I thought you were Patrick. Betrayal like that can actually destroy a person. I felt my heart being ripped from my body." Puma hugged Rory and smoothed his hair. Rory patted her stomach and said, "Are you ready to have some breakfast?"

"Oh yes, we are very hungry. Rory, I am so glad I found you and Beth and the children."

"I'm glad too, I want to hear everything you can tell me about Patrick's years on the frontier, it sure sounds like he found the adventure he craved.

Beth said, "Have a seat on our log, and I will bring you my special breakfast of ham, eggs, biscuits, and gravy. Bought the eggs and ham just yesterday from a farm we came across, you want water or coffee?"

"I would like some of each, please. Can I help you?"

"No, you stay seated, it's no trouble."

While Puma devoured the plate of food, Rosemary and Heath sat on each side watching all big eyed. Rosemary squinted her eyes and asked, "Are you an Indian?

Beth spoke up and said, "Okay, let your Aunt Puma enjoy her meal. Yes, she is a Cherokee. Isn't she beautiful?"

The children nodded their heads and repeated the word, "Beautiful."

Beth continued, "And she is very nice, you will see. She has a little girl about your age Rosemary."

Puma corrected Beth by saying, "I am related to the Cherokee, but I am actually Tsalagii of the Thunder Clan. Our customs are different, but our language is mostly the same."

Puma acknowledged the children's interest by interacting with them. She swallowed the food in her mouth and said, "Yes, Little Doe is your cousin."

Rosemary asked, "Do you mean like a deer?" Beth said, "Shush, let Puma finish eating." After a short pause Rosemary asked Puma, "How'd you learn to talk English so good?"

Puma smiled and said, "I was born with special skills bestowed by the Great Spirit, Kanati. I was born with a gift, or you could call it a special kind of hearing that helps me to imitate animal sounds, bird calls, and even foreign languages. And remember that I had years to master English as your Uncle Patrick's wife. I learned to imitate English very quickly. This is my angry jaybird, — —, and now a crow, - - - see if you recognize this one, — — —;" Rosemary excitedly shouted, "that's an owl." Next Puma gave her best version of a wolf howling at the moon. Rosemary was somewhat frightened by the sound and moved closer to her mother. Beth said, "Puma, you are amazing, what a talent." Puma was silent for a thoughtful moment and then answered, "It is a gift that I treasure."

After finishing the meal, Puma walked into the woods north of the wagon trail. She bathed in the stream and changed into a spare doeskin tunic and leggings. She needed to think. She was eager to get back to the Otter Clan, and reunite with Little Doe and Trotter. A part of her wanted to spend time with Rory and Beth, but she had vowed to revert to the ancient ways of the fathers and shun all whites. She mused that the spirit of spirits frequently changed her plans. A thought formed in Puma's mind, and she seated herself under a massive oak. Partly reclining on a bed of dried leaves and grass, Puma drafted a plan that excited her. "What if Rory claims our farm land? Oscar Jackson is an invalid or possibly dead and can't dispute Rory and Beth's claim." Puma decided to discuss her plan with them. It would be their decision.

Puma walked back to the wagon and sat down on the log. Rory and Heath had gone after more firewood. The girls were picking flowers in a grassy area down by the stream. Beth was heating a big pot of water and asked, "Puma, I'm doin' some wash this mornin' you have anything to be washed?" Puma was lost in thought and failed to hear the question. Beth stopped her work and went to place a hand on Puma's shoulder. "Puma, are you alright?"

"Sorry, Beth, did you say something"?

"Would you like me to wash some of your clothes?"

"Oh, thank you, but not now."

Beth asked, "Puma, your ability with the English language is so unexpected, you truly have no accent."

Puma nodded and said, "Patrick was a good teacher, but I do slip back into my halted dialect when I am stressed." Puma made the sound of a wren and smiled.

"Puma, you are more than amazing." To finish the demonstration, Puma drew a deep breath and made the sound of a screaming puma followed by some realistic and frightening bear growls. Puma's wrinkled face and wide-open mouth took on the look of a lion, and her hands raked at the air. Even Beth was frightened and stepped back. Annie started to cry, and Beth held her on her shoulder until she calmed down. Puma apologized and thought to herself, white people, what scaredy cats. Several dogs from the nearby camps started to bark. A neighboring camper came running with his musket, ready to defend against a lion attack. Beth was dumbfounded and just stared at Puma. Beth understood what an appropriate name Puma-Woman happened to be.

Puma said "I didn't mean to frighten you. Shortly after Patrick was killed a great lioness chose my spirit to inhabit, and I changed my name to Puma-Woman. The lion is my medicine animal, and I take my strength, both physical and spiritual from the great cat. My spirit speaks to the unseen spirits. It is all too hard for white people to accept."

Rory and Heath walked back into camp, dragging several large dead limbs. Heath was talking to Rory, "—oh come-on, Dad, let me try my luck, looks like the perfect spot, bet there's some big ones in the deep part? I been hungry for catfish. I found where a beaver dammed the creek just a little ways downstream."

Rory said, "Heath, I thought I told you to stay close by. Don't be wondering off by yourself, it's not safe."

Beth interrupted. "I need these buckets filled, Heath, Rose."

Rory looked at Puma and recognized that she wanted to speak with him. Rory looked at Heath and said, "Maybe later this evening. Fish bite better in the evening." Rory said to Puma, "Why don't we take a walk." Puma rose from the log and started down the rutted wagon trail beside Rory. Heath and Rose swinging the two wooden buckets, headed to the stream.

Puma said, "Rory, during the night an idea came to me. What if you and Beth claim the farm? The whites will have no legal basis to deny Patrick's rightful heir. The land was a wedding gift from my clan. You couldn't find any better farmland. Rich soil, shallow water table, borders a year-round stream. I visited the cabin a few days ago and found a family living there."

Rory looked at Puma with shock and said, "You want to give the farm to us, but why?"

Puma replied, "Georgia passed a law. It is not legal for me to own land, but you can. I want you to have it. I will take you there before I continue on my trip. You and Beth can decide if you want to settle there."

Rory said, "Yes, take us there, but it should be yours."

Then Puma spit a reply from between clinched teeth, "The whites around here would never allow me to own the land. They want to drive my people from the area. They hate us. Savages they call us. Treat us like animals!" Once she started with the narrative it was as if a dam had burst. "How did Jackson know where our farm was located? Why did he single out Patrick? Though we mentioned nothing about the golden necklace, he asked to see it. Why did he ask to see the place it was found? The answer to these questions is easy to figure, Oscar Jackson had included him in his conspiracy to steal our land. It is likely that Oscar has powerful friends in the Georgia State Government and supported laws to prevent Indians from owning land or bringing law suits against White people. If Patrick maybe returned from Alabama, he be jailed for teaching the two black children to read and write. Oscar Jackson using inside connections, he greedy man. As long as Jackson make paper or was on record he first white man filing homestead paper on our farm he own it. Uncle say Oscar Jackson and men chase us in the night. Kill me and Little Doe. I say, no what I say, Patrick ball of musket in back at fight, of Horseshoe Bend? My uncle witness crime. Oh, I have the events all out of order, — sorry, when I am this upset my English not good, forget to say right words. I speak no more of killing." Puma retreated into the woods to regain equilibrium.

Later that afternoon Puma asked Heath if she could go fishing with him. Heath's mouth opened, and his eyes sparkled. The idea of fishing with a real Indian brought a rush of words, "Wow, with me, sure, bet you Injuns knows how to fish." Rose wanted to go, and Puma gave her a hug and said, "Only if your parents agree."

After Puma and the two oldest children left for the creek, Beth and Rory were able to discuss Patrick's farm. They concluded that there was no harm in seeing the land. Rory's eyes became glassy, and he told Beth that he wanted to construct some kind of a memorial to Patrick somewhere on the property.

On the way to the fishing hole, Puma and the two children came upon a cottontail. She quickly strung her bow and shot the rabbit. Heath sang out, "Good shot, got'em right through the middle." He ran to where the rabbit lay on its side, kicking but didn't touch it. He bent over the animal with a look of fascination. After some coaxing Puma convinced Heath to pick the rabbit up by the hind feet and carry it to the creek. Rose refused to even look at the poor animal. There was a tear running down her cheek. When they arrived at the creek, Puma cut open the rabbit's belly and removed the entrails. As she worked, she said, "Good fish bait, here."

Heath asked Puma, "Reckon you could teach me to shoot that bow?" Puma said, "Not now, but maybe some other time." Rose was still upset over the rabbit and turned her head while Puma cleaned it out. Puma didn't think it was wise for a frontier child to be so squeamish. She took time to explain, "We never kill unless there is a need. Rose, you are right to love wildlife, every animal is precious." Puma hugged Rose and flicked away a tear.

Puma demonstrated how to thank the Great Spirit for the gift of the rabbit. She raised her hands heavenward and motioned for the children to do the same. As she lifted her face toward the heavens she sang in a haunting alto key,

"Yah-Hey-Yah-Hey-Yah-Hey-Yah-O
Yah-Hey-Yah-Hey-Yah-O
Yah-Hey-Yah-Hey-Yah-Hey-Yah
Hey-O Yah-Hey-Yah-Hey-Yah-O"

In total awe Rose whispered, "You are a very good singer!" Rose staired at Puma as though she wanted to memorize her image and then asked, "Is the Great Spirit the same as God?"

Puma put her arm around the child and said, "That is a question for your parents not me." Then, Puma clapped her hands together and shouted, "Let's go fishing!"

By the time they were ready to put hooks in the water, it was after 4:30 PM, perfect timing. Puma demonstrated how to cast a fishing line from the bank and told the children to let the bait sink to the creek bottom. She tossed several bits of rabbit entrails into the water to attract fish. As she rinsed her hands in the stream, a large turtle appeared and made a meal on a choice piece of rabbit gut.

Heath asked Puma, "Do you know if that is a eat-a-bull turtle? I heard of eating turtle soup before."

Puma said, "Yes, this little turtle is edible but for my Tsalagii clan, we protect the turtle. We would only eat him if there is no other food available, killing a turtle would anger the small people that roam the forest. My clan has a special kinship with turtles, and the forest is kind by giving us other food."

Heath's line got the first bite, but he jerked too hard and pulled out a bare hook. Puma demonstrated how to set the hook. Rose squealed, "I have one! I have one! She pulled so hard on her line that the small channel cat landed on the sand fifteen feet behind where she stood. Rose dropped her pole and ran to where the fish was flopping on the ground. She stood bent over with her mouth open and pranced with excitement, taking care not get to close to the flailing fish. Puma said it was okay to be afraid of a catfish, "They have sharp fins with poison in the tip. It really hurts when they stick you." Puma walked over and picked up the small fish. "This is the safe way to hold a catfish." She said and placed her thumb into the mouth and forefinger through a gill. Then she said, "I will show you how to clean the fish." Puma slit the belly of the fish and used her thumb to rake out the intestines. "The guts give us more bait."

Rose said, "Heath, You want me to help you catch a fish?"

Heath frowned and rolled his eyes. "You catch one fish, and suddenly you're the expert." Heath caught the next fish, a channel cat, larger than Rose's fish.

Heath dangled the flopping fish in front of Rose, a little too closely, and she screamed, "Stop it, I'm telling on you Heath!" The squabbling children got on Puma's nerves, and she shushed them. Puma handed Heath her knife, and the boy awkwardly cut open the fish. Then Puma told Heath to wash the two catfish in the creek water. The fish were threaded onto a vine and placed in the water.

As the three of them sat on the sandy bank, Heath asked, "Why are you named after a lion?"

"I chose the name when I realized that the mountain lion or puma is my medicine animal. The lion is sometimes called the Stealthy One. Another name is Klandagi, a word that means Lord of the Forest. The great Shawnee Chieftain Tecumseh is so named because at the moment of his birth a falling star streaked across the sky. The word Tecumseh means Panther-Across-the-Sky. My puma imparts wisdom and gives me strength. Studying the puma's ways helps me survive in the wilderness." Heath and Rose looked at each other with raised eyebrows and then stared at Puma with wide-eyed admiration.

Puma and the two children returned to camp with the two catfish and the skinned rabbit. Puma started to prepare the meat for cooking on sticks held over the fire. Beth asked if she would rather have a frying pan. "Oh, sure, we cook your way." Puma pulled the skin off the catfish and cut up the rabbit. She breaded the meat and fried it in a big iron skillet. As she worked, Puma told Beth and Rory, "Heath and Rose did a great job, they are natural fishermen." Then Rose started tugging on

Rory's sleeve, and said, "Guess how Puma got her name? She told us." Rory bent down and interrupted Rose, "Tell me later."

Puma was comfortable sharing the meal with her newly discovered family, and it was a good feeling. Later, the conversation around the fire was spirited, sometimes speaking over each other. Rose insisted on singing a song for Puma. Heath chattered non-stop about his desire to learn how to shoot a bow. When bedtime came, the children resisted, but Beth was firm. "We will be traveling tomorrow, and you need to be rested."

Once the children were bedded down in the wagon, Rory said, "Puma, Beth and I want to go to the farm tomorrow. How long will it take to get there?"

Puma looked at the wagon and mules, and said, "Most of a day. It's about ten miles from here."

Rory said, "We should get an early start." Then he looked at Puma's expression and said, "I'm sorry Puma for your tragedy, we can be a comfort to each other." Rory walked over and placed his arm about Puma's shoulders.

Puma said, "If that family is still living in my house, I will make them move out." Rory and Beth flashed each other a look of concern. There was no mistaking the threat in Puma's words. Rory decided to keep open the option to continue westward if things got too dangerous.

The Larson family awoke to a clear autumn morning. The trees would be turning any day. Tuffs of white clouds drifted across the pink sky. The road to the farm was rutted and rocky, and Rory had to stop and replace a shattered wheel spoke. Late in the afternoon Puma decided to ride ahead. She loped Breeze the rest of the way to the farm. Puma was dressed in the men's clothing and boots. Her identity was well concealed under the felt hat. On the road, she met a rider that looked like the man she saw through the window of the farm house a few days before. He was headed in the opposite direction, and they exchanged greetings in passing.

Puma tied breeze in a hidden shady spot. She approached the farm on foot and opened the gate. Two noisy hounds met Puma just inside the gate. She was surprised at how fast they had been able to replace their dogs. The dogs complicated her plans. Puma spoke to them, and they began wagging their tails. The blond pregnant woman waddled on to the porch of the cabin and asked, "Who might you be?"

Puma with an authoritative tone said, "Hello, I am Mrs. Larson, the owner of this farm."

The woman's mouth dropped open. Then she placed one hand on her hip and said, "I reckon not, me and my husband owns this place. We bought it a while back. Our name is Becker."

Puma asked, "Can you send your husband out here?"

"Ain't here, gone to the Tradin' Post," said the Becker woman.

Puma replied, "Who sold you the place?"

"Oscar Jackson at the Tradin' Post showed us papers and all."

"Sorry, Oscar Jackson never owned this farm. You need to start packing your things." Then Puma removed her hat and said, "I am the wife of Patrick Larson. This is my property. The rest of my family will be here soon. You can call me Puma and your name is?"

"Rona Becker." Suddenly the woman spun sideways and grabbed the muzzle loader propped in the open doorway, but Puma managed to get the drop on her with her fully drawn bow. Rona replaced the gun and stood with a horrified look on her face.

Then Puma said, "Maybe you can get your money back from Jackson and find some other place to settle."

Rona threw up her hands and said, "Ole Man Jackson is dead, some say he killed hiz-sef after being attacked and almost killed. His son says he don't know who almost kilt the old man. Now Miz Puma, we're broke and nowhere to go. And how do I know you're not lying?"

Puma made eye contact with Rona and said, "I do not lie! I do not steal other folks land, and I protect what is mine. Are you sure Oscar Jackson is dead? I heard he was in bad shape but alive." Suddenly Rona paled and had to sit upon a tree stump standing on the porch. She placed her hand on her abdomen and winced in pain.

"Are you in labor Rona?" When she stood her water broke. She looked down at the puddle of water around her feet and almost fainted. Puma thought, oh no, not now and hurried to help Rona to her bed in the house. The poor woman was doubled over with intense pain. "Is there someone around here to help you?" Puma asked.

"No, my kids are gone to help harvest a neighbor's corn crop, I'm here alone. They will be spending the night with the neighbor."

Puma asked, "How strong are your pains?"

"They's awful strong, oh, can you help me, it feels like the baby is coming."

Puma was worried that Rory might take a wrong turn and bypass the farm. "I need to be gone for a few minutes, but I will come back and help you." Rona started begging for Puma not to leave.

Puma ignored Rona and jogged back to where Breeze was tied. After watching Rona go into labor, Puma was having flash backs to her own birthing experience. Just that morning Puma had seen some pink staining and knew her own labor could be soon. She mounted Breeze and as an afterthought returned to the cabin for the gun. Puma rode the mare all the way to the front door and reached inside and snatched the long gun without dismounting. She unloaded the weapon and hid it in a stack of firewood.

Puma clicked her tongue and gave the filly a slack rein. Breeze came from a line of smooth gaited horses that would come to be called 'Tennessee Walkers.' The filly quickly covered the distance back to where Rory and Beth were bouncing along on the rutted road. She rode up to Rory and shouted, "I will mark the turn off to the farm by tying Breeze to the gate post. I must hurry. Keep to your left at the fork and hurry if you can. Puma pulled Breeze around sharply and tapped her sides with her heels. Breeze whinnied and pawed the air as she reared on her two hind legs. Puma removed her hat and used it to whip her into a full run. Breeze' gate was even more level and smooth at a full run. When Puma got back to Rona, she was writhing from late-stage labor. Puma's empathetic response to the woman was what one would expect from the daughter of a renowned healer. Puma got busy preparing Rona for delivery.

Puma asked, "Did you think you could deliver the baby without help?"

Rona said, "I don't know, maybe. I didn't think it was time yet."

Puma addressed Rona, "Are you ready to push?"

Rona moaned, "Yes!" Her face turned pale, and she turned her head to the side and vomited. Puma wiped Rona's face with a towel and covered the mess with a second towel. Puma looked around and found several blankets and pillows and stuffed them behind Rona's back. She gave her something to bite down upon and checked under the sheet. Puma said, "Pull back on your bent legs while you are pushing." Puma looked around and saw a liquor crock setting on the table. She removed the cork with her teeth and poured the whiskey over her hands. According to the Moravian Missionaries washing one's hands in whiskey prevented infection.

Puma placed a folded flannel bed sheet next to Rona for swaddling the baby. A shriek of pain announced that the head was crowning. After a strong contraction Puma reminded Rona, "Remember to pull back on your legs and push the baby out with each contraction. You are almost done, push hard, push, push!" After a long contraction the head was born. Puma said, "Deep breath and push." Once the baby's shoulders were guided out one at a time it was quickly shot forth into Puma's waiting hands. The boy took a breath and loudly protested his new environment.

The two women looked at each other and smiled. Puma began removing the waxy coating from the baby with the flannel sheeting. Then she tore a strip from the edge of the blanket to use for tying off the umbilical cord. She looked at Rona, her color was better, but she looked exhausted. Puma said, "Do you feel like holding your son?" Before answering, Rona was seized with a contraction and expelled the placenta. Puma wondered if Rona's blood loss was normal. She realized that she needed to know more about the birthing process and she—.

The dogs started raising a ruckus outside and before Puma had finished deciding what she should do next, Beth walked into the bedroom. Puma looked at her with surprise, and said, "How did you get here so fast?"

Beth smiled and said, "Like you, by putting my heel into the side of my horse." Beth walked over to Rona, and said, "Hello, I am Beth. Puma, how can I help you?"

Puma said, "He is a fine big boy, why don't you look him over."

Beth walked over to Rona and took the baby into her arms. "What a fine boy you have." Beth unwrapped the baby and looked him over. He turned his face toward Beth. "Hungry, are you?" Beth chuckled at the squirming baby and handed him back to his mother. "Go ahead and offer him your breast. I will bring you a glass of water."

Rona said, "Thanks, I'm awful thirsty, water's in that bucket by the fireplace."

Beth asked Puma, "Is this the same woman you saw that night?"

Puma nodded and motioned for Beth to step out of earshot. Then Puma whispered, "I told her that they will have to leave this property. Better keep a close eye on her and watch for her husband's return. When he gets back, we can try to reason with him, but there might be a fight."

Puma heard the wagon stop in front of the cabin. The hounds were loud and threatening. At the entrance she saw Rory climbing down from the wagon seat. He kicked at the dogs and sent them scurrying. Puma said, "Rory, we need to talk."

Rory said, "Okay." They walked to a shady spot far enough for privacy.

"Rory, you need to take Beth and the children and hide the wagon near the river in dense brush. Then come back here, and we will wait for Becker to return. Oh yes, the horseman that we saw on the road was Becker, and he is not going to like what we have to say. His wife thinks he will be back about dark."

Rory took a deep breath and said, "I'll be hiding out here in the brush waiting for the fellar to return. Is the woman armed?"

"Yes, she was, I unloaded and hid her flintlock. I'll bring it to you, didn't find any other guns. Tell Beth not to light a camp fire until we tell her it is okay."

Puma checked her own weapons and stayed inside with Rona. She hid her pistol under the big shirt. Nothing went as planned. As soon as Becker rode through the gate, the hounds alerted him to Rory's presence. When they ran to where Rory was hiding, Becker pulled his pistol and walked toward where Rory waited. Rory stepped into the open, and he and Becker stood staring at each with their hands on their side arm.

Becker called out, "Rona, I'm back, you okay?"

Rona screamed, "They's robbers! Shoot'em before they kill us." While Becker was distracted with what Rona was squealing incoherently, not at all sure what she was saying, Rory got the jump on him.

Rory spoke up, "Put your hands up and no sudden movements! We mean you no harm."

Becker lowered his gun a little and said, "Speak yore piece Mr."

Rory holstered his pistol and spoke with a slow calm voice. "My friend just helped your wife deliver her baby."

Becker said, "I need to see my wife." Becker backed to the front door obviously forgetting that "the friend" was not in sight.

As soon as he entered cabin, he felt the barrel of a gun against his neck. Puma whispered, "Drop the gun and you get to live long enough to see your son." Becker stiffened and dropped the pistol. Puma kicked it toward Rory, and he placed it in his waist band. The defanged Becker walked to Rona's bed. "You okay Rona? Baby looks good."

Rona nodded in the affirmative and said, "This woman helped me with the baby. Hon, she said that we have to leave. She claims this farm belongs to her. Oscar Jackson is dead, oh my, what we gonna do?"

Becker looked at Puma and asked, "Who are you?"

Puma said, "It might be in your best interest to say thank you for helping with the baby before you start asking me questions."

She paused, and Becker stammered, "Ya, thanky ma'am, good of you."

Then Puma said, "My name is Larson. My husband was Patrick Larson. He was killed fighting with Andrew Jackson at Horseshoe Bend. His brother and I are here to reclaim this farm."

Becker paced back and forth, running his hands through his greasy hair over and over. Behind Becker Puma could see Rory, standing in the doorway. Then Becker said, "But I don't understand? Oscar said this farm belonged to Injuns and that he had legally claimed the property. He showed me a deed. He was going to sign it over to us as soon as we finished paying off the price."

Puma stood and without lowering her gun, searched Becker for weapons. She found a scabbard and knife around his waist and pitched them to Rory. Then she said, "Have a seat on that stool." Becker backed to the stool and sat down. Then Rory entered the cabin and tied Becker's hands behind his back and then bound his feet.

Becker was obviously bewildered. Rory said, "Puma, tell them what happened. They have a right to know."

Puma sat upon a second stool and said, "I am the Indian—" The baby started to cry, so Puma took the baby from Rona placed him over her shoulder and began patting his back. Rona didn't object.

Puma's voice was forlorn, and her expression was so loaded with emotion that the Becker couple was taken aback. "About nine years ago, my tribe rescued Patrick Larson from a bear attack. He was hurt bad, and it took long time get well. He joins my clan; we became close and marry. The Thunder People give this land for wedding gift. Relatives help clear the land and build this cabin and out buildings. After year we get daughter. We worked hard on this place. The bear rug that hung above the fireplace was the bear that attacked my husband and almost killed him. The rack of antlers was from the deer he killed for our wedding feast. I take back this farm, all is mine. You move, find other place."

Becker shook his head in confusion and said, "But why did Jackson take your land?"

Puma said, "He hear about gold in creek. He was mad that Patrick taught two Negro children to read and write. We not know law about slave children. When word of Patrick's death reached Jackson, about the same time that I found out, men come to kill me and little girl. They follow us, but we get away."

Rory spoke up, "Mr. Becker, I am sorry that you have been swindled, but this land never belonged to Oscar Jackson." Becker moaned and shook his head.

Rory and Puma looked at Becker and then Rona. The couple was in total shock.

When Becker raised his head he said, "Rona, what should we do?" He looked at Rory and said, "We have two other youngins. We ain't got no money left. Jackson was murdered. His son will be running the store as soon as he gets it rebuilt. They had a fire and lost everything. That young Jackson is mean and ate up with greed."

Puma handed the sleeping newborn back to Rona and walked toward where Rory stood. "Let's go outside." Puma and Rory walked a few feet from the door, but kept both Rona and Becker in view. Puma said, "I believe him, don't you?" Rory nodded and said, "Maybe we can help them some, to find a new place and all." Puma whispered, "Why don't you stay here and keep an eye on things, and I will go and help Beth get a fire started and the kids fed. Then I will go and see what we can do about Seth Jackson. I might have a talk with him. I should be back by daylight." Rory objected and said, "You are in no condition to go that far tonight, let me go."

Puma pretended not to hear him and headed to where she had tied Breeze. She rode to the camp and found Beth and the children huddled together in the bed of the wagon. Puma called to them and said, "Everything is going good. Come on out here and help me build a fire." Puma started to drag up some deadwood, and Beth piled rocks into a circle for the fire-pit. Heath helped with the wood.

Rose asked for her father. Puma said, "He's busy but will come here very soon." Then Puma told Beth, "Don't wait up for me. It will be late before I get back." You should be safe enough sleeping in the wagon. Rory will come as soon as he can." Puma stuffed a few pieces of jerky and a canteen of water in her saddle bag. She wrapped her extra bow and quivers in a blanket and tied it behind the saddle. She checked her guns, slung the powder horn and bag of shot around her neck, and climbed into the saddle. She urged Breeze into a trot without looking back. The trading post was a few miles to the northwest. A half-moon had risen and helped Puma see the road.

Puma figured Oscar Jackson's demise to be getting off lightly. She thought it likely that he had killed himself. Oscar's son was in charge now. Would he be willing to refund Becker's money? Likely not, without the right kind of persuasion. Puma, weary to the bone, rode with her eyes closed, occasionally nodding off. Breeze stayed on the road and obediently kept up an even pace. When the trading post came into view, it was after midnight, and the house was dark. When a dog started to bark, Puma drew the pistol from her belt. She hid Breeze behind the newly constructed canvas shelter near where the barn had stood. When Puma reached the small cabin at the rear of the property, the door opened, and Seth stepped on to the porch wearing long johns. He said, "Who goes there?"

Puma, in her deepest voice, said, "Hello Mister, My Momma is sick, and I need to buy some laudanum."

Seth Jackson said, "We are all out of laudanum. Sorry I can't help you."

Puma asked, "Got any whiskey?"

"Sorry, we're closed. Come back tomorrow. Till then be on your way." The man started to reenter the house, but Puma said, "Wait." She approached Jackson holding her pistol behind her, out of sight. "Are you Mr. Seth? I got one more thing to ask you. Could you ask your Misses to look at this cut on my arm? It's mighty bad. Please Mister!"

Jackson, thoroughly irritated, said, "Ain't got no Misses. Nobody here but me, and I ain't no doctor." Puma shrugged and turned as though she was leaving and then lunged at Jackson's back as he turned to reenter the cabin. The force knocked him to the floor. His pistol fell from his hand, and Puma managed to kick it out of reach. She forced Jackson to continue into the cabin at gun point. She said, "Now let's talk. Have a seat in that chair." Puma walked behind him and struck him on the head with her pistol. He fell from the chair, unconscious. Puma lit a candle from a coal in the fireplace. Then she quickly pulled a blanket from the bed and tore off two wide strips. In the mean time she called out, "Hello, anyone here?" Silence. She hogtied Seth and left him on his side on the floor. She checked him for hidden weapons but found none. She picked up a bucket of water sitting on a counter and splashed it over him. He woke with a start and thrashed about on the floor. Puma smiled and asked if he was comfortable. He hissed a series of vile curses and said, "I'll kill you, you filthy Injun." Puma pointed the gun directly at his head and said, "Be careful what you say, or a terrible accident might befall you, like the one your father had. How is he doing? I actually heard that he had gone on to meet his maker." Seth's face stiffened with terror.

"We need to talk about my farm that you and your father sold to the Becker family. They are going to have to move on and need their money back." Seth said, "I don't have their money, and I wouldn't give it back if I did." Puma softly asked, "Are you sure? She placed her boot on his neck and jammed the barrel of her pistol into his ear. Becker violently thrust his head backwards into Puma's feet, hoping to bring her down. The jolt caused her trigger finger to contract. The explosion at such close range blew away most of Seth's upper skull. She landed on the floor in a sitting position. Her ears were ringing from the gunfire. She could feel the wetness of blood and brain tissue spattered upon her face. Seth's brain tissue was all around the room. Puma was horrified at what had just happened and frantically scooted, still in the sitting position a few feet away from the lifeless Seth before trying to stand. As she stood, she slipped on the brain tissue and fell back to the floor. She righted herself with care and backed away from the worst of the spatter. The smell caused her to start gagging. Droplets of perspiration covered her forehead. Now what?

She slowly rose and took the candle to where the bed stood. Where was he likely to hide his money? She searched under the mattress and dumped out a trunk of clothing. She checked the pockets of his clothing that hung on nails. She found a few coins and a couple of gold nougats in a drawstring bag. She transferred them to her own pockets. She stood on a stool and ran her hands along the cabin's rafters. That is where she found a cleverly concealed wooden box. When she tried to bring it down the box must have weighed close to a hundred pounds, and it fell to the floor. The box fell, narrowly missing her head and broke open on the floor. A variety of gold and silver coins scattered about the room. Among the coins were Portuguese pieces of eight, Spanish pesos, silver ingots, and gold guineas and sovereigns. Inside the lid of the box was a land deed, with Patrick's forged signature. Then she saw the agreement signed by Mr. Becker. The sale price was fifty guineas. A quick estimate told Puma that at least twice that amount was spread on the floor. She crawled on her knees gathering the coins. She tore a strip of blanket and secured the broken lid. The sickly odor of human blood and bodily fluids permeated the enclosure. She felt nauseous and dizzy. Before leaving the cabin, she splashed whale lamp oil about the room and ignited it. She carried the heavy box to where Breeze waited. The mare pulled on the reigns and nervously tossed her head. Puma knew that she smelled the blood. She spoke to Breeze with a calm voice. Then Puma took down her saddlebag and filled it with the coins and papers. She put the bag back in place and finished filling the two sides with the heavy coins. Suddenly a shaft of pain stabbed Puma in her lower abdomen. She stopped and placed her hands over her stomach. After a moment she felt fine and mounted to ride away. No more lifting for me until this baby is born, she thought.

Riding back to the farm, her mind kept replaying the macabre scene of Seth's accident. She had hoped to avoid more killing with the exception of Andy Jackson. The hypnotic motion of Breeze plodding along the road soon brought back the need for sleep. It was hard to remain in the saddle. Once she roused as she started slipping to one side. After another mile or two, Puma decided to stop and curl up in her blanket for a quick nap. When she awoke, it was getting light in the east. Then Puma felt wetness and looked to find that she was bleeding. When she stood, a labor pain doubled her over. She hurried back to the farm where she would have Beth with her.

The ride was uncomfortable, and the pains were continuing but were still several minutes apart. She rode directly to the wagon and called to Beth. Beth reached her head out of the wagon, and said, "You're back. I was just about to get up."

Puma said, "Beth, I need you, it's my baby." Beth, still barefoot, ran to Puma and helped her from the saddle. While climbing down, a labor pain struck, and Puma would have fallen if Beth had not been there to support her. Beth saw the blood stains on the saddle. It was too much blood. Beth called, "Heath, I need you, come help me." The sleepy boy with hair sticking straight up ran to help support Puma. They walked her to the wagon.

Beth asked, "Do you think you can step on this crate and climb into the wagon?"

Puma groaned, and said, "Yes, I think so." Once in the wagon, she started crawling to the mattress when a pain struck. "They are getting harder. Heath, I need a stick to bite on, and Rose, will you bring me a wet towel. I'm so hot. Beth, you need to protect your bed with canvas and a towel."

Beth said, "Good idea. Puma dear, we are about to welcome this little one into the world a little early, are you able to push? There keep going." Beth placed a square of canvas beneath Puma's hips and then padded it with a thick blanket. "I — drink of water, thirsty!" Puma made crunching noises on the stick. Beth removed the stick long enough to hold a cup to her mouth.

Through clinched teeth, Puma said, "I have the — the Becker's money in my saddlebag. The papers they signed were in the money box. We can destroy them after we convince Becker that they are fake. The box with the coins is heavy, get Heath to help you. Heath needs to give Breeze water. Beth, I-I need to be in a squatting position. Can you help me over to a rib that holds the wagon cover in place?" Beth stuck her head out the back of the wagon and told the two older children to water Breeze at the creek. "Beth, the baby, it is coming. I feel it."

Beth reached into a drawer and removed a folded muslin sheet. She used her teeth to start a tear and removed a generous piece of cloth. Then she found a roll of leather throng in her sewing box. Beth washed Puma's face with the towel and massaged her lower back. Puma groaned, and her face turned a dark red color. Beth looked and saw the baby being pushed out. Beth looked under Puma's tunic and saw the very top of the baby's head. "Puma concentrate on pushing the baby out with each contraction. I am ready to take over once the baby is out." Beth placed the muslin over both arms and caught the baby as it dropped from Puma. "There, good pushing, you have a boy, ah, ah, I will work with him while you lie back and rest."

The tiny infant was not moving. Beth tried to conceal her panic. Puma crawled back to the bed, without taking her eyes off the tiny baby lying in Beth's arms and collapsed.

Beth elevated the baby boy's lower body and allowed the fluid to drain from the child's mouth and nose. Beth patted the boy on the back and waited. Finally, he inhaled and then coughed, expelling some mucus. Puma and Beth smiled at each other. Beth said, "Thank you Lord." Beth gave Puma a look that said, "What do I do now?"

Puma said, "Keep him warm and tie off the cord; here, hand him to me." Puma helped Beth with the cord." Within five minutes the placenta was delivered. Beth used a towel to clean Puma and then rolled up the soiled bedding and replaced it with another muslin sheet. After a few minutes Beth sponge bathed Puma the best she could and covered her with a feather tick. Puma, began dozing off and said in a drowsy voice, "His name is Patrick, Son of The Bear-Wrestler, Yo-Nv-Ayastigi Larson. He will be called Yony."

Many years later Puma, Yony, and Little Doe were among the group that resisted Andrew Jackson's forced relocation to Oklahoma Territory. The clan managed to avoid detection by the authorities by moving their camp sites often. They outlasted the soldier's efforts to capture them. Their desperate life style was physically hard, but they managed to remain free to live out their lives in the most rugged mountainous regions of the Smoky Mountain chain.

Later in life Puma spent her winter months with Rory and Beth at the farm. Little is known of Little Doe as an adult. There are reports that she eventually moved to Oklahoma where she attended the University of Oklahoma. She majored in Psychology and graduated with a master's degree. She made her home in Tahlequah and worked with troubled Cherokee youth. She and her husband reared a son and daughter.

The prematurely born Yony had some catching up to do but matured into a robust and athletic warrior. The year of Yony's birth coincided with the defeat of the British at the 1814 "Battle of New Orleans" referred to as the War of 1812. In retrospect, Puma surmised that the Great Spirit had preempted her need for retribution in favor of Andy Jackson's leadership in New Orleans. There are tradeoffs that change the course of history and that the Spirit opted to spare Andy Jackson would have much more significance than the defeat of the British. The now prominent national hero came to be called "Old Hickory." As his popularity with the masses soared, he was looked down upon as rift-raff by the Washington establishment. Andrew Jackson became the first president to be elected by popular vote. Earlier Presidents had been elected by the Congress. Andy Jackson was a man of the common people and showed disdain for the more genteel political class. He was known to throw open the doors of the White House welcoming all to the people's house, and upon more than one occasion the event evolved into drunken revelry that left the mansion damaged and filthy.

Crushing indebtedness forced the fledgling government under Jackson to some extreme measures. After searching for other alternatives, President Jackson continued the practice of earlier presidents. He justified selling land as the best way to satisfy debt and protect the credit worthiness of the nation. After Thomas Jefferson acquired the Louisiana Territory, the great expanse of land west of the Appalachian Divide came to be viewed as a federal asset and a potential source of revenue. The sale of land paid the back salaries of those that had served in the military and satisfied the large outstanding loans still owed to France. Word quickly spread to Europe, and hordes of adventurous immigrants disembarked daily from the filled-to-capacity schooners that plied the Atlantic.

Sometime during the War of 1812, the leaders of the Cherokee tribe divided into two factions. For the following twenty-two years, the rift grew until the minority group wanted to sell the traditional tribal grounds and move the population to a territory called Oklahoma. While the opposing majority lobbied before Congress, the others met secretly with government representatives and completed a lump sum settlement on behalf of all Cherokee and moved west to the designated land. The hold outs vowed to kill the traitors and following the forced march called "The Trail of Tears," several leaders of the traitors were dragged from their beds in the middle of the night and brutally killed.

A lesser number of the more traditional Cherokee defied the law and fled to the remotest part of the Great Smoky Mountains. Some of that group were never captured, and their offspring now make-up the Eastern Cherokee Tribe. Below is a quote from a website that describes the division and the group that evaded relocation. Among those to escape was Yony, a high-ranking soldier in the band that fought under the revered Tsali. Yony lived out his life in seclusion, secreted in the Smoky Mountains, the sacred ground that held the bones of his ancestors. Almost nothing is known of his life and his burial place remains a closely held secret.

The Supreme Court declined to hear the case because they lacked jurisdiction. President Jackson signed legislation requiring relocation of eastern Indian Tribes, by force if necessary. The native population that refused to migrate willingly were forcibly relocated by the army. No special consideration was given the Cherokee nation's successful efforts at assimilation into the European style culture. Even though the Cherokees' living standard matched that of white society, they were still classified as uncivilized savages. The Cherokee people had been too successful for the whites that took their advances as an affront.

Chapter 3

THE ASA & OLLIE SAGA

Through the years Cheatie and Grandmother Ollie grew to love and admire each other. They cherished the hours they spent reminiscing about the past. Cheatie became increasingly enamored with Ollie and Asa's courtship. She kept digging for more details from Ollie. The following narrative is Ollie's story as told to Cheatie and then retold as part of this book. I have used a lot of humor and whimsy in this lighthearted section of "Cheatiebo." Cheatie has been entrusted with an old courier trunk that is stuffed with family letters, news articles, diaries, and notations in the family Bible. There were items like a pair of tiny bronzed baby shoes, an antique wooden cloths-pin, and a brittle leather strip that held a few sleigh bells that hadn't fallen off. Among these items was Ollie's large family Bible now separated from its wooden oak stand.

Grandmother Ollie's parents, Sam and Elizabeth presented the Bible to Ollie McClarren McCawl upon the birth of her first born son, Samuel. Enlightening notations turned out to be important resources. I only remember Ollie and Asa in their fifties and sixties, but to my delight Cheatie's second hand accounts, paired with the records in the trunk helped me to know them as a pair of talented, fun-loving young adults. There were photographs of them, wonderful pictures that sent me and my active imagination hurtling backward on the time-warp express.

Several months before Asa and Ollie began courting Asa, despite his youth, undertook carving out a horse business. Asa was the "kid" the old timers around Gainesville doted on and loved to tease. The whole bunch were 'ole cowboy types' that frequented the livestock sale barns, roping events, and feed lots. This fragment of Gainesville society had treated Asa like a 'favorite son.' One of the older fellows of the fireside-gents named Calvin Jessop offered to lease him a building adjacent to the downtown livery barn.

The circumstances that transformed Gainesville into a thriving community made it a prosperous place to start a business. Consider the town's proximity to the iconic pathway to the Kansas Railheads called the Chisholm Trail. The following historical reference is copied from Texas Escapes.com.

Red River Station

"Jumping-off point" on the famous Chisholm Cattle Trail, (1867-87), Red River Station was a main crossing and last place on trail to buy supplies until Abilene, Kan.—350 miles north.

During the cattle drive era of Western history, millions of animals swam the turbulent river here en route to Kansas railhead and markets.

An abrupt bend in the river checked its flow at this point, creating a natural crossing which had been used for years by buffalo and Indians. Even so, the water was wide, swift, and sometimes clogged with sand bars. Frequently cattle were so jammed cowboys could walk across on their backs. Besides a cattle crossing, the station was an outpost of the frontier regiment, which patrolled Texas' northernmost border during Confederacy (1861-65). During cattle era, a town began here, its ferry serving drovers, soldiers, freighters, and settlers returning from Indian captivity. Local cemetery (1 mi. SE) contains many graves of these Texas pioneers.

The most eastern branch of the Chisholm Trail, located at Red River Station, a shallow river ford, gave safe passage to the herds of longhorns. Droves of rowdy cowboys were eager to patronize Gainesville's saloons and brothels. The local restaurants and hotels were only a few miles from Red River Station, the best place to cross the river. The town's population doubled within a few short years. With time Gainesville had within its city limits a stage coach depot and the Katy Railway. The discovery of oil there-about attracted the wildcatter industry. Calvin Jessop's first-rate livery-stable and black-smith shop helped bring customers to Asa's barn. He borrowed Calvin's tall ladder and painted a sign on the front of his barn that read,

ASA MCCAWL's SALE BARN

"QUARTER HORSES FOR SALE"

Trained Cutting Horses

Our Specialty

Asa's old-timer buds were affectionately known as his "fire-side gents." The group of aging cowboys had taken on the role of mentoring Asa. Anytime he competed on horseback he was accompanied by a gaggle of buds and of late more than a few cowgirls, a spontaneous fan club of sorts. Asa's status as a heart-throb around town was a source of embarrassment to him. The rumor mill around town had tagged Asa as the "Drover with the handsomest head God ever put on a blue-eyed and sandy-haired cowboy." Of course, Asa pretended not to notice his popularity with the star-struck female admirers. He had a family to support, and courting ladies would have to wait. It was common knowledge that Asa was inexperienced with the fairer sex, and great sport was made at his expense to watch him blush.

Among the ranching community of North Texas and beyond, word of Asa's horsemanship spread. According to his "gents," watching Asa in action on a cutting horse was a spectator sport. The collaboration between Asa and his mount was legendary, and his trophies and belt buckles continued to accumulate. There was a certain mystical quality surrounding Asa's gift for training quarter-horses. In addition to the horse training enterprise, Asa continued to earn part of his living hiring out to ranchers who needed the services of a real cowboy.

Young Asa looked forward to his nightly visits with the town's sages. Over time he had formed a sentimental attachment and sense of community with the elders. Asa had inherited a ready-made family to provide for, namely himself and four younger siblings orphaned during adolescence. Most evenings he presided over a meal with Callie, Zelma, Sid, and John. All four were still in public school but were quickly becoming independent. Asa was proud of the way they were developing into tough, resourceful young adults. At the death of their mother, they were almost split up among relatives and town folk. Asa, only sixteen at the time, begged for the opportunity to demonstrate that the five of them could make it in the world as a family. Since Asa refused for them to be separated and there were no adoptive families willing to take in a family of five, the town looked the other way and left Asa to his own devises. The first decade of the twentieth century did not have the social networks or child service agencies in place. In modern times society would never have allowed the experiment.

On most evenings once the kids were bedded down, Asa would ride over to the fireside meeting. All four of the younger McCawls were doing well in school and contributing to their upkeep with part time jobs. Sid and John could keep up with most grown men when it came to hard labor. Callie and Zelma took care of keeping the place tidy, cooking, laundry, and tended a small garden and hen house. For young women they were physically strong and fearless when it came to helping Asa with the horse training business.

The loyalty and affection the five McCawl youngsters had for each other plucked upon the heart strings of Gainesville. Asa knew he could always call upon his fire side buds in a pinch but felt compelled to prove that he was capable of providing a proper home. He would never give the nay-sayers an excuse to step in and separate his little family.

Callie and Zelma were reaching the age that Asa had been dreading. The girls were according to Asa, "dad-burn purty." Asa bristled anytime he saw how they turned heads among the young single males of Cooke County. So far no one dared to question his status as a father figure. That was one role that came natural to him. After all, he made sure the kids, as he called them, were all too busy to be part of the frivolous social scene. Sid and John were rarely idol, seeing there was always fire wood to be cut and split, and Callie and

Zelma were learning to do the more the tedious paper work associated with running the business.

Each girl had trained their own smooth gaited saddle horse and regularly participated in local competitions for women. Asa with the help of Sid and John kept the little sisters under surveillance and so far had managed to convince the girls and any prospective suitors that they were too young to be thinking about courting.

Asa was showing aptitude in the business world. First his observation skills helped him absorb the western persona and verbiage of mature ranchers. He knew how to favorably impress folks. People were automatically drawn to his personality, a trait that would boost his life-long career as a public speaker.

Asa quickly realized that the cutting horse business was potentially lucrative. His instinctive way of communicating with horses hastened the time and effort required with each cutting horse. Within six months Asa was selling horses as fast as he could get them trained. In north Texas and well up into Oklahoma, the ranching community was starting to depend on Asa for top notch cutting horses. Word-of-mouth was all the advertising he needed.

Asa was a regular at the sale barns of north Texas. He was always in search of prime cutting- horse stock. It was a bright spring day when Asa arrived at the Whitesboro Sale Barn and registered with the desk. He was handed a number to wear in the band of his Stetson and took a seat in the bleachers. No sooner had he taken his seat when he saw a stunning black stallion. Asa quickly asked around about the horse, but all he got was shrugs. Asa decided he would try to purchase the magnificent animal. He bided his time, and as soon as the black was brought into the arena, Asa removed his hat and held it at the ready. The auctioneer announced that the stallion was a six-year-old Friesian from Europe. The owner had fallen upon hard times and was forced to sell. The opening bid was $1000.00, supposedly far below the true value of such a spectacular animal. For once Asa agreed and eagerly waved his hat at the auctioneer.

The nasal drone of the auctioneer said, "I have one thousand, do I have twelve hundred to the black hat, thirteen over here, make it fourteen, one four double O, going, going, fifteen here in front, do I hear sixteen? Sixteen anyone? Yes, sixteen, going, going, I have seventeen hundred, seventeen to Asa here in front, going, going, last chance, sold for seventeen hundred!" Asa stood and waved his Stetson, acknowledging the spontaneous applause he received from the crowd. Asa asked his good friend, the onsite veterinarian to look over the horse for any problems before "ponying" up the money. The vet said, "I almost jumped into the bidding myself. This is some fine horseflesh." The vet inspected each hoof and ran his hand down each leg, examined the eyes, ears and mouth. He said, "Asa, all I would do if he was mine is give him a good worming."

Asa thanked the doc and handed him forty bucks. "I'll bring him by the clinic here in a few days."

Asa was interested in speaking with the seller, a Texas rancher. The fellow introduced himself as Tex. He was decked out in flashy western garb and had a flamboyant personality to match. When Asa tried to introduce himself, the man called Tex interrupted and said, "I know who you are, everbody around here knows Asa McCawl." The two of them began a cordial chat that revealed the following background on the horse appropriately named Ebony. Tex continued, "The fellar I got him from was a German glucksspieler (gambler) named Herr Otto Wendt. He had purchased the stallion from a troop of gypsies somewhere in Western Austria."

The current political atmosphere in Eastern Europe was hostile to Jews and Gypsies. They were an underclass and universally discriminated against. Poor Otto, a half Jew, had long dreamt of immigrating to the United States where there was reportedly much less prejudice. Upon arriving on American soil, a series of events found Otto and his stallion Ebony in Whitesboro, Texas where he found employment at the livestock sale barn.

Asa asked to meet Otto Wendt, and Tex summoned him. Otto's boss was kind enough to give him a break from his duties. Asa asked the German to tell how he came to own Ebony, being a person that routinely filled in any blanks when conducting business. A language barrier presented itself as soon as Otto began his narrative.

Lapsing into his native dialect of German, Otto began his account of events with the following. "Goot day Mr. Asa, Durch Behalten eines niedrigen Profils und Reisen der Nebenstraßen habe ich es geschafft, das Friesian Hengst böse Land zu einem Norweger Seehafen zu fahren, wo er einer Aufgabe auf einem."

Asa held up his hands and said, "Hold on, I only know how to talk English, please!"

That is when Tex interrupted and said, "My mother's family were Germans. Settled in the nearby community of Muenster. You boys want me to translate for you?"

Asa smiled and drawled, "Have at it."

Tex was well acquainted with Otto's story, and instead of translating he began telling the story by recapping and paraphrasing the events that led to Ebony being at auction. He started with, "By keeping a low profile and traveling the back roads, Otto managed to ride the Friesian cross country to a Norwegian seaport where he was offered a job on a passenger steamer set to depart for Boston, Massachusetts the following day. His passage and stable space for the horse would be in exchange for working two jobs. As a janitor between midnight and 6:00AM and in the kitchen from noon to 7:00 PM. Being a fairly intelligent fellow, Otto realized that he would be landing on the shores of a strange continent, with poor English skills, without the support of friends or family, and absolutely penniless. This motivated Otto to solicit odd jobs on the voyage."

"Careful not to run afoul of his supervisor, Otto managed to earn a few coins doing chores for some of the more well-to-do passengers by shining shoes, babysitting, and running errands. Otto's sleep deprivation grew worse by the day. The gratuities would solve two of his problems, namely money and peace of mind. During the nine days voyage, the ship's officers made sure that Otto earned his passage. A longer cruise would have ended in his total physical collapse."

Tex obviously liked the sound of his own voice and continued the detailed narrative. "The first night in Boston pretty much shattered poor Otto's expectations for his new homeland. Suffering from severe mental fog, hunger, and the disorientation caused by unfamiliar surroundings Otto decided to look for a bed for the night in the less desirable part of the city. He was shocked at the prices and decided to find a place to camp on the outskirts of town.

Otto interjected a nod of his head and a sad sounding, "Ya, I dit."

As he rode along his hunger became overwhelming, and he was drawn to the music coming from a British style pub. Otto found the place to his liking and ordered a small bony fish and 2 potato cakes. He decided to eat where he could keep an eye on Ebony. The stallion was tied between two other horses, and the twilight would help to disguise his pedigree from horse thiefs."

"After finishing the meal Otto recalled seeing a poker game in a back corner of the pub. He decided to delay finding a camping place in favor of watching the poker game for a hand or two. For someone with a gambling addiction, this was a poor decision."

This is when Otto stood and shook hands with both Asa and Tex and went back to work.

Tex continuing the story said, "Three of the poker players were me and my two sidekicks, all hailing from the great state of Texas. We were decked out in cowboy hats and wrangler's boots, high lighting the fact that we were from out of town. It was impossible to miss the interest the young immigrant was showing in our game, and I decided to invite him to join us. He was powerless to decline and accepted the invitation by pulling up a chair. He exchanged the contents of his pockets for poker chips, and the game continued."

"Otto had that lucky feeling! Perhaps fate would cooperate, and once he had won a small hand or two, he could bide his time until he drew a winning hand. When he finally held two pairs, he bet his entire stack of chips and lost to a flush. That is when I offered to stake Otto, keeping him in the game for the time being. Otto gladly took my loan since he couldn't bear to leave the game penniless. Making small talk, I asked Otto where he hailed from and he said Berlin."

I replied, "Ah, a beautiful city, I visited there as a teenager."

"Otto lost the latest stake in three consecutive hands. Hoping to keep him in the game, I asked Otto if he had anything of value to secure a second loan. Otto reasoned that his only option to recoup his loses was to put up the stallion."

Otto replied, "My horse is of great value, but I could never part with him."

I said, "Do you mind showing him to me, maybe we could work something out?"

Otto said, "Ya, you can see for yourself my horse." The game recessed so that I could evaluate the animal. At first sight I struggled to disguise my excitement over the possibility of acquiring such an animal. Otto walked up to the stallion and fondly caressed his head. Right away I knew the giant was gentle and affectionate. I calmly circled the animal and said, "Whoa boy, easy now, as I ran my hand over his withers and hindquarters. The horse remained calm and turned his head to look me over. Not one imperfection presented itself, and I grew more excited by the second. I said, "He's big and looks strong, but his musculature is all wrong. This horse will be crippled by any heavy work, and he will eat a lot of oats. No, not worth much in my book. I could offer you, ah maybe a couple of hundred, but he really isn't worth it. Still, I like to treat people right. Otto, so far you owe me forty-seven dollars American and to make a show of good faith, and against my better judgment, I will offer the two hundred plus the $47.00 you already owe me. Take it or leave it. For now, I'm gonna head back to the game and await your answer."

Back at the pub I waited, hoping to see Otto coming through the door. We waited for the longest 37 minutes I ever experienced. When Otto finally walked through the swinging doors, he had a dour and deflated look about him. You could have heard a pin being dropped as Otto pulled back a chair and sat down. We all waited for his answer. And we waited, waited, and still there was no words coming from his humped over form. Otto put his head down on the table and refused to answer my inquiry of, "Otto, you okay? Feeling ill, what's wrong?"

Finally, Otto slapped the table with his right hand, making the poker chips rattle and a few fall to the floor. Then he said, "I take the loan of $247.00, and if I lose this hand the steed is yours." A crowd of interested watchers had gathered around the table. Silence punctuated the tension in the room. It was my turn to deal the cards, and I was unable to control the tremble of my hands. Had Otto's luck changed?"

"One of the players cut the deck. As I slapped the cards face down in front of each player, Otto's nose kept nervously twitching. Suddenly it was over. My three tens beat his pair of jacks. Lady luck had definitely turned her back on poor Otto. Asa, now you know how I came to own the Friesian stallion."

Tex continued, "Otto was so distraught his sleep-deprived mental faculties just quit functioning, and he reacted to his latest misfortune like a mad man. As sometimes happens when people are pushed to despair, Otto became self-destructive. Without signaling his intent in advance, he snatched the revolver from the holster of the man sitting next to him and pointed the gun at his right temple as he rose from the table. His chair fell over making a loud cracking sound that caused the watchers to flinch thinking the gun had gone off."

"Otto's painful expression was grotesque. He backed to the foot of a stair case and began backing up the steps slowly. As he climbed the stairs he shouted, "Aufenthalt zurück oder ich werde mich selbst töten. Ich will nicht leben. Warum macht das Universum heimlich plant gegen mich? Ich will an mein Leben denken und erinnere mich daran, bevor ich sterbe. Ich will nicht Sie verletzen. Abschied!" Several of us followed him hoping to dissuade him from taking his own life. From the upper landing he followed a hallway that ended with a large open window. Still walking backward, he looked out the window and then stepped through to the rooftop and disappeared into a wall of blackness. Otto wanted to have a moment of privacy to reflect on his life before finding solace from fate's retched conspiracy.

Halfway up the flight of stairs, I held out my arms blocking the others from pursuit and translated Otto's very words, "Stay back! I do not want to live. The universe conspires against me. I want to think about my life and remember before I die. I will not hurt any of you as long as you stay back. Now, I say my farewell!"

Tex came up with a plan. He decided to speak to Otto through the window. He slowly approached the second story window and saw that it opened on to the building's gradually sloping roof. Otto was nowhere in sight, but Tex spoke German, loudly, "Otto, before you shoot I need to ask you about the horse. I promise to take good care of him. When did he eat last? What is his name?"

I told the men that Otto was upset over losing his horse. I have an idea on how to distract him from his death wish. Hey manager, I need a pitcher of beer and two steins.

"Hey Otto, how about I come out and sit with you?" I said, "I think I understand how you are feeling."

Finally, Otto spoke from the darkness, "Okay, aber allein und bringen jede Menge Bier. Wir sprechen wie Sie sagen. Ich möchte, dass mein Hengst, gut gepflegt, sie versprechen?"

The Pub owner asked, "What did he say?"

I replied, "Okay, but come alone and bring plenty beer. We talk as you say. I want my stallion cared for to be, ya?"

One of the men barred from continuing up the stairs spoke up, "I say if some fellar don't want to live who are we to force him to continue in his misery." That statement shocked most everyone on the stairs and elicited some hard looks from the tenderer hearted of the group. A bearded man made the sign of the cross and said a prayer aloud. The Pub owner dispatched an employee to fetch the sheriff.

I balanced the tray of beer and walked to where a dormer interrupted the slope of the roof. It had a level window sill just wide enough to hold the tray. I took a seat with my back against the slope of the dormer and waited for Otto. After several minutes I decided to start the party without Otto. My nerves were frazzled, and I needed to relax. After taking a long draw from my stein, I wiped the foam from my upper lip with my shirt sleeve.

The beer refreshed me, and I took a second and a third as I waited for Otto to come out of the dark. "Otto, come and drink with me; it's not good to drink alone." I began to hum a song between gulps, Mummmm, mummmm, ump pa, "Hey Otto do you know this one? Trink, Trink, Bruderlein, Trink, Trink, Trink, Bruderlein, Trink!" Otto came out of hiding and sat down beside me and filled the other stein. We sang together rocking from side to side. Trink, Trink-.

Then Otto began singing a different song, "Zicke, Zacke, Zicke, Hoi, Hoi, Hoi." With each swig of beer, we grew louder. The next song was the German anthem, "Deutschland uber alles."

Deutschland, Deutschland über alles,
Über alles in der Welt,
Wenn es stets zu Schutz und Trutze
Brüderlich zusammenhält,
Von der Maas bis an die Memel,
Von der Etsch bis an den Belt
Deutschland, Deutschland über alles,
Über alles in der Welt!

Then Tex said, "Know this one, 'Edelweiss' my favorite."
Otto said, "Me too. Zi mudder singt it at bed time."

Edelweiss, Edelweiss,
Du grüsst mich jeden Morgen.
Seh ich dich, Freue ich mich,
Und vergess meine Sorgen
Schmücke die Heimat nach Schnee und Eis,
Blüh'n soll'n deine Sterne.
Edelweiss, Edelweiss,
Ach, ich hab' dich so gerne.

I had a mind to stand and would have fallen from the roof top if not for Otto catching me by a leg as I dangled partly over the edge. By this point we were both suffering from alcohol vertigo and lay back on the still warm roof and drifted into a drunken stupor. The next thing either of us knew we were being awakened by the Sheriff. The beer was all gone, and the swiped pistol handed over to its rightful owner. The lawman and the pub owner helped Otto and I through the window and down the stairs. After a few cups of bitter black coffee and some assisted walking in circles, we were deemed safe to ride the distance to lodging. Our suite had a big overstuffed sofa, and Otto was invited to bed down for the remainder of the night.

After conferring, we Texans took pity on the young German and offered to hire him on as a valet and horse handler. Otto was sober enough to recognize a good deal and the chance to stay in contact with Ebony. I elected to ride Ebony to the hotel and was more than pleased with his smooth gait. I handed off the stallion to the hotel livery stable attendant and ordered up a double ration of cracked grain. Otto meekly accepted a blanket and a dose of bicarbonate as he curled up to complete his detoxification.

"On the morrow a hungover Otto Wendt and the stallion Ebony accompanied our group westward across the expansive American plain. Destined for Kansas City, we hitched a ride aboard a freight train used to transport cattle from the mid-west trail heads to the populated eastern seaboard. On the return trip westward, the rail cars were loaded with hay, food stuffs, and miscellaneous merchandise. Otto gladly took over the care of his beloved Ebony. He refused to leave Ebony alone in the boxcar that was partly loaded with hay. I appreciated his devotion and provided Otto a blanket and personally delivered his meals. The rail trip to Kansas City took four days. From Kansas we continued the journey by horseback. Our group's destination was my homestead located near Decatur, Texas. My ranch, passed to me by my grandparents, represented a sprawling league and a labor, more than 4600 acres of grass land settled by my grandparents. They had traveled with other Americans in the company of Stephen F. Austin years before Texas won its independence from Santa Anna. The nearest town is a small farming community called Decatur."

"When my ranch foreman informed me that we had all the ranch hands we could support, I was forced to let Otto go. Once again facing uncertainty Otto was distraught. Out of the goodness of my heart I wrote him a letter of recommendation that promptly got him hired on at the Whitesboro Livestock Auction. I promised to stay in touch with him."

At this point, Tex finished his narrative and shook hands with Asa. A few weeks after Otto met Asa McCawl, he got word that Asa was looking for a stable hand and applied. Asa was glad to hire Otto, and Otto was excited to work where he could care for Ebony.

Following the job interview, Otto and Asa lingered over a cup of coffee. Otto's English had improved, and the two of them sensed that they were kindred spirits as far as horses go. Asa realized that Otto had an emotional attachment to Ebony and would make the perfect groom and all-around handy man. The two men began a friendship that lasted a lifetime. Asa hired Otto and as part of his compensation he would be allowed to occupy a small apartment at the rear of the main structure that housed the horses. Otto had to promise to avoid drinking alcohol and smoking. Asa also banned gambling of any kind. The apartment would be ready to occupy in two weeks. That would give Otto ample time to notify the sale barn that he would be leaving their employ.

Asa asked to borrow the veterinarian's book on the most prominent horse breeds. There in chapter 2 was a detailed history of the Friesian breed. This is when it dawned on Asa what a wind-fall the horse represented. Asa decided against training Ebony to work with cattle. The gentle giant would be his saddle horse and serve as a pleasure mount as well as a breeding stud. Ebony easily stood 17 hands tall and for a stallion was remarkably mellow. Within a week Ebony grew to recognize Asa as his master and with a few miss-communications and getting-to-know-each-other incidents Ebony took to Asa.

The stallion's physical characteristics were straight out of the Friesian specification book. His powerful proportions identified Ebony as a genetically superior specimen of the breed. The glistening black coat and lavish mane and tail made the stallion a show stopper, a vision of sublime beauty. There was something else about Ebony, a unique trait that was not immediately perceivable to Asa.

Once Ebony and Asa had bonded, he realized the horse had a human-like trait, something akin to pride. Ebony enjoyed the grooming required to keep his tail and mane silky and flowing. He delighted in performing before a crowd. Even more unusual was the way he would time his steps to the beat when music was playing. Ebony's uniqueness further convinced Asa of the stallion's superior intelligence.

Folks would stop what they were doing and stare when Asa floated by on Ebony. They couldn't get enough of the beloved favorite son. Asa's natural entrepreneurial aspirations valued popularity and public relations. He figured publicity, notoriety, and flamboyancy just might be a good thing.

Asa read all the printed material he could find on the Friesian breed. The breed had originated in Holland more than a thousand years before, and though unknown to north Texas, the stallion was becoming a phenomenon. Asa learned that Friesians are generally considered to be the most beautiful of all breeds on the European continent. Asa decided to breed Friesians and commissioned Tex and Otto to sail to Europe and purchase three or four pedigreed brood mares. Tex and Otto were quick to accept the proposition and boarded a Butterfield Stage Coach that would eventually take them to a seaport near New Orleans. There they boarded a ship to Amsterdam.

Tex and Otto quickly found that Friesians are a coveted national icon to the Dutch and the breeders they approached refused all offers. After days of searching, they found a breeder in financial trouble who agreed to part with three mares at an inflated price if they agreed not to publicly identify him. Asa would no doubt be glad to have the mares at any price when they explained the situation. Two of the mares were pregnant, and the third was a filly. The three mares came with verifiable pedigree papers and conformed to the breed's physical standards. The full sum for the stock took every dollar of Asa's money plus most of Tex and Otto's personal funds leaving them with insufficient traveling money. Out of desperation Tex needed to find a game of chance where he could increase the small amount of pocket change he had left. Otto objected to remaining at the stable with the mares, but Tex insisted, knowing Otto was not to be trusted anywhere near a poker game. After losing the first hand, Tex placed his gold pocket watch on the table and actually won a grand sum! He promptly excused himself and took evasive tactics on the way back to Otto. He figured the sooner they got out of town the better and moved to the sea port in readiness to board the ship at the earliest possible moment.

It was the stormy season in the Atlantic, and seasickness was an unwelcome traveling companion. The prolonged journey took a full two months, much longer than expected. Asa was sure glad to see that they had arrived safely. The two travelers looked haggard and exhausted. Asa expressed concern and treated them to a steak dinner. The new stock was a real boost to Asa's burgeoning breeding business. Asa posted a waiting list for Friesian colts.

Shortly after acquiring Ebony, Asa realized he would be needing a saddle that fit the stallion's large frame. Asa substituted a quilted horse pad until the problem could be solved. After inquiring among the locals, Asa was given the name of a saddle maker, a Gypsy called Giuseppe Svoboda. Asa did some checking with a few satisfied customers before making an appointment with the leather craftsman. The saddle maker was in his middle twenties and from all reports maintained the highest excellence and customer satisfaction.

Asa's fireside friends filled him in on the man's background. Giuseppe had emigrated from the Slavic nations of Central Europe at a time when Europe was in economic and social upheaval. When Giuseppe was less than a year old, his father, a trapeze performer, fell to his death. His mother, also a trapeze artist continued with the circus where she reared her fatherless son. It was a natural progression for the young boy to learn the craft. The nomadic nature of the circus gave young Giuseppe the opportunity to experience the most populous and scenic cities on the continent. The circus regularly performed for the European elite including royalty.

In addition to Giuseppe's public performances with the show horses, he was trained as a leather craftsman. He directed the horses in their dressage routines in the arena and did trick riding during the shows. When not involved with his primary duty with the horses Giuseppe worked with the leather craftsman support staff. From an early age Giuseppe exhibited a natural love of music and displayed an unusual aptitude for singing. Some of the circus entertainers gave him a basic introduction to reading music and how to play chords on the piano and guitar. That was expanded to the violin and cello. He began finding a quiet and private place for practicing what he had learned. He had a beautiful voice until puberty, but that changed to a gravely baritone that was strangely painful. As he matured his voice became more controlled and pleasant. Practice and determination helped the lad to train the nerve-grating quality of his voice. Young Giuseppe would sneak away and spend hours practicing singing. He loved music and entertaining, and it became an intrinsic part of his persona for life.

Asa rode Ebony to the outskirts of town to the Leather Craftsman's shop. While he dismounted, he heard music coming from the building: soft guitar music, beautifully played. Asa introduced himself to the saddle maker who set aside his guitar and stood to shake hands. Early in the conversation Asa asked to see a catalog with pictures of parade saddles. He was especially attracted to one particularly ornate saddle. It was outlined in silver spot studs, had accents of silver Conchos, and featured intricate carving in the leather. The basic price tag started at the substantial sum of one four hundred dollars. After Asa thought about the large price tag, he convinced himself that it could be justified as a business expense. Giuseppe took out a measuring tape and asked to see the horse that he would be fitting.

When the saddle maker saw Ebony, he stopped and shouted, "Yi yi! Sheibenkleister Dikhen baro, sukar, sukar Gra- cederi Friesian, cushti bast!" (Roughly translated: do I see a Friesian? Yes, what surprise, beautiful horse, stallion of Friesian breed, good choice?) Asa would later learn that Giuseppe's outburst was in Romani, the language of the Gypsy. He was known to lapse into a few words of German or Russian since he had a working command of the most common languages used in Continental Europe. Asa was having a Deja-Vu moment, recalling when Otto began spouting German. Asa patiently waited for the babble to switch back to the English language.

Giuseppe regained his emotional composure and asked, "Mr. McCawl, do you know what you have here? Do you realize that this breed of horse is rare and highly prized? He is a giant, a perfect specimen. Is he gentle? Please, bring him into my corral. I will approach him there." Asa led the docile Ebony by the reigns through a gate into a horse training arena. Giuseppe said, "Okay, now drop the reigns and back away slowly. Ebony stood in place looking at Asa, ready to accommodate his master's wishes. Giuseppe said, "Please continue to reassure him. I'm going to stand here and let him come to me."

Ebony wore a quilted pad with stirrups and a rope halter. Giuseppe said, "Asa, do I need to put a bridle on him or can I control him with just the halter?"

Asa said, "Ain't nothing wild about him, I mostly control him with just my knees."

Giuseppe said, "Not surprising, stay put while I fetch some treats and my riding-crop. I would normally give him carrots, but I'm out so do you mind a few sugar cubes?"

From where Asa had taken a seat on the top rung of the corral fence he said, "A little sugar won't hurt him none since I'm getting ready to worm him anyway." Giuseppe backed to within ten feet of Ebony and stood quietly hiding his face. Ebony began bobbing his head up and down. Then he made some soft whinnying sounds and took a step closer to get a look at the stranger. Giuseppe began to whistle, and Ebony's ears popped up and rotated in the direction of the sound. It was as though he recognized the song. Giuseppe turned partly toward Ebony and continued the song. Ebony inched his way along until he stood next to Giuseppe and waited. Ebony used a front hoof and pawed the ground.

Giuseppe continued to look away but reached an arm toward Ebony and stroked his neck. Then Ebony used his nose to give Giuseppe a little shove in the back. After that Giuseppe turned to face Ebony and began speaking in a foreign language in a calm and low tone. He rubbed the muscular neck and then inspected Ebony's inner cheeks. Giuseppe said, "I found what I was looking for, your horse has a tattoo. It is as I expected, the insignia of the Austrian Crown. If I had the money, I would try to take him off your hands. Oh, by the way Ebony is accustomed to commands in German."

Asa responded, "Well Ebony is in Texas now, and he will have to learn the local lingo.

Giuseppe threw his head back and laughed before imitating a Texas accent, "Hey, yawl horse, Ebony!"

Asa acknowledged the attempt at humor and continued the conversation, "What kind of price would he bring?"

"Oh, likely in the neighborhood of five to eight thousand dollars." Giuseppe pulled the crop from the back side of his waist band. "Here goes, we'll know soon enough." For the first test he gathered the reigns and began to walk slowly in a circle, then he increased his speed and the horse followed his lead. With each increase Ebony matched the pace.

Giuseppe mounted Ebony and had him run around the arena free style. With a nod in Asa's direction, Giuseppe issued the command to back up, and Ebony responded without hesitating. Giuseppe held a sugar cube forward, and Ebony's tongue picked it from his hand. Still speaking in a low tone, he issued a different command to Ebony. The stallion began shifting his weight between his front hooves, lifting them far off the ground while remaining stationary. When Giuseppe touched Ebony's flank with the crop, the horse continued the diagonal prancing but began slowly advancing.

Asa was about to witness Ebony's repertoire of tricks. He noticed that Giuseppe was issuing commands using a combination of voice, touches from the crop and pressure from his knees and heels. Ebony stood on his rear legs and pawed the air with his front-hooves. Asa's stood on his perch and waved his hat. The stallion's powerful muscles rippled and contracted as he raced around the arena free style. His wavy four-foot-long mane and his tail, so long it narrowly missed sweeping the ground splayed out to create a ghostly image of glistening blackness.

Giuseppe gave Ebony free rein, and he cut loose with the most carefree, frolicking backward kicks, playful bucking, and abrupt switches in direction. Then Giuseppe reined him in and had Ebony relax for a moment. He looked at Asa and nodded his head as if to say, watch this! The surprises kept coming for Asa. Ebony began high stepping in place, raising his hooves far off the ground. The horse shifted his center of gravity to his haunches and while balancing in an upright pose, held his front legs high off the ground. With a subtle command Ebony maintained the upright position and completed three controlled hops forward without touching the ground with his front legs. Asa started whooping and waving his hat in the air until Giuseppe silenced Asa's celebration by making a slashing motion across his throat. Asa quickly restrained his exuberance.

Giuseppe continued putting Ebony through the workout, rewarding his obedience with the treats. The next trick was the most spectacular display so far. The maneuver literally took Asa's breath. Ebony started with a rocking motion before leaping six feet into the air. While suspended he kicked outward with his hind legs before landing back on the ground. The spectacular exercise so excited Asa that he lost his balance and fell from his perch. Embarrassed, he stood as he looked about to see who was watching. After dusting his hat off on his pant leg, he resumed his position atop the fence.

Giuseppe dismounted and picked up the clip board he had stashed by the gate and began measuring Ebony. "Asa my man, you have a king's ransom here, no doubt about Ebony's past, he was a former show horse. I feel certain he was trained by the same trainer we used or someone that worked closely with him. Look Asa, he wants to play. He is enjoying our attention. He senses our emotional response to him. With a smile Giuseppe said, "Yes you are a big boy, like your petting and hugging, don't you? We are going to get along just fine."

Asa, did you see the scar on the inner side of his left front fetlock? I think the original owners sold him, assuming that he was permanently disabled. They normally euthanize animals with this kind of injury. It is a wonder that he has survived. You never know, some horses heal up better than others."

Asa said, "I totally missed that scar."

"Easy to do with those Friesian foot feathers," said Giuseppe. "When I check out a horse, I use my fingers more than my eyes. I felt the defect."

The two men walked back into the shop, and Giuseppe wrote up a work order. Asa asked, "How long will it take, sure would like to start riding him on a regular basis, but I need a saddle."

Giuseppe answered, "At least a couple of months for a saddle like this. But in the mean time I have an old saddle that should fit. I'd be glad to loan it to you. Not much to look at but you could give it a good going over with saddle soap."

Asa answered, "How much sweetening of the pot will it take to get the finished product in say a month?"

Giuseppe scratched his curly mop of hair and said, "Oh if you're in that big-a-hurry I can put off some of my other projects and deliver in a month, give or take a few days. This is one saddle I am eager to get started on. Never made one this fancy but I assure you that I have the technique." Then Giuseppe asked for a deposit on the thousand-dollar saddle and matching tack.

Asa had a money clip with a few hundred dollars in the buttoned pocket of his shirt. "Will an advance of two hundred now and a hundred per week be sufficient with the balance upon delivery?" Giuseppe agreed, and they shook hands and then Asa asked for a receipt.

It would be days before Asa's astonishment over Ebony's show-horse training ebbed. For the present Asa wanted to talk about nothing else. The two men lost track of time as they reviewed their surprise over Ebony's past.

Asa checked his pocket watch and said, "Giuseppe, how about you come on home with me. I want you to meet my family." Giuseppe agreed, and along the way Asa stopped by Raul's Restaurant and purchased a ten-pound container of smoky, deep pit pork loin basted with a hot and spicy tomato sauce and two-gallon buckets each of smoky pinto beans and potato salad. It sounds like a lot of food, but the McCawl family was a hard-working bunch of young people with big appetites.

Callie and Zelma were fretting over what to serve for supper when they saw Asa with the containers of food. They hurried to give him a hand bringing the food into the house when they spotted a man walking behind Asa. Both girls were still attired in their red and white stripped uniforms. They both worked a few hours each day after school as nursing assistants at the local hospital and had arrived home just ahead of Asa and the gentleman. Giuseppe got a sparkle in his eye when he saw Asa's sisters. Asa totally missed the sparks and said, "Soon as I put this food down, I'll introduce yawl."

Sid and John had been splitting firewood in the backyard and responded to the ringing of the chuck wagon triangle that hung from a porch rafter. They came stomping into the kitchen from the back porch drying their faces with a towel in time to be included in the introduction. "Giuseppe, meet my sisters Zelma, and Callie, and my brothers, Sid and John. This fellar is Giuseppe Svoboda, a leather craftsman and horse trainer deluxe. He is going to make a custom show saddle for Ebony. He is a very interesting person, and I wanted us to get better acquainted with him."

Giuseppe, bowed at the waist and said, "Delighted." He stepped in front of Callie and raised her right hand to his lips while maintaining eye contact and said, "Charmed" and followed up in the same manner with Zelma. Neither of the girls had ever had their hands kissed before, and it showed all over their blushing faces.

The two girls quickly changed from the uniforms into everyday calico dresses. They set the table and sliced tomatoes, cucumbers, and two freshly baked loaves of sour dough. There was plenty of sweet Texas Tea and cowboy coffee.

The aroma of barbeque that wafted from the opened containers prompted the sliding of chair legs as everyone hurried to take a seat at the long homemade table. Asa poured tea and asked how many wanted coffee before taking his place at the head of the table. It was Callie's turn to say grace. The words of the prayer were lost on Giuseppe who used the opportunity to get a better look at her. During the conversation he would learn that Callie was the older by a year and a half. Zelma was an inch taller and her blond hair a shade darker. The smitten Giuseppe found both girls' thoroughly effervescent personalities utterly alluring.

The conversation around the dinner table was lively and laughter prolonged the meal. One thing led to another, and Zelma decided to share her poem. She said, "I have this kid in my class named Kenny. He likes us girls, calls us 'purty.' He likes to write romantic poems.

The teacher warned him to leave us girls alone. That didn't stop Mr. Romeo." Zelma pulled a note from her pocket and started to read it.

Sid said, "Here let me read it. I know ole Romeo." He stood and did a convincing imitation of the author.

A Poem for Zelma

I'll start with 'Roses are red, violets mostly blue'.
Got you on my mind so I wrote this just for you.

Think I'll call you an angel, you're too pretty to be a human,
After you smiled at me and said hi, I decided to tell you my plan.

Why don't you and me ditch history class and go to a pond near here?
Joining the circus is my plan, see'n how I'm not gonna graduate this year.

In spite of tryin' hard my brain flunked arithmetic and I don't dare go home.
Math is not my strong suit but you must agree, I'm right good at writing a poem.

Ever heard of kids like me catchin' their parents' wrath?
Wish't you'd come along, one plus one is two, hey that's math.

I'll bring a snack; you like shelled pecans, crackers and cheese?
I cain't eat some stuff, gives me pimples and makes me sneeze.

Stop and pick up your swimming suit, I'll bring poles for fishing.
It's likely to take all day before they figure out we're missing,

There's a rope swings out over the water, I'll do my Tarzan yell!
I'll bait your hook with a worm, might catch a catfish after a spell.

*Before its dark and the stars are out, I'll drag up wood and
build a fire.*
*We can take turns telling ghost stories, the winner is the best
liar.*

*When the fire goes out I'll walk you home, holding hands
real tight!*
*I'll say thanks for playing hooky, picnicking, and ask you for
a kiss goodnight?*

By Kenny Coats, the Poet

Asa took the poem from Sid and looked it over. "Zelma, I'm
feelin' bad for the kid. He needs to stay at home and finish school. We
know what it's like to lose our parents. I might try to talk some sense
to the kid. Tell me what he looks like, ah, later. By the way, you did tell
him you're not allowed to date? Make sure he knows that, okay."

Asa was trying to get a few words into the conversation about
Ebony and his background. He gave up and watched the animated
repartee. Callie insisted on telling about what happened in her math
class. Seems a rat ran across the floor and about scared her teacher to
death. She described how funny he looked squatting on top of his desk
with his knees up under his chin. "He had to dismiss the class because
we couldn't stop laughing. You had to be there to know just how funny
it was."

When the food was devoured, Sid suggested Callie should lead
a second prayer since the first only covered a regular meal. The remark
caused the room to ring with laughter.

Once the dinner table was cleared away, Asa tried to engage
Giuseppe in conversation, but he seemed more interested in visiting
with Callie and volunteered to help with the dishes. Giuseppe was
a stocky man that stood about 5'9", his broad neck and expansive
shoulders identified him as a physically powerful person. His full
cheeks and large brown eyes were framed by a mop of curly brown hair.
Giuseppe was naturally gregarious and didn't mind being the focus of
the conversation, a trait no doubt enhanced by years of performing
before large crowds. From that night forward Giuseppe's quick wit

and quirky sense of humor assured him an open invitation at the McCawl dinner table. Asa noticed that Giuseppe and Callie had their own private dialogue going. He decided to forget Giuseppe and relate his astonishing discovery about Ebony's pedigree to Sid and John but found them only mildly interested.

Giuseppe rode home in the dark, deep in thought. He wasn't thinking about the contract to create a thousand-dollar saddle. Nor was he thinking about the Friesian Stallion and the chances of a horse like that showing up in a place like Gainesville, Texas. All of those topics were preempted by Callie McCawl. Giuseppe's recall of the evening was looped in a circular pattern. *Pretty was too mild, more like stunning. Sure, sixteen is young, but a mature sixteen. My mother was sixteen when she married my father. I need to cultivate a relationship. Asa needs my help with the stallion, and that will give me the opportunity to spend time with the family. I will work on the saddle and finish it faster than expected. I'll show Asa how to put Ebony through his paces. Something about Callie's blue eyes, never seen such beautiful eyes, —.*

Giuseppe was a frugal man and had a nice nest egg stashed in the local bank; why not use some of it? It was time to sharpen his public image. His introspection suggested the best way to attract Callie was to present the image of a respected and successful business man. Giuseppe upgraded his gypsy rags and footwear. He would pattern his personal style to that of the business men and cattlemen of the vicinity. He visited the Court House Barber Shop and had his unruly mop tamed. He stopped by the florist and chose a dozen red roses that he would personally deliver to the two McCawl ladies.

His living quarters, a room behind his shop was suddenly inadequate. He needed a respectable residence suitable for a business man of means. He pictured hiring help and hosting dinner parties. After inquiring around town, he was directed to a house that had come on the real estate market no more than a week before. The little house had belonged to a spinster seamstress that had died instantly in a buggy wreck.

The house had lace curtains at the windows, pink floral wallpaper, and a yard full of rose bushes and flower beds, not what most bachelors would choose, but Giuseppe wasn't most bachelors. Besides, he could imagine Miss Callie waving from the porch, holding a bouquet of freshly cut roses in her hand.

The place of his birth was not called the womb of European Romance without justification. Giuseppe grew up amid the fairytale setting of the Danube River region with its ancient Baroque architecture, Dumka violin music, fine wine, and Magyar Hungarian cuisine. The Bavarian culture of elegance and amazing beauty had imprinted the young Giuseppe with a whimsical tenderness.

Giuseppe quietly purchased the four-room cottage fully furnished. It was on a wooded lot in a popular residential neighborhood in Gainesville. He would wait for the right time to announce his acquisition. The décor of the house might brand him as being effeminate unless he was keeping company with the beautiful Callie McCawl.

Asa too was afflicted with a bad case of single-mindedness. For the first two weeks after buying the stallion, he was absorbed in researching the available information about Friesian horses. Giuseppe, eager to accommodate, used every opportunity to teach Asa everything he knew about *dressage* and *airs above the ground*. The saddle maker had his own agenda that dated from the night of the barbeque dinner. Somewhere in the back of Asa's mind he noticed that Giuseppe seemed to be dropping by to visit several evenings a week.

Unbeknownst to Asa, Giuseppe was impatiently waiting for Callie's seventeenth birthday just two months away. Once she was seventeen, he would ask for permission to come courting. The fragrance of romance born on a breeze can be contagious.

Asa wasn't the kind to put on airs and dressed in work clothes seven days a week mostly because he worked seven days a week. He never needed any "nice" clothes until, out of the clear blue, the strikingly beautiful, red-haired Ollie McClarren invited him to a Gospel revival meeting at a local church. Ollie and Asa had been noticing each other around town, and, on this particular day, fate placed them both in the Woolworth Five Cent Store located on the Gainesville town square. Ollie was looking through a stack of lace handkerchiefs when one of them dropped to the floor. Before she could pick it up, Asa just happened to be walking past where she stood and said, "Here let me help you with that—."

Fact was Ollie had seen Asa approaching in the corner of her eye and dropped the handkerchief on purpose, right in front of him. She had been trying to find a way to introduce herself to him for weeks, and this was her chance. For months on end Asa had been the topic of conversation among Ollie's boy-crazy class mates from high school. In their eagerness they were much too forward and had all been ignored by their target. As far as Ollie was concerned, their flirtatiousness made them look desperate and placed their wholesomeness in question.

Asa had no idea that he was wearing cupid's bulls-eye on his back. Finally, the encounter in Woolworth's gave Ollie an opportunity to field-test her approach, a more demure, subtle method. The only point of agreement she had with the tawdry group of silly girls was that Asa was by far the most handsome bachelor in Cooke County. Since he never attended any of the social functions, he would have to be captured in a novel way. Leave it to the ingeniousness of Ollie to devise a way to rise to the challenge.

Ollie snapped shut her paper fan and let it dangle on a strap from her wrist. Her gaze met Asa's as he handed her the handkerchief. It was a "moment made in heaven." To appreciate what was happening between the two of them, one needed to be there. Neither would ever forget the sensation they experienced when their eyes met.

Ollie said, "Oh thank you, Mr. – I don't believe we've met. I am Ollie McClarren" and she extended her white gloved hand to Asa.

Asa cleared his throat and shuffled his boots in a self-conscious manner before replying, "Welcome, Ma'am, I'm Asa, Asa McCawl," calling her attention to his belt buckle that spelled out A S A. After a pause he shook her hand, "Ah, you are sure looking lovely today Miz. McClarren!" While his ears were in the process of turning bright red, he was at a loss of what to do next and just stood there holding her hand much too long. He managed to regain control of his faculties and said, "Welp, I better be moving along, it is mighty nice to meet you Miz. McClarren." Before Asa had taken the second step Ollie said, "Ohhhh, Mr. McCawl, would you like to escort me to a gospel meeting at the little church on North Taylor Street this evening? It starts at 7:30."

Asa's head snapped around, and when he faced Ollie, he was flashing a most handsome full-faced smile. There was something about him that caused Ollie's heart to skip a beat.

Asa drawled, "Why Miz McClarren, I reckon we need to work out the details of this invitation over a fountain drink, that is, if your schedule allows."

Ollie said, "Lead the way." She couldn't help revealing her amusement as she took Asa's extended arm for the stroll through the store to the soda counter.

Asa nervously cleared his throat and attempted to engage in small talk, "My sister sent me to buy her some pink thread and some sewing needles; I reckon they are here about, but I didn't find'em yet."

Ollie smiled and pointed, "One isle over, by those big rolls of fabric. As they approached the soda counter, Ollie spotted Sarah from high school standing behind the counter. Ollie thought, oh no, not Sarah from history class. Sarah was standing behind the counter watching their approach with great interest.

Just as Asa went to occupy the bar stool next to Ollie, a snaggle-toothed, freckle-faced boy around eight years old scooted in front of him and occupied the only vacant bar stool. Asa, concerned that the youngster would make a big fuss if forcibly removed, did some quick thinking and devised a ploy to get the kid out of the barstool.

Asa stood back and with raised voice exclaimed, "There you are, I have been looking for you, young man, you have just been declared the winner of Woolworth's best smile contest! And even better, you won a prize, twenty-five cents to spend in the toy department. But the rules say you only have five minutes to present this special shiny quarter and pick out a toy. Do you agree to the rules? If the time runs out, the judges will choose some other kid in your place." Asa was thinking gosh, this kid is ugly.

The child looked up at Asa with one eye squinted shut, "Are you sure I'm the winner, Mister? I ain't been smiling much since my ma pulled out my two front teeth." Asa considered the possibility the kid was smarter than he looked after that answer.

"You're the buckaroo that won this prize, fair and square! I reckon the judges like kids with missing teeth, and freckles." drawled Asa.

Asa raised his voice and announced, "Attention everyone, here he is, the winner of the smile contest! Young man, if you don't mind, give us a big smile and then mosey on over to the toy department and name your prize!!! Come-on folks let's all show how we appreciate boys with nice smiles." Asa, holding the coin above the boy's head, led the hesitant and somewhat skeptical shoppers in some sporadic applause. As soon as the now smiling lad vacated the stool, Asa claimed it before lowering the coin.

The girl behind the soda fountain bar had an amused look on her face. She asked, "Ready to order yet?"

Asa looked at Ollie and asked, "Miss. McClarren, what can I git for you?"

Ollie thought for a moment and said, "Saspril—or no, I have been hearing about that new drink, cola, ah, Coke Cola, I think I want a Coke Cola with a scoop of vanilla ice cream, please."

Asa said, "That sounds good to me too. Ah, miz, waitress, we will have two large Coke Colas with scoops of vanilla ice cream, make that two scoops."

In a strange turn of events, the teenaged waitress just happened to be a member of the Asa McCawl Fan Club. The unashamedly flirtatious girl had all of her faculties focused on Asa. Of course, he pretended not to notice. Ollie could have sworn that the air currents generated by her batting eye lashes rid the counter of flies. Asa didn't notice the breeze since he was focused on Ollie. When she got no notice from Asa, the waitress turned her attention to Ollie and asked, "Well Ollie, what brings you to Woolworth's?"

Ollie replied, "Oh my, Sarah is that you? I didn't recognize you at first. My, aren't you looking all professional in that cap and apron. How long have you worked here?"

Sarah answered, "Almost two weeks. It's a fun place to work, and I meet lots of interesting people."

Sarah looked at Asa and in an overdone southern drawl said, "It's nice to see you again Asa, would you like to try our spicy crackers, salty nuts, or peppermint sticks?"

Asa said, "Naw, I thank we're good for now. Thanks anyway."

Ollie inclined her head and whispered, "Asa, I suspect you just made up that contest on the spot?"

Asa leaned over and whispered, "Wuz I that obvious? You hafta admit, it worked, and I got the stool. The kid likely has a mother who thinks his smile is cute, I didn't get thrown out of the store for man-handling an innocent child, and I avoided being kicked in the shin. All of that for the cost of a quarter."

Ollie tilted her head in a coquettish posture and said, "That was some quick thinking. You about had me convinced there was a smile contest." Asa and Ollie got their preliminary business out of the way. Ollie suggested they dispense with the formality of referring to each other as Mr. and Miss. Ollie would expect Asa to fetch her at 6:00 PM at her home at the far end of Mulberry Lane.

Asa commented on how much he liked the ice cream float and admitted that he had never had one before, and then Ollie said, "Me either." The admission struck them both as hilariously funny. When they both started to speak at the same time, that was even funnier. During the course of the earnest and candid conversation about nothing of substance, their eyes would meet, and then a line of pink would rise from their chin to their foreheads. The glow from their faces, mingled laughter, and electrical sparks generated from repeated eye contact combined to set the stage for their first date.

When slurping straws signaled the bottom of the Coke-floats, Asa stood and asked if he could escort Ollie somewhere. Ollie said, "Thanks but no, I am here with my sister and a cousin. Our father will be giving us a ride home any time now. I'm looking forward to seeing you tonight. Thank you for the delicious fountain drink. Toot-a-loo!"

When he turned to walk away, there stood the kid with the winning smile. He had one hand on his hip, bottom jaw jutted forward, and was glaring at Asa. "Hey Mister, the man at the toy counter hadn't heard of no smilin' contest. I figger you just wanted my stool at the bar." The kid was holding a small rubber gun with a plunger at the back of the barrel. "This here is the toy I got." Then, before Asa could react the little hellion aimed at Asa's crotch and sprayed him with water. Some of the spray hit Ollie too. Asa and Ollie's happy mood was dampened and replaced with outrage.

Asa inhaled and voiced a holler akin to the Rebel Yell. The chase was on. Asa was out front and had Ollie by the hand as they wove among the aisles of merchandise, not quite catching up to the little rapscallion. Fragments of words rang out that sounded like, "how dare you, you, you little ungrateful mutt, if I get my hands on you—, say goodbye to the rest of your teeth."

Through the cosmetic department, on to the house-shoe section, sewing notions, toy aisle all the way to the gold fish tank the chase snaked through the store forcing customers to jump out of the way.

Then the "Winning Smile" found what he had been searching for, namely a six-foot-tall person wearing a high visibility chartreuse sun bonnet and matching calico dress and attached himself to a leg beneath the flowing skirt. A rather rotund and athletic person, possibly a woman, had her eyes fixed on where "the apple of her eye" was pointing, straight at Asa. Asa followed by a breathless Ollie had skidded to a halt, just inches from the woman now comforting the little rapscallion. Asa's eyes adjusted to the sunbonnet shaded face and recognized a strong family resemblance. For a moment time stood still, and the only sound was heavy breathing. Asa's adrenaline-fueled frontal cortex was having a premonition. The message was warning him of a clear and present danger.

Asa seated his hat more firmly on his head and tugged on Ollie's hand just as he yelled at the top of his lungs, "Fire, fire, get out! Run everbody!" The sound of his voice rang loud and clear, and the store's shoppers all surged toward the front entrance. Asa and Ollie managed to work their way to the middle of the mass of frightened customers worming their way to safety.

Once outside the store's doorway, Asa went to the left and Ollie tried to turn right. Since they were still holding hands, they created a temporary obstacle for a few evacuees who managed to go under or in some cases jump over their arms. Asa paused long enough to help two frail ladies to their feet before he and Ollie high tailed it from the site. When Asa looked back over his shoulder, he realized that they were being chased by the woman in chartreuse and a very angry looking store manager. Physical agility and youthful athleticism gave Asa and Ollie the advantage. They hid in a clump of heavy vegetation in the back yard of an abandoned house down a side street. After a few minutes of muffled snickering, Ollie and Asa determined the coast was clear and casually strolled from seclusion and went their separate ways. They noticed that the fire wagon with bells clanging had pulled up in front of Woolworth's, so they both wisely avoided the spectacle.

Though there are other similar incidences on record, this seemingly minor event is cited as the historical basis for amending the criminal code of Texas. Within a few months the Texas State Legislature moved to list, "Yelling fire in a crowded building when there is none" a third-degree misdemeanor punishable by one week in jail.

Asa's life was about to get interesting. As for Ollie, it was plain as daylight that young Asa was smitten with her. *We girls just know this sort of thing*, she thought.

Asa hurried to find his sister and made his plea for help. "Callie, real quick, I need some help! I reckon you know who Ollie McClarren is, well she just up and invited me to go to church with her tonight. I'm thinking I need new shirt, hat, and trousers, you wanna help me git presentable? Here is some money and please, no razzin, I'll get enough of that from the old barber and his gang."

Callie said, "Asa, me, and Zelma both know Ollie. The kids in high school think she's stuck-up because her poppa owns half of Cooke County, but she is just a little shy. I think she is one of the nicest girls in school." Callie was glad to hear that her big brother was ready to have a social life. "Of course, I will help you with a new suit of clothes. You go on and get a haircut and shave while I pick out some new clothes for you."

It just happened to be Callie and Asa's grocery shopping day, and the encounter with Ollie McClarren had transformed a common day of chores into a "memorable event." Asa told Callie to hurry and, "Don't buy nothing fancy, just plain, you know what I like in clothes." Callie had always wanted Asa to dress nicer, and this was her chance to pick something really nice. Callie hurried to the Men's Haberdashery with Asa's sizes written on a scrap of paper. Asa double timed it over to the Court House Barber Shop located in the basement of the imposing landmark. The store manager had seen Asa about town and helped her choose a blue shirt, brown dungarees, and a black felt Stetson hat.

The old court house building had three stories or four if you count the basement. The grey granite municipal structure housed all of the governmental offices: the jail, litigation chambers, office of Vital Statistics, the Cooke County Sheriff's Department, and a small branch office of the Texas Rangers. Asa descended the steps that led to the Barber Shop and passed by the familiar symbol of barber shops, the red and white stripped caduceus.

Asa hailed the gray-haired barber with "Howdy" and shook his hand. He found the barber to be a likable sort of fella. In fact, Asa pretty much liked everyone, being a people person. Just like the celebrity, Will Rogers, Asa claimed to have never met a man he didn't like.

In a matter-of-fact tone Asa asked for, "the works: yep, haircut, shave, and boot shine." Asa took a seat in the revolving chair but declined to have his fingernails trimmed. As soon as Asa got seated in the barber chair, one of the regulars burst through the entrance saying that something was going on over at the Woolworth Store. "The far-wagon jus' pulled up in front, not mor'in a minit ago, and the farmen's running ever which aways." That reminded Asa to check his lap under the cloth drape, and he was relieved to see that the wetness from the water gun had dried.

The usual Ty Cobb fans and barber shop loiterers interrogated Asa as he sat perched atop the revolving chair until he admitted he did have plans to spend the evening with a young lady. Asa withheld her identity and other details to the boys' chagrin. Even the scant amount of information was enough for the buds to engage in some merciless teasing. Asa felt his face growing warm with a blush, but the barber unknowingly covered the evidence with a thick layer of lather. Putting on an air of calmness, Asa leaned back in the barber's chair, put a boot on the opposite knee, and drawled, "If I didn't know better, I might think you boys is a mite jealous."

Asa and Callie rode back to their rented cabin on the edge of town, a primitive old shack with a leaky roof. So far Asa had managed the leaky roof with strategically placed buckets, re-shingling would have to wait for cooler weather. Asa jumped from the horse and carried the box of groceries and other purchases into the house and without pausing grabbed a bar of soap, a long-handled brush, and a towel. With no time for heating water, Asa stripped to the waist and headed to the creek. Callie offered to put away the horse, and he thanked her with a pat on top of her head. Asa trotted down the path that led to the creek behind the cabin. Once back from the creek he brushed his teeth, combed his hair, and changed into the new outfit. He took a quick look in the mirror and grimaced. Callie, "This shirt is awful bright, like birthday gift wrappin, and the buttons, I don't know—."

Callie interrupted, "Oh hush, you look very handsome. Take my word for it, Ollie will melt when she sees you in that blue shirt, we girls just know these things." With no time for eating, Asa snatched a left-over biscuit, gave Callie and Zelma a threesome hug, and flashed them a quirky wink on the way out the door. Within minutes of Asa's departure, Giuseppe arrived and spent the evening with the McCawl kids playing a cut-throat game of "42" on the kitchen table.

Asa hurried to saddle Ebony, but despite his haste took a moment to consciously admire the exquisite Friesian stallion. Ebony would transport Ollie McClarren to her church in fine style. His flashy new parade saddle, the creation of master leather artisan, Giuseppe Svoboda would add to the specialness of the ride. Still new to the area, Giuseppe was an immigrant from Eastern Europe and spoke with a slight Slavic accent. He would not remain an outsider for long; fate was working in his favor.

The rich nutmeg-brown saddle with its long skirts, matching reins, and martingale were all stamped and carved with an intricate floral pattern and accessorized with silver concha embedded with turquoise. The entire saddle was outlined with silver spot studs. He wondered if Ollie appreciated fine horses and parade tack.

Ollie took all afternoon dressing for her date with Asa McCawl. Well before six o'clock she was ready and quelling a case of nerves. She pulled a chair to a window where she could see the lane that led to her house. A series of short baying howls brought Ollie out of her day dreaming. It was Blue announcing a visitor. She cracked the screen enough for the hound to squeeze through and said, "Here Blue, you're such a good dog." The huge 85-pound blue tick coonhound took his own good time rising from his rug. Blue gave Ollie a mournful look as he slunk toward his bed near the living room fireplace. Ollie couldn't resist that look and knelt to caress the beloved pet. Blue was thought to be 16 years old and had earned his arthritic joints and a road map of claw marks. A small oil painting of Blue hung on the wall of "Duard's Gun Shop and Pool Hall" located down on the town square. It hosted the Coon Hunter's Club on Monday nights come rain or drought. Blue was at the top of the Coon Dog Memorial Wall. Next to his portrait hung three blue ribbons displayed on a certificate with a big gold seal.

Ollie told Blue to keep quiet and ran her hand over his eyes. He obediently put his head down on his paws and pretended to be sleeping. When Ollie walked away, he opened one eye but quickly closed it when she saw the movement. No ruckus Blue, you hear?

Within a couple of minutes, a rider appeared on the lane, and she wondered who could that be? The face was hidden by a big black Stetson. Surely it wasn't Asa. As the rider entered her yard, she decided it was Asa. *Why was he on horseback? She thought, surely, he doesn't expect me to ride behind him. That's it, he expects me to ride astride behind him. No, he wouldn't.* She decided to send Hazel out to meet him. She moved back from the window and called her sister from the kitchen. "Hey, git over here. Asa's here, go find out if he expects me to ride behind him. Gosh, I hope Poppa doesn't see this."

Hazel started to speak, and Ollie put her index finger across her lips and shushed her.

"Oll, you want me to do what?" whispered Hazel.

Ollie waved her hands out of frustration and whispered, "Just tell him I'm running late and see what he says." *Mean time Ollie was thinking of her alternatives. I can tell him I can't go with him and lose my chance to go on a date with him, or I can change clothes and jump on. I can always beg for forgiveness later.*

Hazel was confused, shook her head, and said, "What do I say?"

"You heard me, ask him to wait on me."

"Ollie, you're gonna git us both in trrrroooouuuuble. Are you really goin' to ride on the back of that stallion?"

"Hazel, I don't have a choice. I'll never see him again if I hurt his feelings."

Asa sat atop Ebony and tried to relax. Poor Asa was suffering from an adrenaline overload that had his heart thumping. His new clothes were stiff and scratchy and smelled like the department store. At his waist he wore his black leather belt with a polished silver buckle engraved with a diamond encrusted "ASA." He liked that nobody had to ask his name when he was wearing it. He'd won the buckle for placing first in a cutting horse competition.

Asa was proud to transport Ollie atop Ebony, no doubt the most beautiful steed in all of Cooke County. He was not aware that propriety dictated that a fine lady like Ollie should be transported in a buggy. Besides, Asa didn't even own a buggy. He had other things on his mind like hoping Ollie would like him. He was rehearsing being a gentleman in his mind.

Hazel knew their father would not approve of Ollie riding astride behind Asa, but like the loyal sister she was, she took a deep breath and calmly said, "You must be Asa, I'm Hazel. Ollie is running a little late." Hazel felt a tingle of excitement just speaking to Asa, and she felt rather important to be running interference for her big sister. She was thinking, Ollie is going to owe me for this.

Asa doffed his Stetson and with true laconic style said, "Mighty nice to meet you, Hazel. Tell her to take her time."

Ollie decided to change into her brand spanking new riding habit. She figured the present was as good a time as any to take her stand against that "side-saddle" nonsense. Feeling a little naughty, Ollie took a moment to admire Asa from behind the screen door, before rushing up the stairs, two steps at a time.

Hazel went back inside, ran up the steps, and whispered, "You're gonna be in troooouuuuble, but it might be worth it, just cry and beg for mercy, you're good at that."

"Stop it, admit you are good at it too."

"I guess, forget I said it. Oh Ollie, Asa is even handsomer up close! Hurry and I'll go back to the kitchen and stall Momma and Poppa long as I can."

Ollie knew not to dilly dally and plotted to set her hook into Asa before her father, the gruff, no-nonsense Sam McClarren scared him off.

Asa lowered his chin and removed one leg from its stirrup and placed it in front of the saddle horn while he waited. From under his wide brim, he was checking out the McClarren property. The two-story house was freshly painted, windows sparkling clean, and the yard perfectly mowed and weeded. It was a perfect example of highfalutin homes. The yard was planted in grass and outlined with flowers and rose bushes.

While Asa was distracted with the McClarren home place, Ebony helped himself to a mouth full of nasturtiums, petunias, and periwinkles located in a flower bed only inches from his nose. By the time Asa realized what was happening, it was too late. He looked around to see if anyone was watching, squeezed the horse with his knees, and said, "Nein!" Then Asa said, "Back, back up, good boy, good Ebony!" Asa verified that the flower bed was only slightly damaged. Ebony had been a bad boy and still had bits of evidence sticking out of his mouth. Asa resumed wondering what it would have been like to grow up in a home like this. It never occurred to him that his future would find him living in a home of equal grandness.

The race with time was on. Ollie threw off her floor length go-to-meeting dress. She shucked her gloves and removed her little straw bonnet. With not a minute to spare, Ollie ran to her closet and snatched a white starched shirt from a hanger. She dug in the back corner of her closet and removed the box that secreted her pair of black flared-thigh Jodhpur pants and knee-high paddock boots. Ollie, for the sake of saving time, pulled off a tricky maneuver. Being fit and trim, she defied gravity by putting on the trousers, both legs at the same time. It was a leap for the history books. That she pulled it off without breaking her neck is remarkable.

For months she had been watching the girls' high school riding club called, "*The Buckaroo Belles.*" Every bone in her body was aching to participate in the practice drills. She had secretly purchased jodhpur riding pants and paddock boots to have on hand when and if she got permission to join the group.

Ollie never missed a chance to go along with Auntie Velma on one of her trips to the fashion center of downtown Dallas. The most recent shopping trip to the city with Velma had been to check out the newly opened Neiman Marcus store. Velma and Ollie shared an interest in fashion and always had a good time shopping, experiencing exotic cuisine at upscale restaurants and attending live entertainment venues. Another favorite thing to do was to spend an afternoon at the Dallas Zoo. The Zoo's gift shop is where she purchased her hat with the zebra hide band. She swore Velma to secrecy regarding the riding pants. Ollie was confident she would eventually prevail and be allowed to join the girls club. Becoming a Buckaroo Belle was one of star-struck Ollie's favorite fantasies.

Chapter 4

ASA & OLLIE'S FIRST DATE

Ollie had hoped to gradually introduce her parents to the idea of her and Hazel riding astride. Having such old-fashioned parents made Ollie a little resentful even though she adored them both. She planned to bring them into the new twentieth century gently, sparing their sensibilities as much as possible. That was before the one and only Asa McCawl showed up. It was a dilemma of the first order. It would have never occurred to her that he would expect her to jump on behind him and ride astride.

There Asa sat, bigger than life mounted on his black stallion, waiting. For the few people that knew Ollie well, they understood the seventeen-year-old was impulsive and at times even reckless. Ollie was sure this date with Asa was the next step into adulthood. She was ready to start living her life as a woman. She recalled old folks saying we all only get one life to live and most regrets come from things we didn't do. She convinced herself that not riding behind Asa was something she would regret forever. She would bear the consequences later, whatever they turned out to be.

She completed her costume with her favorite jacket, made of soft tan leather. It was beautifully embellished with silver and turquoise beads and lavish fringe. Standing in front of her mirror Ollie unpinned her mane of red hair and brushed through it. She let it cascade down her back. She placed the Australian hat at a slight angle. The bold stripes of the zebra-hide hat band provided the perfect accent. Ollie smiled when she saw her reflection and wandered what Asa would think of her get-up.

Just as Ollie appeared at the top of the stairs, Hazel walked out of the kitchen and reacted to the new clothes. She whispered, "When did you get those clothes?" Then Hazel said in a hushed tone, "Hurry, I stalled them as long as I can."

"Here goes," said a very excited Ollie. "Opps!" wasn't the only sound Ollie made as she lost her footing due to her slick soles. She bounced on her buttocks all the way to the bottom of the staircase making a loud bumping noise. Hazel was horrified over the accident and started over to help Ollie. Ollie was able to jump up and brush herself off. She whispered "ouch" and took an instant to rub her offended body part.

As Ollie walked toward the front door, she heard Hazel say, "Momma, do I smell something burning?" Both Sam and Elizabeth asked what the bumping noise had been. Hazel looked surprised and said she would check it out.

Hazel replied, "Everthing is okay out here, but I smell something burning, better check." Sam and Elizabeth reversed direction and walked back into the kitchen to make sure nothing was scorching. The few seconds of time Hazel's ploy gave Ollie was enough for her to slip out the door to where Asa waited.

Ollie took a deep breath and arranged portions of red hair over the front of each shoulder before opening the screen door. She smiled at Asa, and he smiled back. They both glanced back and saw her parents walking toward the big living room window. Ollie recognized that it was time to make her move or be sent back to her bedroom. He could see the outline of Ollie's family peeking through the sheer living room curtains and decided to take his leave.

It was a comical scene that followed. Sam McClarren could not believe his eyes. What was Ollie thinking? Sam, Elizabeth, and Hazel all inhaled in unison. Asa reigned the saddle horse to the edge of the porch and extended his elbow to Ollie. As though this was the normal way for a beau to fetch her, Ollie stepped forward and hooked her arm through his extended arm. Aided by the momentum of the lunging horse, Ollie sprang to the blanket covered rump behind Asa's saddle. She was forced to steady herself by grasping Asa's waist. Asa turned his head to the side and asked, "You all settled back there?"

Ollie stuttered an answer, "I thank soooo, gee, I've never done anything like that before! Whoopee!" Ebony wanted to run, and Asa fed him some slack for a half mile. It was a good thing Ollie's hat had a chin strap. The trees along the street were just a blur as they raced past.

Asa slowed the horse to a high stepping Spanish-walk. Ollie was squirming around behind him and piqued his curiosity. He asked, "What are you doing back there?"

Ollie said, "Oh Asa, this is the most beautiful horse I have ever seen. And the saddle, it is stunning. And oh my, how handsome you look in blue! I'm trying to get a better look at your shirt. Did you buy that brand new just for our date tonight?"

Asa ignored the question about his shirt but put a mark in Callie's 'I told you so' column. "Speaking of looking dapper," Asa said with his eyes more than his voice as he twisted in the saddle to get a better look, "The riding habit suits you, you're plumb toe curlin'."

Ollie said, "How gallant of you Asa, I always appreciate compliments but this toe curlin' I haven't heard of before. Can you enlighten me?"

Asa ignored the question and said, "Ollie, you should talk to my sisters about joining the Buckaroo Belles. They have lots of fun providing entertainment for local events. Ollie, you do much riding?"

Ollie replied, "I had some riding lessons, but it was strictly side-saddle. Asa, I just love horses and daydream all the time about learning to ride like a real Texas cowgirl, but first I must convince my parents. Listen to this, my riding instructor began every lesson with this quote he got out of an old book from England, 'Riding astride has an aura of indecency and profanes the elegance and poise of femininity.' Asa, don't you think most folks have rejected all that old-fashioned nonsense? That old instructor must have been born with a permanent frown. He claimed that proper young ladies never ride astride to prevent losing their hymen. He read aloud from a book that said the side-saddle was invented in the 1300s in England for that reason. Asa, I asked him what a hymen is, but he ignored me and walked away with his nose in the air. Do you know?"

Asa said, "Is it highman, spell it?"

"No, I saw it in print, it's spelled h y m e n."

Asa shrugged and said, "New to me. Must be something girls carry with them if they can lose it. Tell you what, I'll ask around and see what I can find out."

The bright-eyed youngsters' arrival at the church building ended the discussion. Folks were standing and watching as Asa dismounted, tied Ebony to the hitching rail, and lifted Ollie to the ground. The females were all looking at Ollie's outfit, and the men were admiring Ebony. Before there was time for the usual welcomes and introductions, Ebony began vocalizing and prancing in reaction to the mare tied next to him. Asa headed off an embarrassing incident by relocating Ebony to a tree in the apple orchard across the lane. In addition to the reins, Asa used a lasso he carried coiled on his saddle to double the strength of the tether. Ebony was known to untie knots and unlatch gates.

Ollie met Asa halfway back from the orchard and took his arm. All eyes were on them, and for a moment Asa felt uncomfortable until he took a closer look and realized that he knew most everyone. Amid the hugs, hand shaking, and back slaps Asa smiled and felt right at ease.

The men all stood eying Ebony and began questioning Asa about the horse. A few feet away Ollie was whispering and laughing with the young ladies of the group. When the preacher went to stand at the entrance to the little church building, Ollie fetched Asa away from the men and properly introduced him to the new preacher. He and his recent bride had arrived from Ft. Worth less than a month before. His friendly manner made a favorable impression on Asa. Of course, Asa liked everyone. Ollie had her arm hooked through Asa's, but he was too distracted to analyze Ollie's clinginess.

Back at the McClarren home, Ollie's departure had left Sam stammering and sputtering through his grey mustache, totally dumbfounded. He watched the departure from the porch and literally exploded with anger. When Sam recovered enough to form words he demanded, "Who was that boy? I have to get a few things straight with that young man!" The McClarren family had just witnessed a most unlikely event in the otherwise genteel life of the elegant, beautifully coiffed, and always fashionably attired Ollie.

Hazel attempted to soothe her father by placing a hand on his arm, "Poppa that was Asa McCawl, you know, the cowboy that competes in cutting horse competitions and sells quarter horses. I guess you didn't recognize him? He's got a good reputation, Ollie will be fine with him, and after all, they are going to church."

"Where did Ollie get those clothes, looked like a man's outfit. And jumping onto the back of a moving horse like that, she could have fallen. Elizabeth, I'm feeling sick to my stomach."

The gruff no-nonsense Sam resumed mumbling mostly to himself. Hazel contorted her face and bit her lip to hide her amusement.

Sam in a most emphatic tone said, "I will be having a conversation with young Asa!"

Elizabeth said, "Sam dear, it is time to leave for the meeting. Shall I bring your brown jacket?"

Sam plopped down on the sofa, trying to catch his breath. Huffing and puffing, he said, "Elizabeth, I'm dizzy and sick at my stomach. I don't feel like going tonight. The rest of you can go on without me. It's been a long day, think I'll turn in for the night."

Elizabeth offered to stay behind with Sam, but he insisted that she go along with Hazel. After a few minutes Sam stomped up the stairs to his bedroom where he remained until morning. Elizabeth and Hazel arrived at the church bursting with curiosity. Right away they spied Ollie and a bareheaded Asa engaged in lively conversation with the preacher. All three were laughing and gesturing with their hands.

A buzzer sounded and the entire crowd, minus Sam, found seating in the country church building. His absence brought inquiries of concern for his health all of which were answered vaguely. Sam had been scheduled to lead the closing prayer, and a substitute was quickly appointed.

Asa's prior experience with pew setting was limited. As a child his mother had taken him to visit a tent revival. He was expecting more of the same. His childhood experience had made a lasting impression. The denomination he had encountered was characterized by worshipers who prefer a demonstrative or ecstatic experience including speaking in a prayer language of unintelligible sounds. He remembered being frightened during the outbursts. The service concluded with a song inviting the sick and sinners to come forward for healing of the body and soul. The session was designed to motivate and entertain the audience with spirited songs accompanied by musical instruments. Several soloists sang from the podium. There was dancing in the aisles, shouting, and hand clapping. Passing the collection basket happened after each emotional plea from the preacher. They would empty the basket and send it back around after some spiritual warning about the love of filthy lucre.

The church Ollie belonged to was unusual in several ways. The church goers were reverent, orderly, and the best Asa could tell the sermon came straight from the Bible. The singing was congregational a cappella in four-part harmony. Asa had some money ready for the collection plate, but they didn't take up a collection. Asa whispered to Ollie, "The singing is beautiful, and by the way, when do they send around the collection basket?"

Ollie smiled and whispered, "Relax and put your money away. Members give on the Lord's Day, and we never beg for money from our visitors."

Asa nodded and slipped the silver dollar back into his pocket.

After the closing prayer, the preacher rapped on the podium and invited everyone to his house for cookies and hot chocolate. Asa and Ollie eagerly accepted the invitation.

After arriving at the preacher's house, Asa found himself surrounded by men who wanted to know more about the black stallion. They didn't need to ask twice. Asa began a narrative, using his fireside cowboy persona full of folksy expressions. He told the story of a man named Otto riding Ebony across Europe. "The horse and owner gained passage to America on a ship that carried passengers and freight. The man, named Otto, was hired to work out the cost of his passage. He would work in the kitchen and later as a housekeeper. After arriving in Boston, "He lost what money he had and eventually lost the stallion in a poker game. I bought the horse at auction. Until we have colts out of him, we are keeping the stud fee low so bring your mares by. So far, he is producing sound pregnancies, and we have the first foal due in the next month or so."

Ollie was in the kitchen helping prepare the refreshments and being bombarded with questions, "Gosh I never seen you dressed like that but the outfit suits you. Of course, you would be fetching in a potato sack."

"How long you been knowing Asa? You know Joan Lazenby, well, she confessed to having a big crush on Asa, but I don't think he's ever given her the time of day."

"Are those stories about Asa raising his younger brothers and sisters true?"

Ollie wasn't enjoying the interrogated and said, "Please excuse me ladies, we'll have to finish our chat later." Worried that she might say something she would regret, she went to search out Asa. In the living room she asked, "Yawl seen Asa?"

"Yep, he's out on the porch."

Before Ollie could interrupt Asa's conversation, two ladies rolled a desert cart out the front door. The scrumptious smells coming from the cart quickly captured the focus of the gathering. Warm peanut butter cookies, and soft, moist coconut macaroons got folks lining up to partake. The cart had a steaming crock of hot chocolate with mugs and napkins on the second level. The hostess asked the youngsters to go into the kitchen to be served where food mishaps would be easy to clean up.

Ollie found her buckaroo, and he was definitely in his element, speaking to a circle of men. They were hanging onto Asa's every word. Ebony and the Friesian breed were the topic. No surprise there. He had one foot hiked up on the porch and typical for Asa was using his hands as an aid to his vocabulary. His Stetson was pushed back exposing his handsome forehead and a curly row of sandy blond hair. He had rolled up his shirt sleeves to the elbow and was completely relaxed. He was holding Ebony's reins and preparing to climb into the saddle. He was fielding a question about the stallion's blood line, "Friesians have been a prized breed for centuries, some claim they go all the way back to the days of the Roman Empire." Next Asa launched into a description of the *airs above the ground*, and the whole series of *dressage* moves. "I don't know no French or German, so I call 'em fancy tricks. It takes an expert trainer and years to teach a horse this stuff. Though it is mostly Lipizzaner stallions that perform the *airs above the ground*, the Friesians take to the training and in some cases outperform the Lipizzaner due to their more muscular build."

"Asa," A man known as Ted spoke up, "Did you say something about Airs and Lipizzer somthin' another. I ain't heard of any of that"

Ollie decided to interrupt Asa and whispered in his ear, "Better get some refreshments before they are all gone."

Asa said, "Hold that question Ted, what say we check out the refreshments. Sure smells good."

After a second pass at the cookie and hot chocolate cart, Ollie whispered, "You must be hungry."

Asa whispered with a mouth full of cookie, "Sorry, I didn't have time to eat supper, I'm starving."

Ollie said, "Here take my cookie."

Asa's growling stomach settled down and he resumed the conversation, "Ted, they are just terms we ain't heard of in these parts, they was new to me too so don't feel bad. I'm about to demonstrate the airs, and as for Lipizzaner's, they are beautiful white show horses."

Most of the guests had spilled on to the front porch and were straining to hear what Asa was saying. Once in the saddle Asa did a routine warm-up by racing around the open field adjacent to the preacher's house. It was obvious that Ebony knew he was about to perform and was in an excited state. Asa directed Ebony to the front porch. He began the demonstration with the more common tricks and progressed through the repertoire of *dressage* and *aires above the ground*. The entire group watched intently with great interest.

Asa shouted, "This trick is called the *piaffe*, which is best described as an elevated, majestic trot, that calls for the horse to shift from one diagonal to the other. This'n is called the *pesade*. Next we have the difficult *levade* that has the horse rearing on its hind legs with its forelegs in the air and holding the position." Applause rang out prompting Asa to remove his hat and take a bow from the saddle. Asa followed with the *mezair*, the *ballotade*, and the spectacular *courbette* that featured a series of hops while maintaining the raised position with the front feet held high. Asa raced Ebony around the field to relax his muscles.

A young boy about the age of the Winning Smile was transfixed with the demonstration so Asa lifted the kid up to sit in front of him and had Ebony charge back and forth at top speed stirring up considerable dust, which didn't matter since the cookies and hot chocolate was gone by then. Asa lowered the boy to the ground. The youngster was in a state of bright-eyed awe. Asa ended his demonstration with the most difficult of all the exercises. "Folks, this here is the most tricky and hard to teach of them all. It is the *capriole* in which the horse jumps into the air and kicks outward with his hind feet while suspended in the air." The response was a deafening silence from the riveted watchers. When Asa announced the final trick, the people found the presence of mind to inhale making an audible breathy sound. With his tail at attention, Ebony was enjoying the reaction of the audience too. The term show-horse fit Ebony like a glove. "Ladies and Gentlemen, the *zapateado*! The *zapateado* is a solo dance marked by triple time stamping of the hooves in syncopation. Asa received applause and a few whistles. He gallantly removed his hat and bowed. Asa returned Ebony to the hitching rail across the road and quickly wiped him down with a towel from the saddle bag. Asa had a feed bag of carrots in the saddle bag. Asa returned to the gathering leaving Ebony to enjoy his reward before taking a short nap.

In the meantime, Ollie was set upon by the entire congregation. Everyone wanted to thank her for bringing Asa, but as soon as he returned the focus shifted back to the cowboy extraordinaire.

Ollie looked around but didn't see her mother. She was normally in the thick of food preparation. Elizabeth was affectionately referred to as the mother hen of the church. She had been the one to befriend the new preacher's wife Betty, a twenty-something year old burdened with shyness. Ollie walked through the living room on the way to the porch where Asa was visibly absorbed in the discussion of some subject obviously close to his heart.

Ollie, supposing that she was unobserved, indulged in a few moments to watch Asa from the darkened room. She asked herself, is this what it feels like to fall in love? Ollie sensed that she was not alone and looked around. In a shadowy corner sitting in an easy chair was her mother. Elizabeth was slumped in the chair. Her eyes were red, and she held a handkerchief on her lap. When Ollie saw the expression on her mother's face, she knew something was very wrong.

Ollie knelt in front of her mother and asked, "Momma, are you feeling ill? Are you upset with me for riding behind Asa? I didn't know he would come on horseback, and I didn't want to embarrass him. Elizabeth had been watching Ollie watch Asa and saw how she adored him. She had been Ollie's age once. Elizabeth stood and escorted Ollie out the back door to a bench in the shadows of the yard. "Ollie, my dear, you should know that your father is not well. I think he is having heart trouble."

Ollie reacted by hugging her mother to her breast. "Momma, I want to go home and check on him! Oh, Momma, I couldn't bear losing either of you. How I love you both."

Elizabeth kissed Ollie on the forehead and said, "I checked him over before we left, and he was settling down. I want you to know that he was furious with you when he saw you jump on that horse. We both were! And we were upset with the way you were dressed. You could have been mistaken for a young man, and the fact that you were on the way to worship made it still worse." Ollie began wailing and asked for forgiveness.

"Here now, settle down, we are going to talk this out with your father, and everything will be okay."

"Oh, what have I done to you and Poppa? I love you both so much. I don't deserve you.

I'm so sorry Momma, I was so worried about hurting Asa's feelings. I should have been more concerned about your feelings. Poor Asa doesn't understand about such things. He lost both of his parents when he was just a kid. But I confess, I knew Poppa would stop me unless I hurried. Will you ever be able to forgive me?"

"Ollie, it's going to be okay. I'll smooth it over with your father. I admit that he scared me. Right after you rode away, he became red faced and felt weak and nauseous. We need to keep a close eye on him and try to convince him to see the doctor. Here, dry your face and go and enjoy your ride home. Asa is a fine young man. We'll talk tomorrow. Honey, we love you, and nothing is going to change that."

"Momma, Asa was in such a hurry to get to our house he didn't eat a meal, and he admitted to being hungry despite the dozen cookies he has wolfed down. Can I fix him something when we get home? Maybe a slice of ham and some scrambled eggs. We'll hold down our voices."

"Sure honey, there is a fresh loaf of sour dough in the bread box." They parted with a hug and kiss.

Asa took a moment to check his pocket watch, still another first-place prize from a cutting horse competition and told the loquacious preacher that he had a young lady to escort home by a decent hour. Following a fitting complement to the preacher's wife for the generous hospitality, the preacher gathered the group on the porch, and they joined hands for a dismissal prayer. Asa and Ollie strolled to where Ebony was dozing.

Asa lifted Ollie to sit in the saddle and climbed on behind. His arms slowly encircled Ollie as he reached around her for the reigns. Asa thought to himself, finally, a chance for some time alone with Ollie. He set Ebony's pace to "meander." He chose the less direct route by way of the path that ran along Elm River or Creek, as it was called during dryer times of the year. The heavenly order that arranged for a full moon was obviously in cahoots with Asa's grand scheme to create the perfect evening for courting.

All of Asa's senses were heightened. *Ah, Ollie's hair smells of roses; the lovely tone of her voice was soothing.* It amazed him the way her red hair reflected the light of the moon. *Her laughter is musical, and she was not sparing with it.* Asa thought, *she sure knows how to git me to laughin'.*

They talked about the events of the afternoon at Woolworths and questioned the timing of the handkerchief falling to the floor at the very moment Asa walked by. "I'm minded to think it was fate." concluded Asa.

Ollie cleared her throat and opted to go along with his assumption. "Asa, what an intriguing idea, just think, that means we were destined to get to know each other!" They were both thinking in terms of a future relationship. There was silence while the two of them processed the thought of cultivating an on-going relationship.

Ollie whispered, "My, you were a big hit tonight. I don't recall us ever having so much fun! You and Ebony were spectacular. You really know how to relax and fit right in."

Ollie turned in the saddle and gave Asa a little hug. It must have tickled because he laughed and said, "Oh stop it, — Ah, never mind, hug away." Then he laughed again.

"Watch out Ollie, that kind of encouragement might get me camping out on your door step." The conversation rambled from one topic to another. Ollie was thinking, *Asa is so clever and funny.*

Then Asa said, "Wasn't that Winning-Smile-Kid a little terror, and that Momma of his sure put the fear in me. If he was a man in disguise, he could hurt me bad, and if it was a female, I shore didn't want to git in any fight with a woman. Think how would that look in the newspaper? Talk about a losing proposition."

"Asa, you are so funny." The two of them were laughing so hard they were in danger of plunging to the ground, fifteen hands below. Asa once again mimicked the demonic 'Kid with the Smile.' It was uncanny how he could warp his facial features into an exact representation.

Ollie said, "I would love a tintype with you looking like that kid. When you scrunch your face like that, ya really do look like him."

Asa said, "Ouch, Ollie you got me smiling and laughing so much my jaws are starting to ache, stop making me laugh. How 'bout we git down and sit on the grass?"

It occurred to Ollie that Asa might be building up to a kiss. Was it too early? She sure didn't want him to get the wrong idea about her moral character.

Ollie said, "Fine with me, I think I know how to make your jaw pain feel all better." Asa helped Ollie down from the saddle and the two of them found a grassy place to sit close to the creek bank. Ollie suggested, "I'll bet you are feeling the effects of eating all of those cookies."

"Never mind about me making a pig out of myself, couldn't help it. Ollie are you comfortable?" She nodded. He put his arm around Ollie's shoulders and said, "Listen, I hear an owl, and a whippoorwill. What a beautiful night. Sounds like the big croakers are out, too. We got some big ones here abouts. Good eatin'. J'ou ever eat a bullfrog? We catch 'em and fry 'em in bacon fat, taste just like chicken. Are you having as much fun as I am? Gee, I don't want the night to come to an end. Ollie, if the mood strikes you feel free to sing, quote poetry or howl at the moon." The part about howling at the moon got Asa an elbow in the ribs.

Asa said, "Look Ollie, we're getting moon struck, twice. Gittin' a double dose. See how the moon is shining on Elm Creek and then reflecting right at us. Here let me see your face, yep, just as I thought, come a little closer, now hold real still, I thank I can count your eyelashes. Here, try counting mine."

"Asa, you're right, I can count your eyelashes! We really are being moon-struck. Do you feel it, I do; suddenly the air feels fresher—, like oh it just feels good. But, how is your achy jaw?"

Asa was discombobulated. Was it too soon to kiss Ollie? Desire was working on him, well-nigh to irresistible, and just as he was about ready to place his lips to hers, he thought better of it, he would wait until he was sure she was ready to be kissed. This was one relationship he didn't want to mess up. "Yep, feeling a little better, but still hurts."

Ollie said, "See if this helps." Ollie spun Asa around and pulled his head down onto her lap. She began massaging his jaws and his temples with her thumbs. Then Ollie drew in a big breath and began singing in a lovely soprano voice:

By the light of the silvery moon
I want to spoon
To my honey, I'll croon love's tune
Honey moon, keep a-shinin' in June
Your silvery beams will bring love's dreams
We'll be cuddlin' soon
By the silvery moon.

Asa whispered, "Ollie, sing it again." Using his full voice, Asa joined in: grossly off key and ad-libbing the words.

Ollie patted Asa on the head and said, "Interesting rendition of the song Asa. I've never heard it exactly like you sing it, but variety is the spice of life. Hearing you sing is memorable, that's for sure."

Asa pretended to be hurt and asked, "Was it that bad? Maybe I'll just leave the singing to you. I always liked that song; you did a beautiful job, beautiful just like everything else about you." Asa thought to check his time piece and caught his breath. "Ollie, it's late, we better get you home. Where did the time go? It's after 10:30." Asa helped Ollie up to the saddle and mounted in one smooth motion. He loped Ebony the mile or so to Mulberry Street.

Asa rode Ebony up to the porch, dismounted and caught Ollie under the arms to lift her from the saddle. He set her down in the very place from which she had leapt onto his horse. A starry-eyed Asa said, "Good evening Ollie, I sure did enjoy myself, thanks for the invite."

As Asa turned away Ollie said "Wait, come back." Then Ollie smiled and said, "Asa, I'm hungry, and I know you are, come on in to the kitchen, and I will make us a mid-night snack. We need to be quiet. Tie Ebony to the hitching rail right over there by the crape myrtle bush." Asa followed Ollie on tippy toes up the steps and into the living room where he came face to face with Elizabeth and Hazel. They both shook Asa's hand, said good night, and turned to walk away when Elizabeth stopped and said, "I enjoyed seeing your horse doing all those tricks. I didn't know horses could do such as that."

"Thank you Mamm, glad you enjoyed it all, good night." Both women walked up the stairs, and Hazel looked back and waved and flashed a silly little smile at Ollie.

Ollie beckoned for Asa to follow her to the kitchen. She opened the ice box and set a basket of eggs on the counter and brought out a wrapped ham. Asa said, "Let me help."

Ollie handed him a bowl and whisk. "Crack two eggs for me and however many you want." She set a full slice of smoked ham steak into the iron skillet, and as it started to sizzle, a scrumptious aroma filled the room.

Asa said, "Hand me that knife, I have to sample the ham." Asa cut off a bite size chunk of ham and almost dropped it while he juggled it between hands to cool it down. Then he pitched it into his mouth and made funny blowing noises. "Still too hot." Finally, he started chewing and almost swooned over the deliciousness. Ollie got tickled over Asa's antics with the ham and placed her hand over her mouth to keep from making noise. "Ollie where did that ham come from?" he whispered.

Ollie said, "Ever hear of a Spanish man named Raul? He is our butcher. He makes wonderful bar—."

Asa interrupted, "Barbeque! I know we are one of his biggest customers. I didn't know that he smokes hams too. But it makes sense. This is enough to cause a man to founder hisself."

"Asa, here stir the eggs while I slice some bread and pour the iced tea. Ollie lighted the tall silver candelabra and arranged two place settings across from each other. Asa started to sit down but remembered to help Ollie with her chair at the last moment. "Thank you, Asa."

Ollie reached across the table and took Asa's hands and sang a prayer song very softly.

> *Be present at our table, Lord.*
> *Be here and everywhere adored.*
> *These mercies bless and grant that we*
> *May feast in fellowship with thee.*

During the momentous twelve hours that had just passed, Ollie and Asa had bonded. Comfortable familiarity had replaced awkward shyness and moved the relationship from one of attraction to infatuation. Like the kids they were, they consumed the meal with smiles on their faces, and a lot of eye contact, not to mention muffled laughter.

Following the meal, they cleared the table and did the dishes. Asa insisted on washing. The evening's finale found them sitting on the porch swing listening to night noises. Ollie invited Asa to Sunday services at 10:00 AM, but he was non-committal since he had a client coming from Oklahoma City shopping for a cutting horse. Asa raised an eyebrow and said, "I will try, but if that fellow shows up, I will be busy with him."

Asa slowly stood and walked to the porch steps to leave. Ollie reached out for his hand, and he stopped mid stride. That is when she pulled his head down and from tip toes planted a very sweet kiss upon his forehead. Asa responded by bear hugging her and said, "Ollie, I absolutely adore you! Sleep well. I hope to be see'n you soon, maybe

Sunday." Asa's boyishness got the better of him as he sprang into the saddle. He signaled Ebony to rear and paw the air with his hooves, and then Asa kicked the stallion into a full run. Ollie's cowboy rode away gallantly waving his hat as he disappeared into the waning moon lit night. Poor smitten Ollie stood on the porch staring and listening as long as Asa's departure was audible.

The following evening Asa met up with the good ole boys around the campfire. When he arrived, the old fellows sensed something different about Asa and Riley asked, "What you been up to Asa?"

Asa responded with, "Well for one thing Ollie McClarren invited me to go to church with her. Told me to pick her up at 6:00 PM. Course I got a shave and haircut, got some new duds to wear, and showed up right on time. She was all dressed up in riding pants, boots and hat and raring to go. I spurred Ebony to the edge of her porch, and she hooked her arm through mine and sprang aboard. Boys, I must admit that she is cuter than a bug. We got invited to the preacher's house after church. So, now yawl know what I've been up to."

The boys stopped him and asked him to be more specific, especially the part about Ollie jumping on behind Asa from her porch. Asa, considering their advanced age and trouble with hearing, patiently repeated the tale. Riley asked, "Asa, I'm 'sprized you didn't take her in a buggy? Most fine young ladies like Miz McClarren prefer to go in a surrey of sorts."

Asa was taken aback and said, "Oh! Sounds like I messed up bad?"

Ole Riley tugged at his beard and reckoned, "Now don't go beatin' yourself up, it's a minor error in judgment. Just show up next time in a carriage of some kind and take it from there."

Chapter 5

OLD DOGS & IDIOTS

Suddenly Asa remembered to ask the question. He was all comfortably slouched against a log, soaking up the warmth of the crackling fire when he asked, "Anybody know what the word hymen means? Heard something about it getting lost?"

Asa was expecting a definition of the word, certainly not the reaction he got. The entire cadre of gents were suddenly convulsing as though they were deprived of air. Equilibrium gave way to vertigo, causing staggering, gasping for air, and jerking extremities. The afflicted gents were all slumped upon the ground ever-which-way.

Asa sprang to his feet in alarm and yelled, "What's goin' on?" He was prepared to make sure none of his thrashing friends rolled into the fire. Oh Lordy, did the old boys laugh, tears ran from their eyes, and several of them momentarily lost sphincter muscle control. It must have been the noxious gases being expelled that brightened the camp fire. The gents had "cut loose" from all civility while feeding the fire with clouds of methane and hydrogen sulfide. He was about ready to fetch the doctor when the strange attack dissipated. The old gents were spent by that time, and they all took their leave and wore their smile all the way to their abode.

Asa's earnest lack of sophistication made his ignorance of the "word" hymen his only saving grace. The old men could not contain their sometimes-bawdy sense of humor. It was a case of well-behaved, mature men reverting to an earlier state of mind called 'boys will be boys.'

Once the chorus of howls had died down, Asa stood with his hands out, and bewilderment on his face. Little did he know that he was receiving the reprieve normally reserved for *old dogs and idiots*. "Do I git an answer to my question, or you boys gonna leave me in the dark?" Asa was waved off and decided to drop the subject. The next day he rummaged through his book case and found a dictionary.

A week later Asa had not stopped blushing. Everyone assumed he had spent too much time in the sun. The next time Riley saw Asa he asked if he had answered the question, and Asa was ready for him. "Looked it up in a dictionary so I can enlighten you boys next meeting. Sorry about exposing your lack of knowledge, you cain't help what you don't know."

Riley nodded and said, "Can't wait for you to fill us in on what the dictionary had to say. You comin' over tonight?"

"Spect so. Keep the coffee hot."

That evening before Asa joined the fire-side gents Riley shared a personal observation with the group of old timers. "Boys, we all know that Asa missed out on a lot with his parents dying and all. Ain't no wonder the boy is a might shy on etiquette and chivalry. He's a prime example of how a brilliant mind and hillbilly ignorance can coexist. I figger the kid more than makes up for any short commin's."

The conversation stopped abruptly when Asa arrived on the scene. The reception the old gents gave Asa was awkward and he decided to forget about the on-going matter. The elder of the buds, Ole Josh walked over to shake Asa's hand and congratulate him on his evening with the purtiest girl in the state of Texas. Several others gave him a pat on the back and Riley ruffled his hair. "Boy, I figure we've all bumped up agin ole Sam McClarren one time or nuther and it's not for the faint of heart. Better watch your step son."

During a visit with a longtime friend, Sam McClarren learned a few things he didn't know about young Asa McCawl. The old gent had heard about Ollie showing up at church with Asa and brought up the subject, "Sam, you otta take young Asa under your wing. Yep, he's a fine youngster. I predict he's gonna make his mark on this part of the world. I been watchin' how he takes care of his little sisters and brothers. Fore-shore he's got integrity and is a hard worker, not a lazy bone in his body. Why, when his parents died, he was forced to grow up quick like. Got his childhood stolen from him."

Sam who prided himself in having his thumb on the pulse of Gainesville wondered how he had failed to hear about Asa's tragic life of hard times. "Sam, if I wuz you, I'd overlook the part about not bringing a buggy, he probably didn't know it was the proper thing to do."

Sam practically jumped off his park bench, "How'd ju know about that? Must be all over town, I was hoping to keep it under wraps. It's true, my baby ran back upstairs and changed into riding clothes and jumped on behind Asa without considering what it would do to her reputation or how her mother and I would feel. It's all smoothed over, and we forgave her. We chalked it up to youthful impulsiveness."

The following Sunday Asa showed up at church with his business client. Sam was the first to greet Asa, introduced himself and promptly took him aside. Sam noticed that Asa looked him in the eye, and his handshake was just short of painful for Sam's arthritic hand. "Asa, we're serving up a fried chicken dinner at my house right after church, and we want you and your friend to share it with us."

"Thank you, Sir. Can I bring anything?"

Sam got to the point and said, "Manners, boy, bring your manners. You should know, I was so amind to have you arrested for endangering my Ollie. Having her jump on the back of a moving horse like that was dangerous, you ought to know better. Church is startin', and I got to go, but we ain't finished with this conversation. We'll talk more out at my place. Asa's business client was in a conversation with Ollie.

Asa said, "Yes sir, looking forward to it, sir." Sam gave Asa a look that said tread lightly around me and walked away nodding his head."

That is when Ollie came over and invited Asa and the older gentleman to sit with her. Later at the McClarren home, while the women put the finishing touches on the Sunday dinner, Sam took his guests out to the barn where Ebony was tied to a post in the shade. "Fine horse you got there. What would you take for him?" The business client asked to walk around and see the corrals, to give Sam and Asa some privacy.

Asa got a concerned look on his face and said, "Mr. McClarren, there is not enough money to buy that horse, sorry but I can't consider selling him, not even to you."

"I understand completely, he is a beaut! So, this saddle and tact is the work of that gypsy named Svoboda, it's a fine piece of workmanship. I have been looking for a good leather man." Asa faced Sam straight on and said, "I'm ready to finish that talk you started.

Sam began with a sad look on his face. "Reminded me of a terrible accident that happened when I was a kid. My older sister tried to jump on a moving horse from a corral fence and fell. Broke her hip and arm and messed up her back. Her bones never mended right, and she was a cripple. Got around in a wheelchair the rest of her short life. She almost died from the injuries she suffered. She had lots of complications and died in her twenties. Asa, I felt like it was happening all over again when I saw Ollie that evening. Come on and walk over here with me." Sam led the way over to the other side of the barn. "Asa, over in this part of the barn is my box buggy, just sits there most of the time, and I want to offer it to you when you take any of the female members of my family for a ride. Just feel free to make yourself at home and use it anytime. The two draft horses trained for the buggy are the matching sorrels with front stockings. Once you show'em who's boss, they settle down and do a good job."

Asa broke eye contact and blushed, "Mr. McClarren, I sure do appreciate the offer, and I might just take you up on it. How about this evening? I figure Ollie might enjoy a ride. Would you and the missus like to come along?"

Sam declined the invitation and mentioned something about a roundup and said, "Maybe another time, but you're welcome to use the buggy."

Asa completed the sale by mid-afternoon, and the client was on his way back to Oklahoma, leading a fine cutting horse. Asa was back as soon as he could manage. He hitched the two sorrels and drove the wagon to the front yard drive. Ollie had changed into a blue calico prairie dress and sun bonnet and was toting a picnic basket. She had watched Asa in the barnyard from the porch swing. Before Asa and Ollie left in the buggy, Sam invited Asa to come out for his round up scheduled for the following day.

Asa said, "I'm happy to come and give you a hand, daylight here at the barn then?" Sam agreed. He had in mind Asa coming to observe, but if the kid wanted to pitch in all the better; Sam would have a chance to judge Asa's work ethic, see him in action. He would know if the kid had potential.

Asa showed up at Lazy Σ Ranch first light on Ebony, leading a powerfully build sorrel quarter horse. Asa's arrival was announced by Blue, the McClarren's blue-tic coonhound. The old dog walked beside Asa all the way to the barn. Asa stepped out of the saddle and spoke to the dog. He held out his hand and after a respectful interval was able to pet the animal. Blue voiced the usual two or three short howls and then stayed with Asa.

Asa wanted to make a good impression on the old man in the worst way. He figured Sam could use his help, so he jumped right in and worked with the hired hands. They were branding and castrating the latest crop of calves. He volunteered to cut the calves from the herd so that Sam could see the cutting horse in action. If Sam liked the horse, Asa planned to leave it behind. After a half hour of impressive performance, Asa rode the horse over to where Sam was perched on the corral and offered him the reins. Sam climbed into the saddle without a word and put the gelding into play. It was apparent that he was impressed with the horse. Sam smiled and gave Asa a thumbs-up.

Asa amazed Sam by the way he knew how to read the crew and anticipate what he needed to do, the way a hand would do after working as a team. The boys on the crew didn't know why Asa was working with them, but they all knew who he was. When it came time to cook up some grub, Asa volunteered to help. He offered to mix up his special dutch-oven biscuits. As usual, Asa's biscuits were melt-in-your-mouth perfection.

Sam remained guarded and aloof with Asa. He would make a good ranch hand, but courtin' Ollie was something else. Sam determined to do what he could to discourage the relationship. A push over Sam wasn't. Ollie deserved a real gentleman of means.

One would think Asa had been a long-time member of the crew the way he meshed with them. Sam was a big believer in hard work, and the calluses that covered Asa's hands did not go unnoticed. Sam likened Asa to a diamond in the ruff. Make a good foreman for my outfit.

Once the last of the calves was branded and castrated, Asa handed the sorrel's reins to Sam and said, "Keep him and if he works out for you just put in a word for my operation ever chance you git. I'll send over the paperwork on the transfer." That got a raised eyebrow from old Sam, known for his business savvy.

"Asa, you got yourself a deal," and they sealed the agreement with a handshake.

The day Asa gave Sam a hand with his roundup Elizabeth, Ollie, and Hazel asked Jolly to drive them into Gainesville to stock up on staples. When Ollie saw Callie and Zelma walking on the square, she rushed over to say hello. The Five of them went to the Woolworth soda counter and ordered Coke Floats. (There behind the counter was a sheepish Sarah, avoiding eye contact with Ollie.) Ollie made a point of being polite and impersonal. There was some discussion as to whether Ollie and Asa would become an item, and Elizabeth interjected, "You girls are speaking out of turn. Now, I'm right proud of my daughter for inviting Asa to church services, but this other talk is goin' too far. As for me, I want to invite the rest of the McCawl family to worship with us anytime."

Zelma smiled and said, "Thank you Mrs. McClarren, we just might take you up on the invitation."

After Elizabeth left the quartet, the conversation turned back to Ollie and Asa. Callie said, "Ollie I can tell that Asa is really taken with you. He doesn't have much experience with girls. Just the mention and he blushes. I figure me and Zelma can hint around about him asking you for a date, that is if you want us to."

"Well, I reckon!" Ollie continued, "Asa is the handsomest Stetson rack in these parts, but what really matters is that he is an all-around nice fella too. I wish he wasn't so bashful. Hey, I have an idea. Would the two of you like to sleep over at my house? We could stay up late and tell ghost stories or play games." Both McCawl girls were quick to accept the invitation.

Unbeknownst to Callie, Zelma, Ollie and Hazel, the last thing poor Asa needed was a ratcheting up of his fixation on Ollie. The love-sick fool was already full of Cupid's arrows, smarting from ecstasy, and drowning in a quasi-pool of bottomless essence of Ollie.

Ollie opened the conversation with, "Callie, I have been watching you and Zelma practice with the Buckaroo Belles, and it looks so fun. I would love doing something like that. And to be honest, I want an "Annie Oakley Outfit" so bad I can taste it. Where did you get them?" Callie indicated a local seamstress named Rosa Mendez.

Ollie and Hazel went to the next practice session of the Buckaroo Belles. Being denied the chance to participate was a huge disappointment. The performance was all they could talk about, that and Asa of course. Privately the McClarren girls confided that the problem was with their parents. It was going to take some time.

Chapter 6

ORDER IN
THE COURT

It took a week for the Sheriff's department to track down the culprits that yelled "fire" in the Woolworth incident. Of course, it was the fountain girl named Sarah that offered her witness of the crime and named the offenders. Asa was interrogated and issued a citation and court date. Ollie was called as a material witness. The morning of the hearing Asa bathed in the creek, pulled on his buffed boots, and donned his freshly laundered blue shirt.

News of his scrape with the law had spread like wildfire. On the hearing date Asa could have sworn half of population of Gainesville had entered and when filled to capacity stood on the grounds converged on the courthouse. Most of the crowd had come hoping to appear as character witnesses on behalf of Asa. Asa was taken aback by the show of moral support, since he was not yet aware of his status as a favorite son. Asa's fan base was made up of area ranchers, former school mates and teachers, business associates, and the unofficial fan club of teenaged girls that called him "the handsomest head God ever put on a cowboy."

The hundreds of rowdy locals mobbed Asa at the hitching rail. He dismounted and began shaking hands with men and hugging women.

He picked a well-known and trustworthy fan to lead Ebony to the livery stable. Asa interacted with the crowd like a seasoned politician. Upon entry to the hall of justice Asa was asked to wait in the foyer until called by the bailiff.

The ten-minute wait seemed much longer, but finally the bailiff's summons came. Asa removed his Stetson and entered a totally silent chamber, so quiet the proverbial falling pen could have been heard. Asa scanned the court room looking for Ollie. He spied her near the back nervously fanning herself. He paused and said, "Mamm" and raised the Stetson as a salute. The only sound was Asa's foot falls accompanied by his jingling spurs as he sauntered to the witness stand. The bailiff pointed to the chair in the criminal box.

Without any heeing and hawing, Asa began speaking to the assembly, "Hello friends, how is everbody?" The audience response was deafening. Some answered with "Howdy Asa," others "Mighty fine," some unintelligible. I'm here under my own volition, and—." The bailiff held up his hands and said, "Hold your horses Asa, the Judge ain't out here yet."

Ollie's arrival had been "an arrival" worth comment. The impeccable business suit she wore definitely made a fashion statement. Her eye-candy image dazzled the crowd. The ensemble she wore had just arrived from Paris the week before, barely allowing time for alterations. She was hoping to dazzle Asa. She could hear him calling her "toe-curling." Secondly, wearing such a proper business suit would make her father proud. He was still sensitive over her wearing a riding habit to worship service. The McClarren family's comportment in public was of great importance to her parents.

Ollie's haute couture was inspired by the latest Paris fashion. The two-piece business suit and matching parasol were fashioned of brown and black satin brocade. The floor length A-line skirt was enhanced with a flirty bustle. The fitted jacket was detailed with rows of buttons and bows. Ollie's hair was caught up into a mass of red curls, crowned with an off centered, wide-brimmed straw hat embellished with a black and brown striped ribbon. Ollie McClarren was unchallenged as Gainesville's stylish dresser. Unlike most local women, Ollie had the poise and graceful carriage to pull off wearing the latest avant-garde attire.

The courtroom was packed and overflowed to the lawn outside. Spectators had opened the windows and were sitting in the window sills. The only thing missing from the circus-like atmosphere was a concession stand. Even the standing-room was crowded.

The judge assigned to Asa's case was the "wash-board and jug playing" Judge of Cooke County, the venerable Judge Roy Pinto, a recent immigrant from Kentucky and son of a Hatfield Clan patriarch of Hatfield and McCoy notoriety. Judge Roy was a former Justice of the Peace and part-time member of Asa's good ole fireside buds.

The Judge's comportment did not fit that of an officer of the court. He stood well over six feet tall and had the physique of a string bean. His face was dominated by his eagle's beak nose, a grey, foot-long beard that fanned out over the front of his black robe, and a pair of bushy grey eyebrows that slanted up and outward giving him a permanent expression of surprise.

The bailiff shouted, "Hear Ye, Hear Ye, please stand as the Honorable Judge Roy Pinto, magistrate of Cooke County, Texas takes the bench." The Judge took his seat and used his gavel to bring the court to order. The Judge said, "Will the defendant please stand and state your name for the record."

Asa slowly rose and turned toward the judge and pointed to his belt buckle. He looked at the judge and said, "Your Honor." The judge shook his head and said, "We are asking for your name, not mine."

Asa's expression turned to embarrassment and he said, "Oh, yes, ah, Asa is my name, but Sir Judge, you all know my name already."

The judge ignored the fact that the kid left off his last name because it would have been superfluous. "Asa McCawl, do you swear to tell the truth, the whole truth and nothing but the truth, so help you God?"

"Yes sir, I do, I absolutely do!"

"Mr. McCawl, how plea you?"

Asa slowly rotated his head, encompassing the court room while making eye contact with many of the faces that intently looked back. It appeared that most of the local population was crammed into the courtroom. Asa, still holding his Stetson, placed it over his heart and bowed to the audience before turning his attention to the Judge. The expression on Asa's face was painful to behold as he carefully enunciated his memorized plea: "Guilty as charged, your Honor, and members of the community. I petition to waive my right to counsel and ask the court's permission to represent myself." To fully comply with legal protocol, he raised the Stetson over his head and waved it back and forth. He laughed along with the audience, refusing to reveal that he didn't see what was funny about sanctioning an oath by waving one's hat. He reckoned, *even the Bible talks about wave offerings and such.*

Before being seated back in the criminal box, Asa pitched his Stetson at a knob on the railing, and the hat spun around once but stayed in place. Judge Roy said, "Good Shot."

"Your Honor, I'm here to take responsibility for my actions and *partition* the court for a bench warrant proceedings."

The judge lowered his voice and addressed Asa directly, "Son, are you sure you understand that a bench trial leaves the decision in this case exclusively to me as both judge and jury?"

"Yes, your Honor, I read a paper on bench warrants and agree for you to decide." With full voice Asa addressed the silent courtroom, "I admit I done it folks, but I didn't mean nobody any harm. That huge woman dressed in greenish-yeller scared me, of course that's a pitiful excuse, but it's true. I'm awful glad nobody got hurt much. I'm here to throw myself on the mercy of this court."

The outcome of the trial depended on how Asa's guilt or innocence resonated with Judge Roy. The prospect of being branded a convicted criminal was weighing heavily on the young defendant. Asa wasn't sure how credible his defense citing trauma-induced delirium would sound. He had read up on jury nullification, but that didn't apply in a bench warrant proceeding, so Asa contrived his own brand of persuasive argumentation that amounted to *judicial nullification,* a unique pairing of non-sequitur terminology.

Asa's 'Rags to Riches' life closely matched Horatio Alger's fictional "Ragged Dick" character. Young Asa had never heard of Horatio Alger, but Judge Roy was well versed in the American Classic, and the comparison was inescapable.

A quick analysis of Asa's ability to connect with people indicated that the attribute was intrinsic. Asa's innate ability for dissolving resistance, building consensus, and enlisting collaboration would serve him well in his defense before the court. Folks in the court room had arrived with a pro-Asa bias that became increasingly apparent as the proceeding progressed. Asa was ready to state his defense. And so, he did in a most stirring and eloquent manner.

Asa had prepared for his court hearing by reading up on court room parlance including protocol and common phrases. He knew it was no time to come off dumber than a doorknob. Judge Pinto asked that the charges be read by the clerk of the court. Next, he nodded at Asa and said, "You may begin your defense."

With obvious trepidation Asa settled into the chair and raised one foot over the opposing knee. He began his side of the story by saying, "When I take an oath to tell the truth, the truth is what you're gonna git."

Asa began the narrative sitting down but early on rose to address the court in order to clearly demonstrate the details. He confessed right off that he had been pierced through the heart by Cupid's arrow. Asa paused to glance at Ollie and the entire audience followed his line of sight to where she sat demurely fanning herself. He placed his right hand over his heart and smiled as he stated for the record, "The only role Miss Ollie McClarren plays in this here inquest is as a totally innocent witness. She just happened to be at the scene when it all happened." Asa raised his hand to hail Ollie, and she responded by standing and doing a sweet and saucy curtsey and then blew him a kiss. The court room erupted with laughter when Asa turned beet red.

Asa painstakingly described the entire Woolworth debacle using his folksy cowboy lingo. He apologized for not knowing the child's name and referred to him as *the kid with the Winning Smile.* He explained his ploy to bribe the child into relinquishing the bar stool next to Miss. McClarren. Asa did an excellent job at pantomiming the story as it had unfolded. He mimicked the squinty eyed "Winning Smile" and demonstrated how he made sure to be in possession of the bar stool before handing over the quarter.

Since it would be less than gentlemanly to accurately describe the boy's mother, he tried to be kind, not an easy task. "She was a statuesque woman, you know like well fed, wore a colorful calico frock of a greenish, yeller color. At first, I figgered anyone dressed like that must be a female. I couldn't see the top half of the face, but the bottom half was purty hairy. With the sun bonnet obstructing a clear view, there wuz somethin' about the build of the person that didn't look right, and then it hit me what I was looking at. I reckoned the person to be a man, in disguise, doing an undercover investigation, likely a Texas Ranger, or something like that. I normally wouldn't question if the person was a woman, but by gosh that was the biggest woman I ever seen!" Asa had his hands extended and was looking up. The chamber of listeners chuckled but was quickly silenced by Judge Roy's gavel.

Asa was unaware that the crowd reacted to his description of the woman in chartreuse because she had preceded Asa on the witness stand dressed in the same chartreuse sun bonnet and matching calico dress. It quickly became apparent that Judge Pinto was struggling to maintain judicious professionalism.

Asa said, "Roy, ah, Judge, I was confounded by duress, and I want to accentuate how scary the threat wuz at the moment I yelled 'fire.'" Asa described the confrontation with the boy's mother as scarier that facing a longhorn bull on foot. "I skidded to a stop right in front of what turned out to be the boy's momma, and I had an apparition of accidentally walking into a corral with that mean bull. I reckoned at the time I saw smoke coming out of its nostrils. It wasn't until later I spied the lit cigar in her hand. By that time, I had fantasy and reality all mixed up and in my mind. I was lookin' at a creature dressed in calico, pawing at the ground, and preparing to charge. The mystery person was in protective mode, ready to rescue the sweet child attached to "his 'er her" leg from the likes of me. Folks, I've always heard to yell "fire" if you want to get people's attention. So I yelled "fire," and by golly it worked. Everbody forgot all about me and headed for the exit. It was like being in the middle of a herd of thirsty longhorns on the way to the river."

"Folks, I was in fear of serious bodily harm, and not only me, I had a lady to protect. Ever thang was happin' so fast, I only had a split second to choose making-a-stand or hightailing-it-out-of-there."

The Judge lost his struggle to remain circumspect and burst out laughing. That unleashed the crowd's restraint, and they joined Judge Pinto in a prolonged belly laugh. The onlookers noticed that the judge was using the sleeve of his robe to wipe away tears, and when they realized the tears had blinded him, they roared even louder. Watching him feeling around for his gavel stalled the proceedings for an inappropriate "time-out."

When the bedlam mostly died down, Asa gestured inevitability and said, "What would all of you do? You're Honor, I ask you, sir, and the court to consider the boy's act upon my person and that of Miss McClarren an assault. We had no way of knowing what he sprayed on us, and with that scowl on his face, even bein' so young, well, that boy had the look of someone demon possessed." Asa, before he thought better, gave his imitation of the kid's expression. The impersonation was so demonstrative that the folks looked at others in surprise before reacting. Asa was forced to wait for the ruckus to die down before continuing.

"I figger Miss McClarren and I are actually the victims in this case. I have since heard that the boy was seen filling the water pistol in the goldfish tank. Take my word for it, that fish tank water smelled turble. How would any of you feel to be in the company of a beautiful lady and have a kid squirt nasty water all over the front of your trousers? And think what all those folks thought when it looked like I wet myself. Anybody would be embarrassed, right? Me and Ollie wer'nt gonna hurt the kid, we just wanted to give him a talkin' to. That little—ah child got Miss Ollie's beautiful gown wet. Pert near ruined it. And that really got me riled up."

"Since I cain't undo nothing. I'm asking for the mercy of this court and my fellow Gainvillans, no Gainites, oh Yawl, bein' up here's in front's got me flustered."

"Mr. Slinkert, I am offering to work off any damages to Woolworth's by washing windows or sweeping floors, whatever you need done, two nights a week for a period of one month. I feel real bad about the disruption to your business. You're Honor, to sum up my defense, I had a good reason for my act of desperation. How would it have looked if I defended myself against a woman? But it sure peared to me that Ollie and me was in danger of bodily harm. For the first time in my life, exceptin' when I was a kid, I was scared of someone dressed like a woman. Being peaceable and all, I reckoned fleeing to safety was the thing to do. For some reason Asa was reminded of the newspaper article about Tom Dula's court trial. Just like Tom, Asa hung down his head and cried. After a period of silence, Asa looked the judge in the eyes and said, "Roy, ah I mean Judge, I rest my case."

There was applause at first, but then the sad figure of Asa slumped in the witness chair with his head hung down conjured up the legendary Tom Dula's (Dooley) prosecution. Years later the story would be revived by a hit musical recording sung by the Kingston Trio titled "Hang Down Your Head Tom Dooley."

Asa's whole-hearted remorse was undeniable. Silence reigned in the crowded hall of justice. Hiding his face in his hands, Asa continued to sob. His powerful defense had successfully garnered the sentimental compassion of the pulsating assembly. Though subtle, the essence of righteous indignation scented the air and permeated the environment.

The chanting revived, accompanied by rhythmic stamping on the floor: "Not guilty, not guilty, not guilty—."

It may have been his imagination, but Asa looked around to discover the source of a faraway song that floated into the court room.

Hang down your head Tom Dooley,
Hang down your head and cry.

Ollie lost her composure and could no longer keep her distance. She sprang from her chair and ran toward Asa. The sound of her dress shoes clicking sounded loud because silence had descended over the assembly. When Asa saw her coming, it was as though the moment was unfolding in slow-motion. Asa stood and trance-like advanced toward Ollie, also in slow-motion. He converged upon the vision of loveliness floating toward him. The tightly packed spectators parted like water being commanded by Moses. Twenty feet in front of the bench Ollie and Asa embraced.

Judge Roy put down his gavel and enjoyed the spectacle along with everyone else. Murmuring from the audience went something like this, 'Oh my, look at that, what a handsome couple they make.' The two youngsters enveloped each other in an embrace, and Asa impulsively lifted Ollie off her feet and swung her around in a circle. When he went to kiss her on the cheek, she was in the process of turning her face toward him and the kiss connected with her mouth. They both drew back in surprise and embarrassment. The crowd, voyeurs everyone, savored the mishap. From Asa and Ollie's burst of color, it was plain that they had inadvertently shared their first kiss with hundreds of onlookers.

Ollie quickly recovered and continued consoling Asa. She ran her hand over Asa's unruly hair and tilted his ear toward her mouth, whispering inaudible bits of encouragement. The crowd responded by cooing, "Ahhh."

Asa set Ollie on the floor, and the two of them stood holding hands, facing the Judge. The crowd restarted the stamping of feet while chanting, "Not guilty, not guilty, not guilty!" The entire court room reverberated. Judge Roy, in an effort to restore order shouted, "Order in the court" while pounding the bench with his gavel. The chanting continued and grew even louder. It was nothing less than anarchy in the chamber of justice that refused to be quelled by a pounding gavel.

The Judge stood and waved his arms. The stress of the moment transformed Judge Roy into a likeness of the legendary Ichabod Crane, doing a stomp dance. After the release he directed the bailiff to clear the courtroom, but of course no one could hear what he was shouting including the bailiff. About that time the clerk of the court handed the Judge a cone shaped megaphone, and Roy blasted the chamber with, "Order in the court! Aw, come on folks, settle down. I am ready—, I'm ready to render my decision!" Roy continued pounding the bench until the gavel handle broke off. He paused long enough to wave the handle before the crowd and then pitched it over his shoulder. "Here it comes, the court's decision in the case of Woolworth versus McCawl— order in the court!" Asa and Ollie approached the bench and leaned toward the megaphone.

"It is the decision of this court—." Roy stretched out his hands, palms down in a last-ditch effort to quell the pulsating mob. He replaced the broken gavel with his own boot and beat upon the bench. How dare the spectators ignore his sanctions. Out of total frustration he hurled the size 13 clodhopper through an open window, narrowly missing a child seated on the window sill. The boy was smiling. A closer inspection, and then a second, revealed the boy was none other than the lad with "The Winning Smile" and next to him stood his chartreuse calico clad mother. She had boosted her son up to the windowsill from outside the courtroom and was watching the fiasco from outside. She had ducked just in time as the humongous brogan went whizzing past her head. The boy's "Mother" raised her arm with a clenched fist and shouted something that an interpreter would replace with 'expletive deleted.' The moment Roy saw the roiled facial expression on the mother, he experienced the most primordial terror reserved for mortal combat and felt a sudden urge to flee for his own safety. The woman was in the process of hoisting her body up to the windowsill, intent on settling up with the judge once and for all. Just like Asa a few days before, Judge Roy felt the urge to defend his life and limb by whatever means. Legal terms such as *escalation of force, clear and present danger, officer of the law, justifiable self-defense* were dancing around in his head. The judge tasted fear up close and personal.

Judge Roy climbed atop the bench and held the megaphone before his mouth. The strange spectacle of the judge hoisting his gangly torso and daddy-long-legs appendages to the elevated bench quieted the chanting crowd. Judge Roy was having an epiphany, fate had predestined him to walk in Asa's boots at the critical moment of decision. That is how Judge Roy Pinto is believed to have succumbed to "*judicial nullification.*"

Whatever he had in mind for a verdict before his awakening, this is the one he handed down. With a rasp in his overtaxed vocal cords, the Judge croaked, "Asa McCawl's guilt is not in question and complicates a bench trial decision. Mitigating factors further complicate matters. Asa's infraction was committed without malice of forethought and falls short of costly damages to personal property or significant bodily injury. It is my considered opinion that harsh punishment in this case would be a miscarriage of justice. Furthermore, the charges are without legal precedent in the annals of jurisprudence. Therefore, as a duly appointed officer of the court exercising the powers vested in me, I declare Asa McCawl innocent of all charges. Mr. McCawl, you are free to go." Roy slammed his fist down, absent the gavel, to signal finality.

Roy then privately addressed Asa. The courtroom was now completely silent. "And, ah by the way Asa, it would be straight up of you to give the manager a hand as you suggested, as a good-will gesture of restitution. I think the community of Gainesville agrees with me: we all know you to be a fine young man, and we regret the mental duress being hauled up on these charges may have caused you."

Asa had a bout of weak knees and had to sit down, "—free to go—"? His mind was still in defense mode, and the verdict had not yet penetrated to the seat of his intellect. Had he imagined the words, free to go, go where, to jail? Ollie was smiling, and shaking him, "Asa, are you okay? Here, look at me, take a deep breath, Asa, you won your case! You're free!"

Asa hid his face in his hands, totally overwhelmed with emotion, lots of different emotions. The cheering crowd spilled out onto the town square. A town wide celebration and hoedown broke out at the city park. Asa and Ollie made the rounds on foot, thanking everyone for their moral support. Back at the livery Asa tied Ebony to the back of a borrowed surrey and transported Ollie to her home. Ollie poured two tall glasses of lemonade and carried them to the porch swing where she had left a recovering Asa. Ollie scooted closer on the seat and motioned for Asa to rest his head on her shoulder. A few minutes later Elizabeth walked to the swing and invited Asa for dinner. After the screen door closed, Ollie whispered that they were having ham and beans. Asa nodded his head and said, "One of my favorites."

The "Woolworths' Trial" would be the talk of the town for months. Texas history recorded a couple of "firsts" on that day. The hallowed halls of Justice in Cooke County, Texas would go down in history for rendering the precedent setting landmark decision against creating a panic in a crowded area. Woolworths' versus McCawl sparked the Texas State Legislature to pass legislation creating a law against knowingly inciting panic. The statute passed and became known as McCawl's Law. The penalty for placing the public in danger was set as a class three misdemeanor. Secondly, in response to Asa's bench warrant hearing, from that day forward, in legal circles, the un-official term *judicial nullification* was coined.

Chapter 7

"BACK AT THE RANCH"

Ollie was excited about hosting Callie and Zelma McCawl overnight. They were kindred spirits in so many ways, and though she didn't realize it at the time would eventually live together like sisters. Dinner was served shortly after Callie and Zelma arrived. When desert was being served, Callie took a moment to hand Sam and Elizabeth a sealed envelope. Sam looked it over before opening the elegantly embossed envelope. Inside was a formal invitation and complimentary pass to the Cooke County Fair, Rodeo, including a VIP pre-event buffet. A self-addressed RSVP envelope was tucked inside. The front row tickets were just behind the master of ceremonies and the judges. The buffet would be an opportunity to socialize with the town's dignitaries, rodeo contestants, stock owners, and notable attendees. Sam's was obviously surprised, nodded his head in respect and said, "Well thank you! Sounds like something both Elizabeth and I would enjoy. We will plan on being there." Neither Sam nor Elizabeth would mind doing a little hob-knobbing. Smoozing with the elites of the area opened doors to Sam, and he could certainly hold his own at such gatherings.

Callie and Zelma's sleepover at the McClarren home happened a few days before Asa's janitor duty at Woolworth's. Elizabeth and Sam were both early risers and were headed into town by the time the four girls awoke. First thing after breakfast the foursome headed for the horse stable. Ollie introduced Callie and Zelma to the McClarren stable of horses and vice versa while the girls pulled grass and fed it through the corral fence. Jolly, the ranch hand walked up behind them and said, "Moan'n ladies, you're up early see'n as how you wuz up all night. I could hear you singing, beautiful voices and great harmony by the way. Sounded like 'The Glow Worm Song.' Reckon you wuz hav'n too much fun to waste time sleepin'." Jolly was a fixture around the Kneeling Σ Ranch. He was the descendent of African slaves and had genuine affection for the entire McClarren family. He loved to tell about the time the girls were born and how he stood at the bedroom door and prayed while his Millie, the area's midwife, delivered each of the two girl babies, spaced two years apart.

Ollie set out to convince Jolly to saddle up four horses for a trail ride. She got straight to the point and told Jolly, "Me and Hazel want to practice riding astride western style." Jolly put up his hands, took a step backward while rolling his eyes and said, "Reckon we should wait till Mr. Sam is here?" Jolly was more of an uncle than employee. He was devoted to the man that had taken him in and finished raising him.

A young Jolly, thought to have been about nine years old, had been abandoned and was trying to survive on his own when Sam found him camping out in the cross timbers of north Texas. Big hearted Sam invited the boy to live with them and gave him the only spare bedroom, which happened to be in the basement. Sam had given Jolly a puppy to care for and provide some companionship too. When Jolly grew up, he moved into an apartment next to the cowboy bunk house. Jolly was willing and even eager to do what he could to help, ever mindful of his good fortune. Jolly's loyalty to the McClarren family led to him serving as the self-appointed guardian of Hazel and Ollie and he pretty much kept tabs on the mischievous pair. He also had a hard time saying no to their requests. The girls cajoled and begged saying please, please. Soft-hearted, Jolly decided to accommodate but saddled four of the calmest plow horses in the stable. The girls took their ride along a dirt road with Jolly trailing behind on an aged Morgan. Nothing bad happened, and the horses were put up before Sam returned from his trip to town.

Hazel and Ollie would have to be patient and hope that Elizabeth and Sam would have a change of heart after seeing the Buckaroo Belles perform at the rodeo. The day of the rodeo took forever to arrive for young Ollie.

The sport of rodeo during the first decade of the 20th Century provided a wholesome environment in Gainesville. Ollie and Hazel knew that the Belles met and trained at Asa's arena at 3:00 PM most days and they became regulars.

Callie said, "Ollie, you and Hazel may have missed the shindig this year, but we can start getting you ready for next year.

Asa said, "Ollie, once your parents see that riding astride can be ladylike, they are likely to come around. In the meantime you can get started practicing on our obstacle course and learn the various exercises. I will be glad to help."

Sam's ears caught the buzz caused by Asa's day in court. Everywhere he went he heard folks talking about the McCawl kid. Asa McCawl was so popular he could easily be elected for an office and win by a landslide. Sam had missed out on the court room scene, but the firsthand accounts were all similar enough to be credible. He actually admitted he was sorry to have missed the "trial of the year." He learned that the rumors about Asa were true even the part about Asa raising his four orphaned siblings.

Asa's plan for doing clean-up at Woolworth's got around town due to his sisters' loose lips. Starting on the next Thursday night, each Thursday and Tuesday for a full month he would do janitor and maintenance work just as promised. When Asa arrived at the back entrance to the store, he found a small group of friends waiting for him. The helpers included the four girls, Giuseppe, Tex, Otto Wendt, Judge Roy, ole Riley and by golly, ole Sam McClarren. Asa did a double take when he saw Sam. He rushed over to him and exclaimed, "Sam, good to see you Sir, what brangs you here?" Asa, with an inquisitive grin, grabbed Sam's right hand and began pumping it up and down, and up and down all over again.

Sam was obviously amused and spoke through a smile, "Well Asa, I'm here to give you a hand like the rest of these friends and cohorts of yours."

"Thank you, sir, friends are sure good to have, I don't know what to say, I will be available if you ever need me to give you a hand."

Then Asa greeted the other men with his overly affectionate handshake.

Roy said, "Boy, it's rare to find young people like you, willing to take responsibility for yore actions and all. To reward your ethics we'uns got together and decided to give you a hand here at Woolworths."

Otto said, "Asa, sollen wir hier Unterstützung und Freundschaft zeigen. Die Welt ist glücklich, Sie zu haben." (Asa, we come to show support and friendship. The world is happy to have such boy as you too.)

As the group tackled the tasks enumerated by manager Slinkert, it was a busy scene. While pushing a broom Riley entertained the group with some cowboy poetry and fireside songs. He recited one of the oldest poems on record by an unknown author. It began like this:

In the reaches of the western wind
Erasing boundary lines again
Imprisoned by the force that sets him free
A cowboy's life is like the tumbleweed

Callie, Zelma, Ollie, and Hazel had all practiced singing the "Glow Worm Song" in their high school chorus class for the past few months. Callie started singing the song first, and they all joined in. Callie sang alto, Ollie took soprano, with Hazel and Zelma completing the close four-part harmony. Included in their musical repertoire was, 'Row, Row Your Boat.' Soon the entire group was belting out the lyrics in full voice. Downtown Gainesville was a merry place to be that evening, as it would be for many evenings into the future.

The blended voices filled the air of the town square as the four girls washed the big exterior windows. When Asa decided to sing along and begin heartily belting out his revised version of the lyrics, Ollie ran to him and said, "Asa, quietly, okay?" Asa grabbed Ollie and threw her over his shoulder and started walking away singing, "Glow worms glitter, glitter," but abruptly stopped in his tracks when he saw Sam walking his way.

Samuel McClarren with an authoritative voice said, "Asa, its glimmer, glimmer not glitter, glitter." Asa gingerly lowered Ollie to the floor and began straightening her frock. Sam spoke up and said, "Youngman, Ollie is fully capable of smoothing her dress without your help."

Asa jumped back with his hands in the air and said, "Yes sir, I mean sorry sir, I didn't mean—."

Sam interrupted Asa and said, "Yes, Asa, I know, you meant well, but I think you get my point without saying more." The bearded patriarch put his head back and laughed with a bombastic roar and gave Asa a slap on the back.

Thanks to Asa's boyish exuberance and coaxing, a once young and vital Sam McClarren re-emerged, a Phoenix from the ashes. Ollie glimpsed her aging father's youthful self and ran to hug him saying, "I love seeing you like this!" The once robust sandy haired Sammy of yesteryear joined in the singing and even quoted some poetry he had learned from his groomsman, Jolly.

A Cowboy's Love Song

Oh, the last steer has been branded
And the last beef has been shipped,
And I'm free to roam the prairies
That the round-up crew has stripped;
I'm free to think of Susie,—
Fairer than the stars above,—
She's the waitress at the station
And she is my turtle dove.

Biscuit-shootin' Susie,—
She's got us roped and tied;
Sober men or woozy
Look on her with pride.
Susie's strong and able,
And not a one gits rash
When she waits on the table
And superintends the hash.

Oh, I sometimes think I'm locoed
An' jes fit fer herdin' sheep,
'Cause I only think of Susie
When I'm wakin' or I'm sleep.
I'm wearin' Cupid's hobbles,

An' I'm tied to Love's stake-pin,
And when my heart was branded
The irons sunk deep in.

Biscuit-shootin' Susie,—
She's got us roped and tied;
Sober men or woozy
Look on her with pride.
Susie's strong and able,
And not a one gits rash
When she waits on the table
And superintends the hash.

I take my saddle, Sundays,—
The one with inlaid flaps,—
And don my new sombrero
And my white angora chaps;
Then I take a bronc for Susie
And she leaves her pots and pans
And we figure out our future
And talk o'er our homestead plans.

Biscuit-shootin' Susie,—
She's got us roped and tied;
Sober men or woozy
Look on her with pride.
Susie's strong and able,
And not a one gits rash
When she waits on the table
And superintends the hash.

Anonymous

When Sam finished the poem, the entire work brigade applauded, and Asa asked, "Sam, you recon I could have a copy of that poem. Anonymous huh, too bad the fellar didn't sign off on it."

The singing continued, and everyone seemed to be having a great time. Never was work so much fun.

Shine little glow-worm, glimmer, glimmer
Shine little glow-worm, glimmer, glimmer
Lead us lest too far we wander
Love's sweet voice is calling yonder
Shine little glow-worm, glimmer, glimmer
Hey, there don't get dimmer, dimmer
Light the path below, above
And lead us on to love!

Zelma started a novel ditty and sung it as a round. Everyone, even Mr. Slinkert joined in. Asa held out his hands to Ollie questioning if he could sing along and she mouthed, "Sure, go ahead."

Row, row, row your boat,
Gently down the stream.
If you see an alligator,
Don't forget to scream.
Row, row, row your boat,
Gently down the stream.
Throw your teacher overboard
And listen to her scream.
Row, row, row your boat,
Gently down the stream.
Verily, verily, verily, verily,
Life is but a dream.

Once the singing started, Giuseppe jogged to his nearby cottage and brought back his guitar. He took time away from window washing to accompany himself to several romantic ballads, his baritone vibrato settled over the workers like perfumed incense.

The Judge, now just plain 'Roy' had a big smile plastered on his hillbilly face. It was a moment he couldn't allow to pass without adding a bit of humor from his reservoir of modified idioms, "We are all having *"more peep than funnels."* The group paused and looked at him and then each other while mouthing 'peep than funnels.' Then Sam yelled, "Come on folks, you know, like *more fun than peoples*, only backwards!"

When the windows were all washed, floors swept, scrubbed, everything feather dusted, Asa and Ollie took over the cleaning of the fish tank. Their personal experience with the putrid water was a strong motivator. After dipping out the fish, emptying the tank and scrubbing the inside walls, the freshly filled fish aquarium was sparkling and easily passed a sniff test.

What would have taken Asa, working alone, a good six hours was finished in about the same amount of time by the dozen volunteers. Of course, on that particular occasion, the mission had evolved into a group project that seemed to lack much organization. An outsider might have described it as a party or celebration of some kind. Not even the stern Mr. Slinkert seemed to mind the lollygagging and merrymaking that permeated the worksite. It turned out that the store manager, underneath his "professional persona," was a regular fun-loving gent, and a generous one too, as demonstrated by the complimentary coke floats he served up for the whole crew. A little beyond bedtime for the group of workers, they took their time saying their good-byes. The lady reporter wrote, "Before drifting off to their various homes Asa's work crew parted wearing big smiles."

The local journalist, well attuned to the town's rumor mill, had decided to cover the continuing saga of Asa's brush with the law. She and her photographer mostly kept to the shadows but managed a few short interviews. The event was printed in the Saturday Issue of the Gainesville Post. The Post was glad to have something interesting to write about that would be likely to attract subscribers. The previous day had been a slow news day for the social section of the paper. The local crime section had only one report, a case of grand larceny. A hotel guest had absconded with a pillow and towel. The thief was put on notice that she had a week to pay for the property or have her name revealed in print.

The previous days front page story was that the "Welcome to Gainesville" city limit sign had been vandalized and altered to read "Welcome to Hangesville" a reference to the Civil War Era's mass hangings that saw more than 40 Yankee sympathizers hanged from one of Gainesville's giant trees. A kangaroo trial found them all guilty of spying and sedition. Just the mention of Gainesville's darkest moment stirred up raw feelings among the old timers. The white citizenry preferred to forget the incident, but when forced to give a viewpoint, some defended the guilty verdict as justified and lawful. Many of the local black people were still intimidated and resentful.

The next item on the Buckaroo Belle's agenda was to help organize the Cooke County Fair. Callie and Zelma McCawl quietly promoted Sam McClarren for parade marshal and nominated him to lead the opening prayer at the rodeo. Ollie got the coveted assignment to lead the parade as flag bearer. The Belle's matching costumes would be patriotic red, white, and blue Annie Oakley split skirt ensembles. The big question remained, would Ollie and Hazel be riding side-saddle or astride?

During the choreography sessions and rehearsals, Sam and Elizabeth realized that Ollie and Hazel were being sidelined due to the side-saddle issue. After a long conversation with Elizabeth and only days before the event, Sam chose dinner time to grant permission for Hazel and Ollie to join their peers and ride astride.

Sam waited until the dessert was being served. He interrupted the conversation by tapping his glass with a fork. "After considerable thought you're mother and I have decided to allow you girls to fully participate in the Buckaroo Bell Performances. You will be able to ride astride and wear the costumes if they are modest and clearly designed for women. You are to conduct yourselves in a lady-like manner as befits Christian young women. Any unseemly behavior and this decision will be reversed. Understood?"

Ollie and Hazel squealed and rose to hug their father. "Thank you, thank you! We promise to make you proud of us." The girls turned to their smiling mother and hugged her too. Finally, Ollie and Hazel could ride with the Buckaroo Bells and wear trousers in public. For members of the traditional community like Sam and Elizabeth the changing times were uncomfortable and would take some time to fully accept. Welcome to the twentieth century.

***

The biweekly Woolworth cleanup eventually morphed into a recurring social event, and the number of helpers grew. Once Asa's month elapsed the group decided to continue as a community service organization. They planned beautification projects, held gospel music singings on the steps of the court house, and assisted the elderly with property maintenance. Just the after-hours presence discouraged crime, which was actually rare. Gainesville's crime report mostly consisted of public drunkenness, bar-room brawls, ladies of the night soliciting, and an occasional burglary. Ollie was elected project chairman of the planning committee. She submitted the name 'Gainesville's Glow Worms' for the organization and it was adopted unanimously.

The Gainesville Glow Worms Association remains as one of Texas' oldest community service organizations. At first its scope was limited to promoting local pride, community beautification, and crime prevention. By the beginning of the 1918 Influenza pandemic Callie and Zelma were both Registered Nurses and felt the call to provide overflow emergency care. They received permission to set up an emergency field hospital at the Cooke County fairgrounds inside a large pavilion normally used for cook offs, quilting displays and talent competitions.

Chapter 8

THE HONEYMOON HOME

Asa's hard work was paying off, and it was obvious that he had a business head on him. He insisted on personally learning to navigate the statutory requirements and tax regulations. Asa was a "hands-on" man.

As the summer wore on Asa and Ollie grew closer. Asa had mostly forsaken the fireside buds in favor of spending time with Ollie. After much rehearsing before the dresser mirror, Asa approached Sam to ask for Ollie's hand in marriage. The two men took a long ride along the river, and Sam probed Asa on his world view, got his take on the sanctity of marriage, and on the responsibilities of parenthood. Asa answered as honestly as he could, and Sam came away satisfied that Asa would do right by Ollie.

Elizabeth and Sam planned an engagement celebration and cookout. They invited about a hundred people. Sam had the event in his backyard and hired Raul to cater the food. Giuseppe volunteered for the entertainment. He loved to be in the public eye and never missed an opportunity to play and sing for gatherings. Sam and Elizabeth gladly took him up on his offer.

Ollie asked, "Callie, Zelma, in view of our friendship I want you to serve as bridesmaids in our wedding." Hazel, the best sister a girl could have, will you be my matron of honor?"

The three girls squealed and converged for a group hug. Ollie was silent for a few moments and then said, "Ya know, I really want to keep the wedding ceremony small and private." The four girls responded by excitedly speaking over each other.

Zelma said, "Do you know what kind of dress—?"

Callie interrupted, "When can we start shopping?"

Hazel blurted out, "I see Ollie in a beaded sheath, and a full long veil, that style is so popular right now in Paris and London."

Ollie's sparkling eyes and ear to ear smile reflected her passionate state of mind to Asa. Callie looked at Ollie and said, "Hush, girls, we need to let Ollie tell us what she wants. "Okay Ollie, describe the wedding you want us to help you plan. We are your worker bees."

Callie spoke up, "Yawl come on over to the dining table and bring paper and pencils. We need to make notes and lists. Like, who does what."

Hazel brought glasses and a pitcher of lemonade to the big round pedestal table. Ollie said "Wait, where's Momma, she'll want to be in on this. For now, we'll just sit and chat. Momma deserves to be in on the planning." Ollie sat with her hand supporting her chin, a dreamy look plastered on her face. She said, "I love white flowers, especially roses, and gardenias. Yawl remember that fashion magazine called 'Here She Comes'? It features all the latest bridal designers' advertisements. Remind me to buy the latest issue next time we are out shopping. Auntie Velma was telling me about a new department store just opened in down town Dallas, called Newman Markus or something like that. It is supposed to be very hoity-toity if you know what I mean.

Callie said, "I will ask Asa about a shopping trip to Dallas."

Chapter 9

A LIFE WELL LIVED

Sam had been looking back over his life. The Lord had blessed him and his business dealings. He and Elizabeth had always been charitable and donated to about every worthwhile cause that came along. Sam had been thinking that the time had come to do more. It was mid-afternoon, and he was breathing hard for some reason. He happened to be crossing the town square and was walking past a shady bench. The ancient oak was shedding it acorns, and they crunched beneath his work boots. *Think I'll set a spell and catch my breath.* Along with his shortness of breath, Sam had been feeling melancholy. A few tears found their way to his chin. *Ever since I've been having these chest pains and being out of breath, I get all sentimental for some reason. I reckon I need to tie up some loose ends.* Sam began to pray, *Lord, I know you are letting me know I'm not long for this world, and I appreciate you giving me a heads up. Thank you for hearing my prayers, this will be a short one. I've got a few things to talk over with you. You know where my sentiments lie and know what to expect as far as my requests. For my family, Lord do what you can to motivate them to be faithful short of violating free-will. And give them good health and happiness in this life. You know my long list of friends, watch out for them much as fits in with your plans for ever-thing. Lord, I sure hope*

Ollie is making a wise choice for a husband. I think Asa will pan out okay with a little help from you and me.

Sam was sure it was his heart causing him to feel bad, but he had been keeping it to himself since Elizabeth would panic if she found out. He figured to drop by Doc.'s Office and let him listen to the old ticker. *Not that he can do anything other than put me to bed and that ain't happening.*

On the day after the slumber party Elizabeth and Sam went into Gainesville to shop. The road was rough and dusty. After a period of being lost in their own thoughts, Elizabeth broke the silence by saying, "Those girls were having a good time. Could you hear them singing? They are good singers, woke me up several times. You tired like me? Maybe we can go to bed early tonight." Elizabeth asked Sam to stop by Doc.'s office. She was helped down by Sam and strode into the office and said back over her shoulder, "I'll be right back, Dear. Please don't leave, I'll hurry"

Sam grumbled a little after Elizabeth was out of ear shot. Right away Elizabeth walked back out and motioned for Sam to come in. "Doc wants to talk to you." Elizabeth had quickly told Doc about Sam's spells and that she was worried. Doc excused himself from the two patients in his waiting room and said, "Looks like I have an emergency. Feel free to wait or come back another time. Tell my receptionist if you want a drink or snack, and she'll get you something.

Sam set the brakes and tied the lead horse to the hitching rail. He was grumbling as he strode to the office entrance. Once in the presence of the Doc, Sam shook hands and asked after his family. Then Sam looked at Elizabeth's face and then back to Doc's face, and he knew he was being tricked into a doctor visit. Surprisingly, Sam didn't argue. The Doc led him and Elizabeth into his examination room and seated them on a sofa.

Doc began by saying, "Sam, Elizabeth tells me you have been having weak spells. Tell me what they feel like."

Sam cleared his throat and said, "Yep, it's true, I had already decided to sneak in here and see you without Elizabeth knowing. The worst part is that I get out of breath and feel dizzy and sometimes it hurts right here in the middle. Once I looked in a mirror and my face was red. I have decided it is my old ticker acting up, and medical science can't do much with that ailment, right, so this is likely a waste of yours and my time."

"Sam, if you think diagnosing yourself before I do will save you the cost of an office visit, think again." Sam, Elizabeth and Doc all had a good laugh.

Doc asked Sam to remove his shirt and used his stethoscope to listen to Sam's heart and breathing. He took his pulse and looked into Sam's ears and mouth. Then Doc knelt down and removed Sam's shoes and socks. Doc saw deep grooves where the socks and shoes pressed into Sam's puffy ankles and feet. "How long your ankles been swelling, Sam?"

"Oh, it started about two or three years ago. It seems to be getting worse."

Doc gave his diagnosis, and it was mostly what Sam expected. "Sam, pears you're suffering from early-stage heart disease." You must slow down, rest often, and cut back on food. Elizabeth, try to coax him to take a nap in the afternoon and hire a couple of extra cowboys to take over the physical chores." Elizabeth's lip was quivering when she said, "Doc, Sam has never taken orders from anyone and sure not me. I've been try'n to slow him down."

Sam and Elizabeth walked back to the buckboard and headed for the Farmer's Market. On the way Elizabeth asked, "Sam, you know, I think I would enjoy just the two of us taking a little vacation. You think we could take the stagecoach up to Turner Falls and rent a little cabin. Call it a second honeymoon, just two or three days. Must've been almost 20 years since we went up there, back before we had kids. Remember how romantic it was?" Elizabeth moved closer to Sam on the buckboard and hugged him. He reached over and kissed her on the mouth.

The exchange was a wake-up call for Sam. Suddenly he felt like he had been a disappointment to Elizabeth. Women like romance, and I've let her down. Sam thought, what good is wealth, just sitting in the bank? Right there in the light of day ole Sam took Elizabeth in his arms bent her back and gave her a lingering kiss. He said in an emotional tone, "Elizabeth, there is nothing I would like better. I feel bad I didn't think of it myself. We can be lazy and enjoy the mountain scenery. The way I feel right now we could spend some extra time in bed if you know what I'm gittin' at."

Elizabeth said, "I would like that, but for now behave yourself. Folks will talk."

That evening Sam and Elizabeth lay in bed and talked. They needed a plan for spending down. They both wanted the joy of watching the recipients. First on the list, they committed to doubling the size of the church building's auditorium. It was always crowded on Sunday morning and needed remodeling. Replacing the old song books and installing a new modern baptistery with a water heater was on the list of up-grades.

Second, Sam wanted to donate to the local hospital. Because of hard times many patients had defaulted on paying their bills, leaving the hospital in a pinch. Third, he wanted to surprise Hazel and Ollie with brand new houses when they married. They also divided some of the ranch land among the two girls.

Within the week, Sam and Elizabeth hired an architect, got estimates from builders, and purchased property within the city limits. Ollie and Asa would have a whale of a wedding surprise.

One of Sam's longtime coffee shop acquaintances sat down next to him and opened the conversation by saying, "I hear your daughter is being courted by young Asa McCawl."

Sam admitted, "I didn't take to the boy at first, seemed a little too rough around the edges. Well, right away it was apparent that my Ollie was smitten with young Asa, so I decided to take a closer look. That's when I got an ear full. Ever body I asked spoke highly of him, in fact I didn't hear one bad report. I started thinking that young McCawl might have a political career ahead of him. Asa grew up poor and short on manners, but the kid is growing on us. I reckon Ollie could do worse, he is a right polite and likable buckaroo."

The romance of Giuseppe and Callie was the talk of the town. They were frequently mentioned on the social page of the local newspaper. In fact, they were up-staging Asa and Ollie, who preferred to avoid public attention, having had enough to last a decade. World affairs were troubling for those in touch with news reports. Articles covering world events were only mentioned and were mostly skipped over as "boring." Asa was unaware of the rumblings of war coming from the European Continent. The United States was experiencing smooth sailing before the proverbial storm.

Several weeks before Asa proposed to Ollie, Giuseppe asked Asa for permission to marry Callie. She had turned seventeen and had her high school diploma. Asa had already seen the sparks between them, so it was no surprise. He had gotten to know Giuseppe well and trusted that he would make a good husband for Callie. In response to Giuseppe's question, Asa drawled, "If Callie is so a-mind to marry you, far be-it for me to stand in the way. Promise you'll always be gentle and provide her a prosperous life-style, be a good father to any little ones and you have my blessing." Giuseppe grabbed Asa and gave him a bear hug. "I will, I do, Yes, yes! The love-sick fool went on and on about how he planned to propose. "I have the perfect place to pop the question."

Asa said, "Whoa, I have to get back to work, we'll talk soon. Welcome to the family.

Giuseppe picked Callie up in a brand-new surrey hitched to matching grey dappled mares. All he had told her was to pick a pretty dress to wear and be prepared for a surprise. He whispered to Asa as they left, "We'll be out late tonight so don't wait up."

The secrecy and Giuseppe's strange behavior had made Callie a nervous wreck. She had fussed over what to wear but finally decided on a long sheath. The dress was royal blue with iridescent beading on the high-necked bodice. It had billowy organza sleeves finished at the wrists with beaded cuffs. Callie's beauty stunned Giuseppe. Being in her presence was other-worldly. The blue of the dress brought out the color in her eyes, and her hair reflected the bright sunlight. Poor Giuseppe felt humbled to be in her presence.

On the ride to the new home, Giuseppe tantalized Callie with the mystery destination. They rode around the courthouse square twice, rode by the high school where the football team was practicing, and one final lap around town, waving and shouting hello to everyone out and about. At one point the Gainesville Post reporter saw them. She was so eager to interview them she hiked up her dress, inadvertently exposing her ankles while chasing after them. She was near collapse by the time they helped the woman into the surrey with them. She insisted that Giuseppe return to where she had left her photographer and cajoled them to pose for a picture. They agreed if she would finish up quickly. Giuseppe convinced her to do the interview the following day. He would drop by her office. Giuseppe noticed the photographer's equipment and asked a few questions. Technology fascinated Giuseppe. He noted how the man covered his head with the black cloth and raised the bar that flashed. He claimed he was using the latest in photography technology. Giuseppe was thinking about the modern miracle of photography and how it had changed the world, what would inventers think of next, traveling to the moon?

Giuseppe had exercised patience. He had worked through a list of things to do before popping the question. He was confident she loved him and would say yes to his proposal. His heart was pounding when they pulled up to his little cottage. He had spent days, for long hours, preparing the cottage. He picked up the diamond ring he had been paying out on installments. He had placed an order at the local florist and scheduled delivery. A red carpet was borrowed from a wedding planner and unfurled from the threshold to the street. The player piano that came with the house was ready to play the most romantic music know to the world. He had a bottle of French Champaign on ice. Dozens of beautiful candles were ready to ignite, and the table was set with lace, white China, silver, and crystal stemware.

The previous week Giuseppe enlisted Ollie and Hazel to have everything set up in advance of his arrival. The signal to light the candles was when Giuseppe and Callie passed by without stopping. They would return in approximately five minutes. The burner under the marinara sauce was put on low, they wound and started the player piano playing. When Giuseppe pulled up in front with Callie, both Ollie and Hazel ran out the back door and hid in some bushes to watch Giuseppe escort Callie along the red carpet. The look on Callie's face was one of amazement. Ollie and Hazel could clearly see the sparkle in Giuseppe's eyes. They overheard Callie ask, "Who lives here? Why the intrigue? Giuseppe tell me something, anything, you are driving me mad. Is this house the surprise?"

Giuseppe opened the door and before entering smothered Callie's words with a sweet and tender kiss. "This, my love is my new home. You are my first guest. Please make yourself comfortable, and when you are ready, I'll give you the grand tour. I have prepared a meal for us."

"Oh, Giuseppe everything is beautiful, and so cozy."

"Callie, I must confess, when the realtor showed it to me, I thought of you. I thought you might like it."

They walked into the bedroom, and Callie rushed to sit upon the bed and bounced up and down.

Callie mouthed, "Nice, just soft enough." They walked arm in arm toward the kitchen.

Giuseppe said, "I hope you like spaghetti and meatballs. Have a seat while I put the finishing touches on the dinner."

Callie objected, "No, let me help. I love spaghetti, and I am starving. Opps, I smell the bread, I'll check on it. Um, garlic bread. Giuseppe, did you do all of this yourself?"

"I had a couple of helpers, ah I believe they are friends of yours, can you guess?"

"No, oh I can't wait, tell me."

"It was Ollie and Hazel that were here just before we arrived. But yes, I did most of it."

"Well now I know that they can keep a secret. What sweet friends they are. Oh my, that is a beautiful tossed salad. Ummm, and bread pudding, I love it!"

Giuseppe helped Callie with her chair and asked her to bless the food. They were both hungry and finished their plate of food quickly. Giuseppe offered more pasta to Callie, but she waved him off, so he dished a second helping onto his plate. Callie said, "I'm getting full but give me a little more salad and that little end chunk of garlic toast. Thank you dear."

Callie finished her salad, and Giuseppe rose from his chair and walked around to Callie's side of the table. He turned her chair to face away from the table and knelt in front of her. He grimaced as he struggled to remove something from his front pants pocket. He stood and removed a small box and returned to a kneeling position. Callie stopped breathing; she was being careful not to assume that he was about to propose. "Callie, my beautiful Callie, will you marry me? I can't face life without you! You are my life, since the first time I saw you." Giuseppe opened the box and removed the ring. "Callie, please say that you love me too. Please say yes."

Ecstatic over the proposal, Callie sprang from her chair and flung herself at the still kneeling Giuseppe, repeating, "Yes, yes, I will marry you!" She caught him off balance, and he fell backward to sprawl on the floor. Callie landed on his chest. The mishap caused them to start laughing. They were laughing while sprawled on the floor with clothing askance and legs intertwined. They failed to notice that the lacy tablecloth had caught on the beaded dress. The tablecloth brought the dishes, flowers, and candles with it. There on the floor they embraced and began kissing. All five of their senses were occupied to the extent that the world could have been on fire, and they would not have noticed. At least not right away. After a minute or two of pure ecstasy, they began to cough and could hardly see each other.

The heat from the burning tablecloth, napkins, and floral arrangement broke through their moment of joy. Panic replaced their other emotions! They sprang to their feet and started fighting the fast-spreading fire. Callie splashed the contents of a tea pitcher on the flames, and Giuseppe used a wool blanket to beat the flames. Luck was with them, and they managed to extinguish the flames in time. They could hardly speak from the coughing. The smoke-filled house forced them to dash to the door and open it wide. Next, they opened the windows. They examined each other, "Are you hurt? Here, turn around, whew, that was a close call."

Just as the smoke was clearing a neighbor appeared at the front door; "Hello, everyone okay in here? Need help? I'm Richard from next door. Looks like you had a small fire."

"Hello, Richard. Thank you for coming to our aid. This is Callie, and I am Giuseppe. The candles caught the tablecloth on fire. Other than scared to death, we are safe. Close call, but all is well that ends well. Since you are here, stay and have desert with us. It was intended to be bread pudding, but now it is looking more like crème Brule." Callie and Richard found the reference to the flamed dessert somewhat funny, but not as funny as Giuseppe. He had no compunction against laughing at his own joke and blasted the interior of the cottage with his booming guffaw. Laughing always made Giuseppe feel better. "Just kidding, the bread pudding wasn't burned at all." Richard declined the invitation but said, "Welcome to the neighborhood."

Callie collapsed on the sofa and with a deep sigh, held the ring level to her face. To her young eyes it could have been the rock of Gibraltar. "Oh Giuseppe, the diamond is stunning, the most beautiful ring I've ever seen."

Giuseppe interrupted Callie and said if you like it, we will keep it. There is a matching wedding band on reserve. If you want to shop for a different design, we can, I want you to be totally pleased. You just have to say the word. I want you to understand that my love for you has no bounds and price is not a consideration."

Callie cooed, "Giuseppe, I have never dreamt of a ring this fine. Yes, of course I want to keep it. I can't wait to show my family. They will be thrilled to welcome you into our family."

The damage to the little cottage was mostly smoke damage. Giuseppe and Callie spent the next few days washing down the interior and hanging new wallpaper. Callie chose new wool rugs for the floor. She and Zelma made some of the curtains but hired the living room drapes professionally done. There was a silver lining to the fire. Callie got to redecorate the house according to her personal preferences.

With the help of Ollie and Hazel, a wedding ceremony was planned at the little church building on Taylor Street. Ollie and Velma organized a trip to Dallas to shop for Callie's trousseau. Out of Asa's adorable smile came, "I'll be paying for the trip so you girls go and have a fantastic time." The bridal entourage included Elizabeth, Auntie Velma, Hazel, Zelma, Ollie, and Betty the preacher's wife. Jolly was given the task of transporting the women to Hotel Dallas where they had a four-room suite reserved for a week.

After two days of shopping every boutique in downtown Dallas, Callie found the dress she had been looking for. Her entourage was hungry and ready for lunch but first they had to get Callie to take the dress off. She was having a moment but came to her senses and off to a steak house next door. The dress was ivory, a princess style ball gown with a voluminous hoop skirt. with rows of gathered tulle ruffles sewn in swirls and circles decorated the floor length skirt. A section at the back of the skirt had satin bows from the waist to the end of the ten-foot train. Callie was determined to show some individuality in her outfit and for accessories chose rhinestone encrusted, western boots. She completed the outfit with a custom-made white satin Stetson hat with a rhinestone band and an attached tulle veil.

The Gainesville Post included a photo of Callie in her wedding gown.

Her striking good looks and unusual accessories assured her a cover story on the front page, pre-empting news of a disturbing nature, whispers of Marxist' Socialism under Lenin's Bolsheviks. Giuseppe and Callie chose a rustic cabin nestled in a hidden meadow atop the Arbuckle Mountains of Central Oklahoma. Precious, unforgettable memories sanctified their matrimonial union into one flesh. They spent leisurely hours enjoying strolls along pine and juniper forested hiking trails among the unusual rock formations. Cliff diving at Turner Falls swimming hole was a tempting thrill, but the young couple wisely decided to watch the spectacle from the bank.

Chapter 10

PLANNING THE HONEYMOON

About two weeks before Ollie and Asa's wedding, Hazel and Ollie were napping on a quilt spread under a shade tree. They were looking for clouds shaped like objects. Ollie pointed out a giant shoe. Hazel found a sunbonnet and then indicated that she was tired of the game and asked Ollie if she had planned a honeymoon.

"Not really, just spending a night or two at the Red River Inn. Asa may be too busy for a real trip. I will bring it up and see what he wants. Now that you mention it, I will bring it up tonight."

That evening Asa had a buggy ride planned. She suspected that he was under the weather. He was subdued, but it had nothing to do with illness. In a sad tone, she asked, "Asa, do you mind taking me home? I sense that you are not in the mood for my visit."

He read disappointment on her face and knew he needed to share his unexpected news. Asa lifted Ollie down from the buggy and seated her on a blanket. He handed her a letter. The letter was from Marion Frances McCawl.

Dear Asa,

This is your father Marion. I met someone from Gainesville in San Francisco, and he told me what a fine person you have grown into. I am doing poorly, nigh to death, and I need help getting back to Texas to say my farewells. Please hurry to fetch me, there is a lot to tell you. Disappearing was not my fault. I forgot who I was after two robbers tried to kill me and almost did. I was hurt bad. It was years later when I remembered who I was. I have these terrible headaches almost every day, bad ones. I sure would like to see you and the other kids before I die.

Your Father Marion Francis McCawl
Pacific Beach Hotel, Level 5th Floor, Room 505
San Francisco, California

Asa waited for Ollie to read the letter. Ollie lowered the letter to her lap and waited for Asa to speak. Asa was still adjusting to the shock that Marion was alive.

"Look, Asa, what a beautiful sun-set."

Asa ignored the sun-set and said, "How dare he claim innocence. Why did he wait so long to get in touch with us? All those years when we kids needed him, he was off doing his own thing. Just up and disappeared. Well, it's us that don't need him now. He sure didn't need us all those years." Asa started to rip up the letter, but Ollie stopped him. He suggested that it was not an issue of abandonment. "What else could it have been? It sounds like he is making excuses and is trying to convince us he is sick in his head."

Ollie said, "Marion was right, the medical term for losing one's memory is amnesia. Your father sounds desperate, and the longer we fume over this, the more upset you will feel. Asa, something is very wrong, why don't we go on home and get some rest. Sometimes things look better in the morning." Asa had never heard of amnesia, but Ollie was somewhat aware of the malady from her nursing classes.

That night Asa kept replaying the words of the letter over in his mind. The following morning, he went to the hotel where the local doctor eats breakfast and pulled up a chair next to him. "Doc, will you read this letter and tell me what you think."

"Glad to do it, give me a couple of minutes to finish this omelet while it is still warm. Coffee is good this morning. Um, Asa this letter sounds like a trap. It wasn't right what he did to your family and it is not good news. Asa, you are asking for trouble if you try to rescue him. If you want my advice, steer clear, this is more trouble than you deserve. I didn't hear nary apology, did you?" Asa thanked the Doc for speaking to him and paid for the Doc's breakfast on the way out of the restaurant.

Asa went to his office but locked the door. He needed to think. Without notice, the man he once knew as his father is begging him to travel hundreds of miles to California and transport him back to Gainesville. Asa was becoming angrier as the hours passed. The worst part was the pain caused to his mother. She had been abandoned penniless with small children to feed. Anger over being deprived of a stable home life and the influence of a proper role model added fuel to Asa's hostility. He had memories that children should not have, things like dealing with his siblings' childhood illness, missed meals, lack of warm bedding and winter clothing. He was convinced the abandonment had broken down his mother's health, hastening her death.

During the night Ollie hardly slept. She wanted to help Asa solve his dilemma. She briefly thought about postponing the wedding and quickly discarded that idea. She wanted Asa to follow his conscience and do what he felt was fair and kind toward his father. Perhaps he should go to visit Marion. And, what if she went too. A trip to California would be a fantastic honeymoon. She had heard so many exciting things about the Pacific Ocean, the great trees that were thousands of years old, the wildlife, and earthquakes. There had been rail service at one point and then disrupted, but the current status was unknown. Just mentioning the word California excited Ollie.

She knew guilt can wound a person and bring long-term loss of self-respect.

Chapter 11

SOMETHING BLUE & OLD

With Callie and Giuseppe happily married, Ollie and Asa's betrothal and wedding was receiving its due attention. Asa gave Ollie a Friesian filly with leather trappings. The extravagant gift made the society page of the newspaper, but the title embarrassed him. "ASA, WHEN DOES OLLIE GET AN ENGAGEMENT RING?" The little hometown paper devoted half a page to the story. There was a beautiful picture of Ollie brushing the colt.

The wedding planning quickly picked up momentum. Elizabeth and Sam were relieved to hear that Ollie wanted a small, private wedding ceremony with just close friends and family in attendance. The plan was doomed to failure because of Asa's popularity and that he was incapable of telling anyone they could not attend the wedding. Word of the upcoming wedding had spread like wildfire. Asa had a piece of paper in his pocket for adding names to invite. There were the fireside buds, about 20 or so, the owners and employees of the surrounding stock auctions and sale barns, fifty or so, and that is when Ollie threw up her hands and said we can't do this.

Truth be told, the townspeople all doted on Asa and his younger siblings, and Asa admitted he couldn't turn anyone away. Asa suggested,

"I'm thanking we should run away and let a judge marry us." That got Ollie all upset and crying. Sam stepped into the fracas and took Asa aside. He found a shady, private spot under a big tree, and the two men sat and let the dust clear. Then Sam said, "Asa, git used to the cryin' that wimen do. They say it's harmonly or something like that."

Asa responded, "Really, I don't 'member my sisters doin' that."

Boy, "It's likely your sisters didn't git the trainin' from their mother. Now listen up, I have an idear how to please everyone. We can hold the weddin' and reception at the town park. I think I can rent the circus pavilion for shade and their bleachers."

Asa felt like he had just been freed from the squeeze chute and said, "Sam, you are brilliant, what a perfect idea. But this could cost a purty penny. I don't think I have that much saved up yet."

Sam slapped Asa on the back and said, "Leave the finances to me son, we can invite souvenir merchants to put up carts with pictures of you and Ollie, and little bags of rice to throw, and greeting cards, stuff like that. We can charge them a percentage to set up their cart and that can help pay some of the cost of the things we pay for. You can help some if you can afford it.

Ollie was able to cancel the printing of invitations and some of the strictly indoor decorations. In lieu of personal invitations they took out a full-page advertisement inviting the good townspeople of Gainesville to witness the nuptials and celebrate the reception to follow. As it would turn out, the owner of the paper, Mr. Banister, refused to charge them for the add and offered any other publicity without charge.

Sam said, "Asa, we both know that things could get out of hand in a jiffy. We need to set some rules and make sure they are enforced, if you know what I mean. I'm gonna get with the sheriff and his men to post the rules around town, we could put 'em in the paper, and at the entrance to the tent, and park gate. I figure we might need some extra officers for crowd control, ridding the shindig of troublemakers and so forth. This is what I wrote down. He handed Asa this handwritten paper.

ATTENTION ALL RESIDENTS OF GAINESVILLE

Yawl are invited to a Wedding on

October 7, 1905

At 10:00 AM

Mr. & Mrs. Samuel McClarren want to share

the coming marriage of their daughter,

Ollie Jamima to Mr. And Mrs.'s Francis McCawl.

The wedding vows will be exchanged at the

Cooke County Fair Grounds circus pavilion.

A lunch of barbeque will be served at the city park

Admission is free. Locals only. Please RSVP at the Sheriff's office.

You will be asked to present identification

with a valid Gainesville address.

Alcoholic beverages will not be allowed.

Drunkenness will be cause for a fine, expulsion, and/or arrest.

Children aged 16 and under must be supervised by their parents.

All animals must be left at the fairgrounds livery.

Out of respect for the occasion, guests are asked to come nicely dressed.

As soon as the invitation was published, the overwhelming response suggested that compiling a list of citizens that would not be attending would save a lot of time and effort. When the RSVPs exceeded three thousand, Sam and Asa along with Sid and John went back to the ranch and upped the number of slaughtered hogs, steers, and fryers to be delivered to Raul. The needed amount of food was triple the initial estimate. The number of support staff and everything else required tripling.

A large flatbed wagon was chosen for the stage. The elevation and mobility would offer flexibility. A cold-room in the ice company's warehouse was where the wedding cake would be assembled and decorated. The site's location was top-secret and being supervised by Callie and Velma. Auntie Zelma volunteered to design and decorate a two-sided basket to carry the rose petals.

Blue, the family pet was appointed to carry the rose petals to be scattered. The basket would be mounted on the blue-tic coonhound's back. Five-year-old twins, boy and girl 2nd cousins of Ollie's would walk on each side of Blue and scatter the petals.

Sam hired gate attendants from surrounding communities, a half-dozen off-duty police officers, all friends of the family.

Ollie asked Callie to loan her the white rhinestone encrusted western boots from her recent wedding. They were too large for Ollie, but she was determined to use them as decorations. Ollie's love of tradition prompted her to have "something old, something new, something borrowed and something blue." Ollie, being an original thinker recruited Blue as something blue.

Wearing the cowboy hat didn't work with her dress, but she got the idea to use the hat as something borrowed. It would make an eye-catching lid for the main punch bowl. She got help gluing it on a white board. She filled in the rest of the surface with white flowers. The punch bowl in this case would be a barrel filled with Texas sweet tea.

For something old and something blue Ollie decided that her Blue-tic coon-dog could satisfy two out of the four. Blue was both old and blue and would be a way to include the beloved pet as a family member.

Planning the wedding ceremony and reception had taken on a life of its own. Some locals went so far as to predict it would be the social event of the decade, engraved into local folk lore.

Since the entire town of Gainesville was invited to the town park for the reception, and Texas wedding receptions bring the expectation of food, Sam McClarren wanted to roll out a banquet fit for his beloved fellow Texans. It was his way of giving back to a community that had provided a lifetime of neighborliness. Gainesville's love of down-home cooking was legendary and Sam McClarren's menu had "Texas Victuals" listed for the cuisine. Raul, the head cook would oversee the pit barbequed chicken, pork, and beef. His staff prepared tubs of potato salad, coleslaw, ham flavored pinto beans, and corn on the cob. Bushel baskets of cornbread muffins and barrels of sweetened tea completed the menu.

The Wedding Cake would have to serve a community and the design was over five feet tall and required its own re-enforced table. The cake maker, named Lilly Beth Ross was a creative artisan with a talent for carving life-like cake toppers. She had grown up with the McClarren clan and doted on Ollie since day one of her thus short life. Lilly Beth wanted her beloved friend's wedding to be a dream come true. Nothing was out of bounds when it came to conjuring up a magical celebration for Ollie and her handsome cowboy. She would begin by choosing the best piece of whittling wood for carving a show-stopper cake-topper.

Lilly Beth interviewed Ollie and Asa. She asked them to describe their first date. She wanted to know how they were dressed and noted any unusual mannerisms or mishaps. She was especially interested in seeing Asa's black Friesian stallion. She asked Ollie to model the wedding gown. Asa gave her a sneak peak of his black western cut suit. During her joint interview with the bride and groom, she asked them to recite the story behind his diamond belt buckle. Ollie dropped the name of the Paris designer responsible for her wedding dress. When Lilly Beth saw the dress, she recognized its tasteful and obvious opulent style. She whispered, "Truly a dress worthy of you! Beautiful choice!"

As for the wedding cake, it was to be the crown jewel of 'French Pastry', the crème de la crème of epicurean cuisine. Even the cake's name, Dacquoise, sounded French. A favorite of Paris high society, the Dacquoise layer cake uses hazelnut and almond flavored meringue spread between multiple thin layers of cake. The five-hundred-pound cake was assembled and decorated in a special walk-in cooler over the course of a week. It would be transported to the reception in a crate via a flatbed wagon just minutes before it would be served. Rumors of the cake had spawned several jokes. Most of them about the age-old dilemma, whether to eat their cake or keep it.

The artful cake-top carving was kept hidden until time for the reception to begin. Not even Ollie could see the cake topper. The replica of Asa's black stallion measured eighteen inches tall. The recognizable and proportionately sized bride and groom were amazingly true to life. Ollie was riding behind Asa and holding around his waist. The carving captured the prance of the stallion's high stepping Spanish Walk. The bride's lightweight skirt and veil flowed wind-swept over the horse's hindquarters. Asa was looking back over his shoulder and waving his black hat high above his head.

The day before the wedding Ollie was exhausted. Elizabeth banned her from the last-minute fracas and prescribed extra bedrest. The rest of the preparation crew were frantically fielding oversights, correcting miscommunication, and handling last minute trouble shooting. Ollie was having trouble complying with her banishment and was caught peeking out her window, listening through a crack in her bedroom door, and scribbling reminders to a number of facilitators by way of a 10-year-old message boy. For the most part the bride spent most of the day in her bedroom being pampered by her beautician. The woman would return early the next morning to do Ollie's hair and makeup.

The final dressed rehearsal took place after the evening meal. Ollie arrived at the last moment and was escorted away as soon as her part was practiced. Hazel helped Ollie pack an overnight suitcase. Just after Ollie and Hazel managed to lock down the latches, Elizabeth knocked on the door. She had two gift wrapped packages for Ollie. The largest package was wrapped in pink floral paper and had a huge satin bow. Ollie quickly tore open the wrapping and held up a white satin and chiffon peignoir edged with white rabbit's fur. The peignoir she had packed was polished cotton trimmed with eyelet lace, plain by comparison. Elizabeth's gift was fitting for a royal princess. Ollie sang "for I'm a jolly good fellow," held the garment to her body and danced around the room. She tried on the slippers and laughed when her ankles wobbled. The fur covered boudoir slippers had been shipped separately and arrived a few days late. Ollie was kept in the dark to avoid adding to her stress level. The second gift from Sam was a beautifully carved wooden box. When the lid was opened, music played. Ollie smiled and held it to her ear. She had a dreamy smile on her face when she saw the pearl necklace, earrings, and bracelet. A card packed inside the box had a company logo, "Hawaii's Finest Jewelers, Inc." imported from Honolulu, HI. The necklace had three strands, and the cluster earrings had diamond accents. Ollie was accustomed to pretty things but nothing like this. She immediately tried on the jewels for Elizabeth and Hazel. A knock on the door silenced the girls. Ollie said, "Yes."

Sam's voice whispered, "Ollie, it's me, you still up? I need to see you. okay." Ollie sprang to her door and jumped into her father's waiting arms.

"Oh Poppa, Momma, the pearls are exquisite, thank you! Here, please sit down, I want to model the pearls for you. Oh, look at how they reflect light! They are perfection, perfectly matched! Thank You so much. Hazel, how did we happen to have these wonderful parents? I suspect God had a hand in the arrangements." The four of them chatted for a few minutes. Sam wrapped his arms around all three for a group hug and led a short prayer before going back to his bedroom. Elizabeth noticed Sam's expression. She knew he was having a hard time with the prospect of handing Ollie over to another man. Back in his room he had a lot more to add to a private prayer.

Hazel waited until she and Ollie were alone to reveal her gift. Inside a lace drawstring bag was a white satin handbag with elaborate pearl beading. She proudly displayed the label that said made by "Hazel McClarren." Ollie's expression burst with appreciation over the lovely clutch bag. The delicate beading closely matched that of her wedding gown. Ollie encircled Hazel with a bear hug and said, "I love it, I will treasure it forever!" The sisters hugged and kissed each other on the cheek. Right away Ollie transferred articles from her everyday handbag to the little clutch bag. Items like a compact with mirror, a lace handkerchief, and a few coins. She added a scarf, a glass vial of cologne, and a tin of lip rouge. There, she was packed. It is likely Ollie was the only McClarren to sleep well that night. About marrying Asa, she had no doubts. Asa was the man for her. She fell asleep after a rambling, emotional prayer.

Chapter 12

WEDDING DAY

First in the wedding procession were the twins with Old Blue. The organizers were questioning if such an elaborate event go smoothly? Just as the wedding procession started down the aisle, Blue decided he wanted a drink of that tea he was smelling. Unlike most coon hounds, he loved iced tea and was accustomed to tea in his drinking bowl. Right on time the wedding procession got started. Blue, a good ole dog most of the time, caught a whiff of the tea only a few yards away. He jerked away from the flower children and plunged his nose under the lid and started lapping tea as fast as possible because he intuitively knew the handlers would pull him away. Sadly, Blue had upset the rose petals. Hazel took control of the situation and brought Blue back to his station. The cook shack was notified to brew more tea, and the rose petals were gathered from the ground, soggy and bruised, but recognizable as rose petals.

The carpeted path led up to the back of the flatbed where the preacher would stand behind a pulpit. The now un-nerved man-of-the-cloth was eager to get to the business of marrying the two lovebirds before anything else went wrong. The String Quartet began playing the Wedding March, the que for the bridesmaids and groomsmen to saunter their way down the path. That the twins had failed to keep

Blue under control was a minor mishap that added some levity and actually settled some nerves.

Giuseppe took center stage and tuned to face the guests. His mop of curls had been cropped, and he was dapper in a black tuxedo. Callie couldn't take her eyes off him. He accompanied himself on a guitar and sang a romantic Hungarian aria. As he commenced to sing, the nods of approval encouraged him to pour great passion and tenderness into the operatic piece. This is when Blue heard the call of nature. He hiked a rear leg and sprayed the wheel of the flatbed wagon, causing a couple of women in the front row of the choir to hop backwards to avoid the splatter. Ollie and Asa's facial expressions wilted. They were thinking that having Blue in the wedding wasn't such a good idea after all. Asa seized the moment and turned to face the guests. "Sorry folks, please excuse Blue, looks like he drunk too much tea." Asa felt better when thunderous laughter rang out. Not that the thought was expressed openly, but at a later date several attendees admitted that the actual exchange of vows was slightly anti-climactic.

The minister's body language indicated an eagerness to hurry along the ceremony. "Do you, Ollie and Asa, agree to be wed forever and remember how God hates divorce, joined in matrimony in the sight of God and all these witnesses?" Ollie and Asa looked up at the preacher and moved their heads in a manner that indicated they agreed. "What God has joined together must stay together. Please say, I Promise." The couple spoke in unison, 'I Promise.' Please exchange rings, careful now, don't wanna drop'em, and now you may kiss your bride." This was the second time Asa and Ollie had entertained the town of Gainesville by kissing. The designated violin player stepped forward and played the Wedding March. The melodious tones blended to produce a beautiful sound to the human ear, but the effect on Blue's auditory nerves was so painful the poor creature raised his nose to the sky and drowned out the violin with a sound so mournful it likely awakened some residents of the nearby grave yard. That brought a premature end to the violin solo.

Mealtime was announced by the tantalizing aroma of barbeque. A boy cut in line and grabbed a roll and drumstick. The lightning speed of his escape left the adults with open mouths. After some speculation on the identification of the child's parents, they all wagged their heads and remained in line, lest they lose their place.

The poor shaken fiddle player rosined up his bow and commenced a lively tune. He thought 'good-riddance' when he saw the dog take off after a rabbit. Unveiling the wedding cake was reaching high anticipation accompanied by fiery explosions. No, the explosions were firecrackers thanks to the machinations of a few teenaged boys. The sound of the explosions hurt Blue's ears and led to more howling. A stern woman grabbed a boy preparing to light more firecrackers. She had him by his shirt collar and held him suspended above the ground until he dropped his burning match. Sam happened to be near-by and took control of the apple of his parent's eyes.

Genuine, copious appreciation was expressed for the workmanship and lifelike portrayal of the Bride, Groom, and the Friesian Stallion. Not only was the cake topper masterfully carved, but the cake was a work of art, ornately speaking. The flavoring was neither overpowering or bland.

The wedding party was seated at the head table. Ollie fed Asa a mouth full of cake just as he inhaled, and it went down wrong. He coughed, turned red, and coughed more. White crumbs rained down like snow. After being slapped on the back by the preacher and Ollie lifting his arm above his head, he recovered. He pulled a handkerchief from his pocket, and Ollie used it to clean the spots from Asa's suit, from her own bodice, and then passed the kerchief around for anyone that felt the need. Blue thought the cake smelled good and helped with the clean-up. Asa's second bite managed to descend the esophagus instead of the trachea. Just as Ollie took a small tidbit from the fork Asa held, Callie and Giuseppe abruptly hurried them to the dance floor for the bouquet toss and first dance.

Ollie closed her eyes and faced away from the young ladies in contention for the bouquet and, of course the reward catching it brought. Ollie threw the clutch of flowers so high a gust of wind carried it out of the perimeter of the dancefloor and dropped it in front of Blue's place of repose under a giant oak. Blue knew better, but he had always liked the taste of flowers, so he seized the opportunity. Before he had finished two mouthfuls, Hazel yelled, "No, Blue, give me the bouquet, thank you, good dog." Blue lowered his eyes and took on a guilty-as-charged expression. Blue's sad look signaled his feelings of discrimination for being a dog. He snapped at a fly crawling on his paw and went back to sleep.

Ollie picked up what was left of the bouquet and re-enacted the bouquet toss. It was flicked over her shoulder, and the trajectory took it past Woolworth's Sara at knee-cap height. This time Sara jumped sideways and dove under the "pinto beans" table in time to grab it before it landed. Sara heard a cheer go up and realized she was the object being cheered. That is when she realized she was in a most un-ladylike position. The crowd only seemed interested in the fair catch. Mrs. Smithers, a known football fan, acting as a pro-bono referee held up both hands and yelled, "score." The only problem was that Sara's landing revealed her "Woolworth" step-ins. Nothing was left to the imagination. The un-mentionable was yellow with white lace. One of the middle-aged ladies spoiled everyone's curiosity by holding a table cloth between Sara and the gawkers while she righted her skirt. The look on Sara's face said she preferred to stay under the table, but she crawled out on all fours and wiped the mud from her sad face. The flowers were ruined, and her yellow dress had green grass stains on every part that touched the ground. She offered the flowers back to Ollie but was told to keep them. With Sara's new frock spoiled, she wanted to disappear to the privacy of her bedroom. Despite her caustic personality, folks couldn't help but feel badly for her and turned away to spare her further humiliation. She pitched the bouquet at Blue and almost hit her target. The kind lady told her to wrap the sheet around herself and run along home to change her outfit. From that day forward Sara was never seen in Gainesville, Texas. A rumor circulated that she took the stage to Houston to live with an aunt.

Word got around about a spur-of-the-moment black market that sprung up when some of Gainesville's teenaged entrepreneurs went back for second helpings of cake and proceeded to auction them off at a price that the market supported. A few takers paid full price, but most got by with paying the sale price of a dime.

The musical entertainment was crowd pleasing. Three bands took turns playing. There were three genres, Rhineland polka, Western two-step'in, and Dose-E-Dough square dancing. As expected, the two-step'in got the biggest crowd.

It was a little after midnight when Sam and Elizabeth ended the band music and dispersed the crowds. They had plenty of help hauling away the leftover food. That is when the clean-up crews took over. Sam had hired a janitor service out of Sadler. They had orders to work all night if necessary to restore the grounds.

Chapter 13

THE RED RIVER INN

Ollie asked Asa what kind of honeymoon appealed to him, and he slowly looked her up and down and said, "Being with you."

"Oh, Asa you are such a jokester. Be serious. We should think of something that will make great memories and be adventurous."

Asa said, "Let me think on it. For right now, bring me a glass of tea and clime up on my lap. There, I was thirsty for your sweet tea, now come a little closer, shoo that fly off my nose, thanks, back to the honeymoon."

The newlyweds were too enraptured with each other to recall that the world was still out there somewhere. The three days they spent at the Red River Inn fused them into "one flesh." Asa and Ollie were inexperienced but willing, eager but awkward, and completely overcome with "being in love."

The first day back from the Red River Inn is when Sam and Elizabeth introduced the newlyweds to their new home. It was set up with linens, the most crucial furniture, and the kitchen was stocked with groceries. The master bedroom was made up and ready for occupancy. Ollie and Asa were about to receive the wedding gift of wedding gifts.

Sam and Elizabeth met up with Ollie and Asa as soon as they arrived at Asa's house and loaded them onto the buckboard wagon. When Sam stopped at a home on South Taylor Street, Ollie asked, "Who lives here?"

Elizabeth answered, "You'll see when we get inside." Asa commented that he had noticed that a house was being built on the property but had no idea who owned it. It was a spacious two-story clapboard painted white with dark brown trim. A covered porch stretched across the entire front of the east facing home. Asa noticed a small barn and corral at the back. As soon as the four of them entered the living room a huge crowd shouted "Surprise!" There didn't appear to be a single missing family member or friend. The men raised Asa to their shoulders and paraded him around the room. The women handed Ollie a dozen red roses and engaged in a hug-fest. Sam stood in the center of the room and bellared out, "Welcome Home Ollie and Asa!" Shock registered on Asa's face, and he turned toward Ollie. "What's goin' own?"

"Asa, I 'm just as surprised as you are. Poppa, thank you, but the house may be more than we can afford. Oh, it is beautiful! Maybe, one day in the future we can have one like —."

Sam interrupted Ollie and said, "We can talk finances later, for now, just enjoy your home." Asa was wondering about Zelma, John, and Sid. Ollie was thinking about them too and rushed to welcome them to their new home. She started the conversation with them by saying, "It looks like there are enough bedrooms for all of us to have our own room."

Sid looked at Asa and then said, "No more buckets when it rains?" A big laugh cleared the atmosphere of any awkwardness, and Velma, Sid, and John were smiling from ear to ear. Callie let loose of Giuseppe's arm long enough to join in a big hug with Asa and Ollie's ready-made family. The McClarren family was so genuine with the invitation that the three young McCawl youngsters felt welcome to call the house on South Taylor Street home. Hazel reminded the group that John and Sid are staying out at their bunk house and helping with branding the new calves. Hazel looked at Ollie and said, "If you want, we can help you move out of the rental house."

Ollie said, "That would be a huge help. Thank you." Asa and Ollie spent about two weeks settling into the home. Elizabeth, Hazel, and a few ladies from church helped Ollie sew curtains, make decorative pillows, and hang some hand-me-down wall decorations.

Not long after the wedding a friend struck up a conversation with Sam. "Sam, that was some weddin' reception you threw for them kids. Wish I could have been there. I heard the fiddle music had ever body up and dancin', and the food was as good as it gits. That party was one for the record books!"

Chapter 14

CELEBRITY HAPPENS

Later in life, Asa McCawl was a regular attraction at the Cooke County Fair. Early on he would say his piece before reporting for the cutting horse events. Word of Asa's story-telling talent spread and eventually led to an invitation to speak at the Texas State Fair in Big D. The resulting celebrity and face recognition caused Asa to spend some of the "easy money" the fair organizers paid him. He hitched a ride to Fort Worth and upgraded his wardrobe with a few gaudy cowboy shirts, leather chaps with fringe, and a pair of fine alligator boots. From then on Asa was one flashy "cowboy."

The fearless Asa, seemingly unaware of his mortality, had gained recognition for some daring skills he used for rounding up cattle. He knew how to get meanest feral bulls out of the brush. He designed some protective equipment and hired Giuseppe to construct the leather body armor that resembled the protective gear used by bull fighting lancers called picadors. The gear included narrow sleeves that wrapped the fore legs of the horse, pads to strap around the flanks and underbelly. The equipment was quite successful at shielding the horse from snake bite, bull nettles, thorns, and horns. Asa found the market for the protective gear to be lucrative and used every opportunity to showcase it at county fairs and local parades.

Asa had a striking appaloosa gelding that was gated and could do a spectacular Spanish Walk. Local parades gave Asa the opportunity to promote his celebrity and his product line. The crowd was dazzled by Asa's stable, but there was no doubt that Ebony was the crowd's favorite.

Asa's skill for spinning a good yarn brought him considerable fanfare. At first, he enjoyed the attention, but he soon discovered the downside to celebrity. Folks wouldn't leave him alone, and he eventually yearned for more anonymity.

Chapter 15

"BACK WHEN"

When looking at the old photos of Grandmother Ollie's sweet countenance, I understand why she was so special to her parents, and I am not one bit surprised by her ability to capture the local heart-throb bachelor. An unnamed confidant of Sam McClarren's revealed that Sam doubted Asa's ability to provide for Ollie and her offspring in the style and luxury of her earlier life. Asa's transition into a husband and head of his own household started on a high note, and here is what the Gainesville old timers had to say about his legacy. As the husband of Sam McClarren's first daughter, Asa was known as "Sam McClarren's son-in-law," but that changed; within a relatively short period of time Sam McClarren became known as Asa McCawl's father-in-law.

Asa didn't set out to impress people, and that is part of the reason he impressed people. It helped that his mind was uncluttered with feelings of guilt. That and a host of positive characteristics contributed to Asa's popularity in Gainesville.

By middle age Asa had added a paragraph to his resume. He joined the Cooke County Sheriff's Department as a deputy where he served his community until the limitations of age and poor health forced his retirement.

Chapter 16

THE SMITHSON
CHILDREN

The two-minute warning sounded in the halls of the nursing home, "Time for Lawrence Welk, everyone ready?" Cheatie pointed her remote at the T.V. and changed the channel. P.B.S. would be showing another re-run of the Lawrence Welk Show. The highly anticipated program was the favorite at her nursing home. Cheatie had spent the afternoon speaking into the video camera, spinning another of her yarns for our book. As a backup to the word-of-mouth stories, Cheatie's old trunk was overflowing with supporting documents for many of her stories. It was up to me to merge the various sources into a cohesive narrative.

Digging for information in the old trunk was never disappointing. The Smithson family ancestors were on Grandfather Asa's side of the family tree. The next item out of the trunk was a stack of brittle and yellowed handwritten pages bound with twine. The top page caught my eye. The date was August 5, 1845 and beneath that, was neatly printed, 'The Journal of Mary Elizabeth Smithson.' The first paragraph stated that Ida and Jonas Smithson and their four children lived on a remote homestead west of the Cook County line in north central Texas.

The Smithson homestead was located on arid mesquite and prickly pear strewn terrain west of what is called the Cross Timbers, a heavily wooded strip of land that stretches from southeastern Kansas and covers the midsection of Oklahoma and terminates in central Texas.

After the first two or three pages, the narrative became so compelling, I finished it that same day. Lizzy began by describing her day-to-day routine. When the imagery became violent and troubling, I was compelled to keep reading. My bed was left unmade, and the sink of dirty dishes were left to soak a while longer.

I realized early on that this child of 14 was a good writer with the vocabulary of an adult, an educated one. For the 1840s her narrative was surprisingly descriptive. As I read along, I kept asking myself, how would I have fared in the same circumstances? Her "Mother-Hen" protectiveness made her a sympathetic character from page one.

As a family, the Smithson's were champions of resourcefulness. The four kids worked hard even for those times. Their callused hands were badges of honor. They were accustomed to eating what was put before them. The youngsters were no stranger to discomfort, and that included hunger. When left to their own devices, they knew how to analyze, make comparisons, and be willing to adjust plans as needed. Defending the family name was ingrained from the time they had been toddlers. Thanks to wise parenting and their disciplined hard scrabble life the four Smithson children were physically well equipped for trying times, but nothing could have prepared them for the challenge that awaited them.

There were a few dangerous encounters described in the opening pages. One close call was when Jonas was almost bitten by a diamondback. The diary recorded Jonas' bouts with malaria, a severe thunderstorm that spawned a funnel cloud, and ferocious growls coming from the pig pen and hen house. Lizzy's father Jonas referred to their drought-stricken vegetable garden as a patch of weeds with a few garden plants. He believed the weeds were the consequence of Adam and Eve's original sin and subsequent expulsion from the Garden of Eden them.

> Because thou hast hearkened unto the voice of thy wife,
> and hast eaten of the tree, of which I commanded thee,
> saying Thou shalt not eat of it: cursed is the ground for

thy sake; in toil shalt thou eat of it all the days of thy life; thorns also and thistles shall it bring forth to thee; and thou shalt eat the herb of the field; in the sweat of thy face shalt thou eat bread, till thou return unto the ground; for out of it wast thou taken: for dust thou art, and unto dust shalt thou return.

The dry spell had forced the carnivorous predators like puma, fox, wolf, and coyote to lose their fear of humans and become unusually aggressive and threatening.

It was early August, the time of year for gathering wild food like prickly pear apples, acorns, mustang and post oak grapes, a variety of nuts, honey, and wild plumbs. Lizzy was up early to prepare for a day of foraging the wild plants and animals. They were about to walk to the plum thickets and bring back a load for canning when Lizzie yelled, "You boys ready? Don't forget your bags and a bottle of water." The plumbs grew along a deeply carved arroyo a little over a mile from the family homestead. In broad daylight the four of them didn't worry about animal attack and the Comanche had been peaceful for a year.

A few days earlier Jonas had traded for a bag of raw brown sugar, a necessary ingredient for preserving the plums. The fruit made great dumplings and pie, especially appealing during the bleak winter months.

Ralph said, "Hey Liz, we're waitin' on you, let's go. Pete, did you decide to go with us or stay here with Momma and Poppa?"

Peter responded by putting his hands on his hips and squinting his eyes, "Ralph, I'm big now, and I work hard like the rest of youins. Course I wanta go." Because the Smithson family supplemented their diet with wild food, it was a common event for them to go into the surrounding hills to gather nature's bounty. They extended flour and cornmeal by adding a bland powder made from acorn meats. Prickly Pear and Yucca plants were used for food and medicine. Other species of cactus have special uses such as medicine and food.

Each spring Jonas and Ida were quick to plant garlic, onion, and marigolds around the perimeter of the vegetable garden for their insect repelling properties. For warding off animals, they ladled dissolved dung of lion and wolf around the plants. The child that drew the short straw got that task.

On the walk to the plum thickets, Lizzy was on alert for things like snakes, bees, and poison sumac. She had trained herself to be watchful. She enjoyed observing the mischievous boys' antics and wasn't beyond jumping into the fray. Under her watchful eye, the boys skipped and scuffled the entire way. 12-year-old Ralph was a smaller version of his father Jonas. Next in line was James, a tall and serious nine-year-old. The baby was five-year-old Peter, a chubby, good-natured child with a cherub face.

All four Smithson children were intellectually bright and handsome children. Descended from Scandinavian ancestors, they had the characteristic blue eyes and curly blond hair. The boys were sturdily built and tall for their age. Lizzy had a more delicate frame and was maturing into a stunning beauty. Her angelic facial features reminded one of a porcelain doll.

The Smithson children would be competing with birds and vermin for the fruit. They each carried a cloth bag. First, they picked what they could reach from the ground, eating as they worked. Their faces were stained with juice as they munched on the tart fruit. When the most accessible fruit was gathered, Lizzy spread an old blanket under the tree, and Ralph or James or both would climb up in the branches and shake the tree. Their bags got heavy fast. Peter remarked, "Momma and Poppa is gonna be mighty proud we got so many plums."

Suddenly Peter began crying but refused to say why. He was hiding something in his hand. Finally, Lizzy pried open his fist and found a squished plum. That is when Peter said, "Can you see it? Right there! I ate half a worm, and I can feel it in my tummy. This part is still moving too. It tasted like plum, but it is making me feel like—." Pete began gagging and heaved up the entire contents of his stomach. The eruption narrowly missed the blanket. Lizzy used her apron to wipe his pale face and helped him to rinse his mouth with a swig of water. Immediately Ralph and James began examining each plum for worm holes before placing them in the bag. Lizzy decided that they had sacked up enough of the fruit and called it quits. It was almost fall, and Lizzy was planning a foraging trip for nuts soon. From the look of the trees, it was a good year for nuts, both pecans and black walnuts were starting to blanket the ground.

On the way back Lizzy gathered a few ripened prickly pear apples. The fruit made wonderful jam and juice, and new growth paddles served as a last resort green vegetable. Lizzy carried along a separate leather pouch and a pair of tongs for harvesting the fruit and paddles. The spines would be singed over a fire and then scraped away with a dull blade. A buzzing sound attracted Lizzy's attention to a newly established beehive, and she marked the location with an arrow formed with stones. Poppa was the only one that dared to gather honey. He had sewed himself a special leather suit and a helmet inset with a fabric mesh over the facial opening. Earlier in the year Jonas consented to Lizzy observing him harvest a large hive. The hive had inhabited a hollow tree trunk. He insisted that she stay back at a safe distance. He used a torch made of dry grass and oily rags to smoke the bees into a state of inactivity. Next, he used a machete to reach into the hollow tree trunk and carve the comb into blocks. Jonas knew how to dislodge the sleeping bees by tapping the comb against the tree trunk before loading the combs into a couple of small covered barrels. Collecting honey from wild hives was not a chore for the children.

The young Smithson children were about to experience a horrific shock. Unbeknownst to the Smithson family, the Nokoni Comanche had resumed their raids on the most isolated settlers, and even a few farms and ranches close to settlements. The homesteaders in the area had been free of Indian attacks for more than a year. There had been a few brawls and sniper incidents attributed to Indians but nothing serious. The Texans had been living with a false sense of security.

The children were headed home, and Lizzy was singing a song called "Turkey in the Straw." The boys joined in.

"Turkey in the straw, turkey in the hay.
Turkey in the store got nuthin to say.
Jump down, turn around, get in the way.
If you're gonna feed a turkey gotta feed him every day."

By the third verse Lizzy abruptly quit singing. She was looking toward the farm where there was a column of smoke rising. She stepped up the pace and told the boys to hurry along because they might be needed to help fight a wildfire.

An hour before a war party had suddenly appeared at the Smithson farmhouse. The braves were not the usual beggars. He made the usual overtures of friendship and offered them a piglet from the sty. An Indian dismounted and snatched the pig from Jonas without making eye contact. He noticed the war paint, the sight of which made the hair stand up on the back of his neck. The surly demeanor of the braves told Jonas that this visit was far from a routine shake down.

When one of the braves attempted to enter the cabin Jonas shouted, "No" and barred the door with his arms. He said, "Ida, we have a problem out here, you know what to do." The brave shoved Jonas out of the way and brandished his axe. Jonas lowered his gaze and allowed the intruder to enter.

One of the Comanche understood Jonas' warning and immediately rode his horse to the rear of the cabin in time to catch Ida climbing through a window. The brave lassoed her and dragged her to the front of the cabin. A couple of men searched the cabin. Once they were satisfied that the man and woman were alone, the leader gave the order for Jonas to be killed.

A hideous brave made more so by the striped black and white face paint threw his lance at Jonas with such force that the tip penetrated his torso. Jonas screamed and grasped the spear with both hands as he crumpled to the ground. Despite the rope Ida crawled to Jonas' side. Her hysterical screaming disrupted communication and irritated the attackers. The men stopped what they were doing and glared at the crazed white woman. The leader held up his hands to pause what was being said and slapped Ida across the face. Her head snapped backwards violently, leaving her stunned. She was shaking as she hunkered over the unconscious body of her husband, in order to shield him from further injury.

The Indians whooped and raised their fists in a show of bloodlust. The brave that had thrown the spear dismounted, and sauntered stiff legged to where Jonas lay. He placed a foot on Jonas' chest, and removed his lance. Jonas revived to scream out in agony. When Jonas saw Ida, he tried to stand. The sullen brave kicked him in the face and then turned to bask in the adulation of the war party. The preening sadist shoved Ida aside and drew his knife slowly, in a ritualistic manner. There was a hushed anticipation as he bent to slice a circle around the circumference of Jonas' balding head. Jonas tried to resist but fainted when his scalp was ripped away. The brave took Ida by the hair and dragged her into the cabin. Her crys were high pitched shreaking that could have awaked the dead.

The leader took Ida by an arm and flung her upon the bed. He violently removed her clothing and delighted in her anticipation of what would come next. Her frenzied resistance further excited the aroused brave. Ida fought back with every ounce of strength she could muster. The man was enjoying the fight until she bit down on his arm so hard, she tore away a chunk of flesh. That is when he knocked her unconscious with a fist to the face. After he finished with Ida, a succession of braves each took a turn ravaging the fortunately comatose Ida. When they were satiated, they cut her throat, removed her scalp, and ended by mutilating her private parts.

The marauders propped up the bodies, side by side next to the door stoup of the cabin. Before torching the cabin, the Indians stripped the farmhouse of food, implements, and anything else that caught their fancy. One half-gown pig escaped, and the chickens scattered into the brush. The raiders decided to move on. They whooped as they rode away in a cloud of dust.

On the way home, Lizzy noticed the billowing smoke toward the cabin and sensed trouble. She considered the likelihood that a grass fire had broken out. They would be needed to help fight the fire. Lizzy, who carried the heaviest bag of fruit, rushed ahead of her brothers. She had an eerie feeling that something was terribly wrong even before she saw the orange flames that engulfed the cabin. Her first thought was an Indian attack. She decided to hide the boys in thicket of brush before going ahead to investigate.

Through the haze of thick smoke Lizzy could barely make out her parents lying in front of the cabin. They were motionless. Fear stricken, Lizzy checked for Indians before approaching through the choking smoke. She had the presence of mind to place the bag of fruit on a flat rock well away from the heat. She could see the broken ground churned up by the Indians' horses. Satisfied that the riders had gone, Lizzy tried to approach Ida and Jonas, but the heat forced her back. She sensed that they were already dead, but because of her tender age she was unable accept the obvious. She was determined to launch a rescue. She lifted her skirt to shield her face and dashed toward the bodies. She retreated in a state of mental shock. The scene had been staged for the maximum macabre affect. Her first thought was to protect her brothers from the trauma of seeing what had happened. How could this happen? What about the peace treaty? Poor Lizzy staggered backward for a few feet, to where she had dropped the heavy bag of fruit. She grabbed the fruit and ran back to her brothers. She hissed in an excited whisper, "Shoo, be quiet, we got to stay hidden! Injuns been here." Lizzy led the frightened children to a better hiding place in a distant ravine, "Look for rattlers and fire ants and then hunker down under these bushes. Stay here, ya hear? Don't move a muscle. I'm gonna sneak around the backside of the hill and see if the Injuns is gone. I'll be back as fast as I can."

Ralph asked, "But wher's Ma and Pa?" Lizzy pretended not to know and gestured with a shrug. Lizzy walked through the brush, maintaining a low profile. She circled the burning farmhouse and returned to the spot where the corpses lay. There were no Indians in sight, but she thought they might be hiding. As she carefully approached where her parents lay, she wept, silently. When Lizzy approached, the intense heat blistered her face and singed her hair. She was forced to step back. She removed her petticoat and rushed in to cover her mother's nakedness. Above the roar of the burning cabin, she heard her father groan. "Poppa, you're alive! It's Lizzy; I'm here!" She embraced him, and then her mother.

Her young mind could not grasp something so terrible. Lizzy took her father by the feet and pulled him about fifteen feet from the fire, far enough to allow her to kneel beside him. The skin of his forehead had fallen over his eyes. Blood was flowing from the bare place where his scalp had been and from the wound in his abdomen. Flies and ants began claiming his body now that the heat no longer repelled them. Lizzy's soft voice was repeating, *Poor Momma and Poppa.*

Tough as nails, Jonas revived once again as he fought off the grim reaper. With a labored attempt, he whispered, "Ida, — help——Ida." Then Jonas stiffened, and stopped breathing.

"Please God, bring Poppa back." Lizzy placed her ear over his mouth, he had stopped breathing. She knew they were both gone. She pulled both of their bodies further from the heat. Lizzy turned around and walked slowly back to where the children waited. The look about her startled them. Big eyed and whimpering, the boys were startled by Lizzy's blood-streaked dress, hands, and face. The children stood up and started to bolt toward the cabin.

Peter screamed, "Momma, Poppa!"

Lizzy sunk to the ground, and moaned, "Quiet, stop, come back! The Injuns may still be about." The children returned to where Lizzy knelt. She placed her arms around them. They all clung to each other, shaking from shock and fear. Lizzy drew a big breath and said, "Momma and Poppa, well—, the Injuns killed them both, they are gone to heaven."

Ralph said, "Let me go git Papa's gun, I'll show them Injuns—."
Lizzy placed her hand over Ralph's lips and shushed him. She said in a slow calm voice, "Wait, we have to think this through."

Lizzy wiped at her tears with her sleeve and looked around. She sat on the ground and moved Peter to her lap. She held him in an embrace until he fell asleep. Ralph whispered, "Okay if I walk around and look for Indians, I will stay hidden?" She agreed and handed the sleeping Peter to James. She rose and walked away in search of a better hiding place farther away from the cabin. When Ralph returned from his scouting trip, Lizzy suggested that he and James hang the bags of plumbs from a sturdy mesquite tree limb.

Lizzy bowed her head and prayed. "Dear Lord, Momma and Poppa is up there with you in heaven now. We kids need your help. Please keep them Injuns away. Help me to keep these boys safe. Amen." Lizzy had been taught to carry on and do what must be done. She and Ralph decided to split up and look for Indian sign. She told James to stay with Peter who was sound asleep lying on a sandy spot in the shade. Watch and move him if ants start crawling on him. She followed the trail of the departing Indians for a few minutes and found Ralph in the top of a tree. "See anything?" Though the tree tore at Ralph's clothes, he hardly noticed. From the highest branch capable of supporting his weight, he looked in the direction of the tracks. Far away, and barely visible was a dust cloud.

Ralph dropped to the sandy ground and said, "Looks like they are gone for now." Lizzy and Ralph walked back to where James and Peter were hiding. Lizzy told James to break off a cedar limb and sweep away all footprints to their hiding spot. Lizzy stressed how important it was for them to stay hidden. She walked back to the tool shed located about seventy feet behind the burning cabin. She looked for anything useful.

Lizzy needed to fix a platform up off the ground for the children while there was still some daylight. That meant rigging a sleeping platform in a tree. She spied a big mesquite tree with sprawling branches. It was far enough from the burning cabin to not be seen by the Indians should they return. She recalled that her father had stored some lumber underneath the back porch, just what she needed. That side of the house had not completely burned. The boards were hot and were starting to smoke on one end. It took Lizzy and Ralph three trips to haul the lumber to the tree. The boards were hot but not enough to blister. As they worked Lizzy said, "Being off the ground will help keep us away from the ants and spiders that come out at night."

Lizzy returned to Peter and James. Peter was awake and so frightened he was squeezing James' neck too tightly. James croaked, "Pete not so tight, you're choking me." The little fellow was scanning the landscape with unnaturally wide eyes. James looked frightened too but held back his emotions for the sake of Pete. It was touching the way James was lovingly patting his little brother on the back. He figured he could be scared later, but for the time he would concentrate on being big for Peter.

Thirst drove Lizzy to draw water from the cistern, and just as she was ready to drink some it occurred to her that it might be poisoned. Indians were known to poison wells and food. First, Lizzy sniffed the water. It smelled okay. She looked to see if it was clear, and it was. She dipped her finger in, and it tasted the same as usual. Lizzy took a small drink and waited a minute to see how she felt. Lizzy declared the water safe to drink which was both good and bad. Good because it meant survival for the short term. Bad because it meant that the Indians might be planning to use the cistern as a future source of water. Lizzy insisted, "You boys need to be drinking plenty water, don't forgit, okay?" The water was warm, and that reminded her of what the Lord said about luke-warm water. Then she gave the order to eat some plums. "Eat up, we need to keep up our strength." Ralph used a rock and cracked several handfuls of pecans. They ate because Lizzy told them to, not from hunger.

At dusk a distinct feeling came over Lizzy; it was as though a supernatural force was directing her actions. The stars were appearing in the sky one by one. The breeze was enough to keep down mosquitoes. Ralph's hyper-vigilance revealed how frightened he was though he was trying to put on a brave exterior. Hampered by the darkness, finishing the sleeping platform was no easy task. The mesquite branches were warped and twisted. Lizzy worried that someone might fall to the ground in their sleep, so she built up the edges with dead limbs. Though not completely level, the platform would at least provide them an elevated bed. It was the best she could come up with so fast. The blanket from plum gathering was able to cover all four of them. It was hard to distinguish individual bodies, seeing how closely they were huddled together. The night was unusually warm, so the blanket served as a barrier to the darkness rather than a shield from a chilly night.

The platform was only about six feet off the ground, and when the coyotes started their nightly barking, the children became frightened. Lizzy feigned bravery and gave each boy a stick for protection. Ralph backed up Lizzy's bravado by saying, "Those old coyotes would not dare come around us, why, we would send them back to wher they cum'd from." The children gripped the sticks as they lay huddled on the rough hard platform. Peter felt safer with his head covered.

Emotional and physical exhaustion prevailed, and sleep came quickly to the closely packed mass of boys. It took longer for Lizzy to doze off. She was thinking about tomorrow, all the tomorrows. She took stock of their situation. Thankfully, the outhouse was undisturbed and useable. There was water to drink, and pecans and plumbs for food. Lizzy was praying a long repetitive prayer for the Lord's help in burying her parents when she lapsed into a restless cat nap filled with frightening images. The troubled slumber did nothing to refresh Lizzy. The nightmare of their situation was becoming more real by the hour.

The call of a crow awakened Lizzy in time for sunrise. She quietly climbed down from the platform. Lizzy was stiff from lying on the hard surface, but it didn't last once she got moving. She left the boys soundly sleeping and walked toward the smoking cabin. First, she checked for Indians and found none. With the greatest stealth possible to avoid waking the boys, she drank from the cistern and surveyed the area. Lizzy was full of dread as she contemplated burying her parents.

Since the Indians had stolen the tools and implements she needed, she would halve to improvise. First, she looked to see what had been left behind. Not much. She circled the area around the burned cabin and came upon a short-handled shovel sticking in the ground where her father had been using it. The thought occurred to her that he purposely left it there for her to find. As she made her way back, she looked inside the tin implement shed and uncovered a partly buried horse blanket. She felt as though she had been guided to the blanket and the shovel and thanked the Lord. Was her mind playing tricks on her?

Nothing could have prepared her for the shocking condition of her parents' bodies. Lizzy was whispering as she walked, "*Cain't let the boys see Momma and Poppa like this, got to hurry and get them buried —.*"

The smell of death cloaked the area around the decaying bodies. They had been moved about by the animals. Two vultures were fighting over a piece of flesh. The back end of an armadillo could be seen as it feasted inside Jonas' body. The macabre scene struck Lizzy with such force that she fell backward with faintness and began retching. The scavengers brazenly ignored her approach. Several vultures were competing for the remains, while still more of them were circling on the wind currents far above. A pack of coyotes paused to watch her approach. Lizzy briefly indulged her broken heart long enough to weep and pray before commencing the work that no child should have to do.

Anger welled up in Lizzy when the carrion eating menagerie refused to leave their meal. She gathered rocks into her cupped skirt and pelted the scavengers. Poor Lizzy must have not looked very threatening. She continued rock throwing and then resorted to beating them with a broken limb. All but the armadillo moved back to wait for a chance to resume feeding. She was forced to jab at the armor-clad critter repeatedly before it hid under a bush.

Downhill from the cabin soil erosion had carved up the landscape. Lizzy walked past one of the erosion ditches and stopped. It was down slope from the cabin, and she figured it would be perfect for the grave. After she slid to the bottom of the gully, she decided to look for a deeper ravine. Lizzy wanted to check on the children, but had difficulty climbing out of the gully because of the loose crumbling walls. She realized how easy it would be to cover the bodies. She found a much deeper ravine farther down the hillside. It was about ten feet deep and narrow. The sides were crumbly like the other ditch.

Dragging the bodies to the gully would be the hardest part. Back at the site where the bald headed, bloody-beaked vultures were once again squabbling for the best position, Lizzy turned vicious in her effort to drive them away. She turned her head and gagged. "The children must not see this ghastly sight." She tried to roll her father's body onto the horse blanket.

The vultures had hopped a few feet away but refused to take their eyes from their interrupted meal. They were so near their foul smell caused Lizzy's eyes to water.

First, she tried to shove the body of her father onto the blanket with a pole. She pushed with all her might, but his form did not move. She needed more leverage. Her Father was a big man, over six feet tall. Then she tried a maneuver her father once used to move a slaughtered hog. She crossed his feet and twisted. Just like the hog, his body rolled over onto the blanket. Lizzy was glad that he was still wearing boots. A dense cloud of flies hovered above the dead bodies. They covered the exposed skin of both corpses, and to Lizzy's horror they lit upon her face and arms. She ignored the flies the best she could.

The task of burying Ida and Jonas was almost too much for Lizzy. She used a mental device called compartmentalization to complete the task. She visualized Momma and Papa being welcomed into heaven. She pictured God on His throne with Jesus beside him; she imagined the beautiful city and angels escorting Jonas and Ida to a lovely mansion with their names on the door. The diversion worked well enough to get the job done.

The odor of death was a smell she would never forget. She was glad the gully was downhill. It was difficult to keep the bodies from rolling off the blanket while pulling them over and around bushes and rocks. At last she rolled the body of her mother into the ravine and watched as it fell upon her father's body. Lizzy felt weak and thirsty. She took comfort in knowing that their souls were in the presence of God. She said a sad farewell and used the horse blanket to cover them. Lizzy took a break and walked to the cistern for a drink. She thought, *how blessed we are to have parents like them* and then corrected her internal dialogue to use the past tense.

Lizzy was exhausted and rested in the shade for a few minutes before resuming her task. Within thirty minutes she had the bodies hidden from sight and protected from the flying insects, but the lingering smell of death was strong enough to keep the swarms hovering. She knew that it would take several more feet of dirt to block the odor and provide protection from the larger animals. She was determined to finish the job before nightfall.

After the easy fill had been caved off, she started scooping up dirt from the level ground and pitching it into the grave. Lizzy began adding larger rocks to the fill. She decided to ask the boys to help finish adding rocks to the top of the grave. Lizzy stopped, dusted off her hands and went to check on the boys.

Lizzy was coated with the reddish sand. She was itching, and she could smell herself. After another short breather, she walked back to the sleeping platform. She was thinking about the miracle of finding the shovel. Her blistered hands were starting to really hurt. She rinsed them with water, but the warm water didn't help. She wished for some soap. She asked herself what her mother would recommend, and the gel of the aloe Vera plant came to mind. Lizzy went and broke off a leaf and squeezed the cooling gel onto her hands.

Lizzy heard a noise behind her. Her first thought was, "The Injuns' is back." She raised the shovel and jumped aside, striking in the direction of the sound. Luckily, Ralph was able to dodge just in time to avoid the swing of the shovel. A distraught Lizzy dropped the shovel and fell to her knees. Ralph's resolve to be strong quickly dissolved. The two of them embraced and crumpled to the ground. The dam broke, and they were consumed with great heaving sobs. After a few minutes, Ralph stood, and wiped his face on his sleeve and said, "You need to rest, let me finish covering the grave."

What did he say? He knew about the grave. Lizzy asked, "Ralph, did you see them?"

Ralph looked at his feet and shook his head, admitting that he had walked up just as she rolled their mother into the ditch. "Liz, you done good, but you should've let me help. It was too much for you. I know you were wanting to spare me."

Amazingly, both Ralph and Lizzy benefited from the emotional outburst. Lizzy looked at Ralph and said, "We can survive this together with the Lord's help." Ralph looked at Lizzy's hands and insisted that she rest while he added stones to the top of the grave. Ralph gave it all he had and was dripping with sweat when Lizzy stood, and said, "That's good enough. We need to let Peter and James help some, too. It will help them accept that Momma and Poppa are really gone, don't you think?"

Ralph nodded, and they started walking toward where their brothers slept. Then, Ralph stopped and looked at Lizzy, "Ya know, I sure wish we could-a seen 'em one last time, while they were alive—."

Lizzy, said, "Ralph, I know, I feel the same, but it's good we weren't here. We would be dead too or maybe captured like Cynthia Ann Parker. They say she and her little brother have never been found." Ralph averted his gaze and dropped the subject.

Ralph and Lizzy were in a wretched state, gritty with dirt. The original color of their clothing was impossible to determine. "Ralph, you think we could wash this dirt off without wasting too much water?"

Ralph looked at his hands, and said, "For now we should just wash our hands and face. We can leave cleaning up for later." The morning was unusually hot and humid. They walked directly to the cistern. First, they drank their fill, and Lizzy poured water over Ralph's face and hands. Suddenly they heard Peter screaming, and they ran to him.

Peter and James had awakened, expecting to be in their own beds. When they realized it was only the two of them, they panicked and began screaming. It took Ralph and Lizzy several minutes to calm them. Confronted with such a monumental calamity, the immaturity of the Smithson children complicated their acceptance. Lizzy gathered Peter up and he wrapped his legs around her waist. She held him close and murmured, "Here now, we're gonna be okay, we have each other." Ralph put his arm around James and gently patted him on the back. The youngsters were a heart-rending sight that morning. It is easy to imagine the heavenly hosts shedding tears as they peered down from their heavenly abode.

Lizzy felt a great weight of responsibility. Just keeping her brothers sheltered, fed, and protected from insect bites, and sunburn was a tall order. It occurred to her that there were threats and dangers she hadn't yet anticipated. She knew how filth can breed sores and blood infections. She must find a way to bathe away the grime. Lizzy became preoccupied with setting priorities and searching her memory for solutions. She remembered the small spring fed pool about a quarter mile away, a place where they could bathe. If only they had some soap.

Lizzy recalled helping her mother make soap from yucca root. A friend of Ida's, a kind-hearted Apache woman, had demonstrated making the soap when Ida ran out of hog lard, the main ingredient of lye soap. The Apache woman was married to a white man and spoke broken English. The procedure for processing the yucca root was simple but a lot of hard work. Lizzy figured with the boys' help they would end up with something close to soap.

As she and the boys canvased the area for useful items, she spied an old rope swing hanging from a live oak tree. It was a good two hundred yards from the house. She asked Ralph to climb the tree and untie the rope. Lizzy said, "We can use that rope to make a hammock."

James piped up and said, "Let me get the rope 'cause I'm the best tree climber."

Ralph grinned and said, "Oh sure, I can beat you climbing any ole tree if I want to. Go ahead, just don't break your neck."

Lizzy needed fabric to use for the hammock. They still had the blanket they had used to catch the falling plums. As they searched the area, she stressed the need to watch out for snakes. She encouraged the two older boys to forage for anything useful. This is when little Peter whispered in James' ear. James gave a wide-eyed smile and nodded his head. Peter took Lizzy's hand and led her to a secret fort located on the hill just north of the burned-out cabin.

The pretend fort was under a dead stump. A small cave had been hollowed out underneath an old juniper tree. The bared roots formed a structure that resembled the legs of a giant spider. The main structure was disguised as a brush pile. Peter fell on his stomach and squirmed into the opening. Just as fast he reversed direction and crawled back out of the hole yelling, "Tran-tuler, a big black, watch out!" They all jumped back, and Peter made a flying leap for Lizzy's arms. Within a few seconds a large, hairy, tarantula followed Peter out of the hiding place. Ralph gritted his teeth, summoned his manly bravado, and squished the bug with a large slab of sandstone. "Ain't bit, are you?" Ralph asked. Peter was silent; he was too scared to be answering questions. Ralph got on his knees and checked the hole before allowing James to enter. James, determined to be brave like Ralph, crawled into the hole. He quickly squirmed his way out holding onto a tattered blanket, a hunting knife with a missing tip, and a dented dishpan. "Hey, good job, all stuff we need bad!" Lizzy gave them both a big hug.

She said, "Ralph, bring down the bag of plums and the pecans. We need to eat something." James frowned and said, "I ain't hongery for no plums." Pete said, "Me eatter." Ralph climbed up the tree and handed down the bag of fruit. Lizzy placed the open bag on a large flat stone, and the four of them sat in a circle to eat. Ralph went to draw some water from the cistern. Peter said, "Be sure to look for worm holes! Lizzy, I'm gittin' tired of plumbs and pecans."

Lizzy replied, "Me too, don't we wish we had Momma here to make breakfast for us. But since she can't, we have to be brave and eat what we have and be thankful. Are we going to make Momma and Poppa proud of us and do our very best?" The boys shook their heads in the affirmative. Lizzy was prepared to do a lot of cheerleading if it helped. "Peter, I agree, we have to find more food." "Ralph, why don't you take the shovel and bring some coals from the cabin, and we will get a nice fire going. Boys we must keep this fire going no matter what."

Ralph spoke up and said, "I saw one of our hens down by the pecan tree. Maybe we can catch it, ya think?" Lizzy and the two younger boys helped Ralph chase the squawking hen in circles for a few minutes before concluding that the hen was more scared than they were hungry.

James commented, "That is the scartest chicken I ever seen."

Then Lizzy said, "I know, let's wait till it gits dark and spy out where it goes to roost. That's how to catch it."

Lizzy told the children to sit in the shade of a large mesquite tree. "We have to talk. This morning while you were sleepin', me and Ralph buried Momma and Poppa. The grave is down by that wash. It is important that we give Momma and Papa a Christian funeral with a cross for a marker." The children nodded their little heads.

Pete thought for a minute and then asked, "What is a funderal?"

Ralph smiled, and said, "It's called a funeral, and that is when, ah, ah, what you do when people like Momma and Papa have to go to heaven. We all get to help."

Pete said, "Help do what?"

"Don't worry, we will show you."

Lizzy said, "James, will you climb the tall oak, and watch for Indians and if you see them sneaking up, don't yell, but blow this chicken bone whistle, it sorta sounds like a quail, had it in my pocket. We gotta be ready to run and hide, all the time. The rest of us will look for food. Then we will have the funeral. The grave needs lots more rocks, and don't forget about making a stick cross."

Ralph placed the shovel over one shoulder. He was unwittingly imitating the way his poppa, Jonas would have carried the implement. The weeds were knee high, and he was forced to push them aside to look for any kind of garden produce. After searching a half hour, his eyes fell on two wilted turnup tops. Just seeing the plants triggered Ralph's salivary glands, and his stomach started growling. Ralph suddenly felt guilty for fixating on his own hunger pains. He and Liz had children to feed. Ralph was thinking about how Lizzy would prepare the turnips. He hoped it would be fast. Urgency took over when Lizzy started slicing them for frying. They smelled like food. Something akin to a feeding frenzy possessed all four. Lizzy figured raw turnips would be okay this time and divvied up the banquet. Though the house was mostly burned out, a crude implement shed was left standing. The shed was about eight feet square, had no door, and had a dirt floor. The entrance faced east. Lizzy and Ralph agreed that they should start sleeping inside the shed.

Lizzy looked at the sky and said, "Looks like rain. Maybe we can get a bath in the rain." Lizzy set about hanging an improvised hammock in the shed. Rafters and protruding nails provided plenty of places to attach the hammock. Then she stored what food they had in the dish pan and placed it back into the cloth bag. The pan was stowed on a wide rafter of the shed until the next meal.

The burned cabin had gutters to channel rain into the underground cistern that required replenishing. Some of the gutters were intact. Lizzy stared at the cistern and then at the outbuilding. "Ralph, come help me. We need to move the gutter that fell off the house and see if we can attach it to the shed. That way we can still catch rainwater. Lizzy found a few nails scattered on the dirt floor of the shed. Then she boosted Ralph up to the roof and handed him the section of gutter. After an hour, using a rock for a hammer, Ralph was able to redirect much of the water that would fall on the shed's roof into the cistern. Lizzy looked at Ralph and brushed the dirt from her hands in a self-satisfied manner, and he grinned. Then Lizzy asked for help bringing some fire kindling into the shed to keep it dry.

The storm came on quickly. By mid-afternoon cloud-to-ground lightening charged the air and made the hair on Lizzy's arms stand up. Loud claps of thunder shook the ground and caused the children to huddle together in the little shed. The rain came down with a vengeance, spattering the inside of the shed. Lizzy stood in the door and peered out into the storm. She stripped to her camisole and pantaloons, and after hanging her dress on a nail at the back of the shed, she walked into the rain and started rubbing her face and wringing her long blond hair. Next, the three boys followed. Ralph and James stripped down to their underwear, but Peter hadn't learned modesty yet and joined the others in his birthday suit.

Just as the dirt was mostly washed off, a loud clap of thunder struck close by and the bathers almost collided getting back into the shed. The downpour was showing no signs of letting up. Suddenly Lizzy glanced in the direction of the grave, and moaned, *Oh no! The runoff from the storm will surely flow into the gully."* A nervous Lizzy told the children that she had to do something. "Stay inside the shed while I'm gone." She grabbed the shovel, and ran into the storm, clad only in her underwear. Before she ran fifty feet, it began to hail. At first the hail was pea size but got bigger. The fearsome lightening exploded over and over. The clouds were churning. Lizzy ran back into the shed, bruised and frightened. The hail grew larger, and its sound was deafening. Lizzy wasn't sure if the roof of the shed would hold up. The ground turned white with hail. The frightened children stood plastered to the back wall of the shed, as far as possible from the bouncing hailstones.

The combination of evaporation and fright chilled the children. Their mother had always managed to sooth them when it was storming. They stood, shivering, and big eyed. With each clap of thunder, they would jump and crowd closer together. Ralph removed his shirt from the nail and wrapped it around Peter. Lizzy said, "Just think how good a fire will feel." Lizzy and Ralph both started to speak at the same time, and said in unison, "The fire!" Then Ralph said, "The rain will put it out!"

Ralph asked Lizzy, "What wus ya 'bout to do?" She leaned to his ear and whispered, "I was thinkin' that the flood might uncover Momma and Poppa." Ralph's eyes got big, and with a knowing look, nodded. Then he said, "Let me take care of it, soon as the hail stops. I will build up the dirt so the water will go around the gully."

Finally, the storm moved to the east, and the sun peaked through the clouds to cast an orange glow across the landscape. Peter pointed at the sky, "Lookie, a rainbow, yea, I saw it first! Lizzy, does that mean that I will git to keep the gold, if I find it?" Lizzy absent mindedly asked, "What gold? Oh, you mean at the end of the rainbow. Yes, you get to keep the gold." Peter turned his head sideways as he stared at the rainbow and said, "I always loved that rainbow story Momma toll us."

Bare chested Ralph ran from the shed with the shovel. He slipped in the mud and fell on his qiester. He realized that Lizzy had been watching, and the embarrassment he felt was written across his face. She asked, "Ain't hurt, are you?"

"Naw, just muddy."

That night Lizzy climbed the tree where the chicken had gone to roost and grabbed its feet before it could take flight. She tied the chicken's feet together and placed it under the old trash barrel. She piled some heavy stones on top of the overturned barrel, to keep any critters from making off with the prize. "I can already taste that chicken." Just the thought got their stomach to growling. Lizzy looked at the three boys and said, "First thang in the mornin' I'll be ringing that chicken's neck. Some meat is what we need."

Morning fog prolonged the misery of the long, cold night. Lizzy walked barefoot to save her shoes from the mud to the fire pit. She ran her hand deep into the now cold ashes. Now what do we do? She sat on the side of the cistern and let her emotions take over, but only briefly.

Ralph walked up. "No fire, huh?"

Lizzy said in a whisper, "It's my fault. I saw them rain clouds, even brought in some wood to keep it dry."

Ralph said, "Stay here, I'll gonna look for something we can eat that don't need no cookin'. Liz, we're gonna make it one way or another. We don't dare give up."

Lizzy decided to check on the chicken under the barrel on the way back to the shed. The chicken was still alive, and she wondered if she should try to give it some water when she heard Ralph yelling. "Liz, Liz, guess what!" Lizzy ran to meet Ralph.

He wrapped his arms around her and said, "I found the tree that got struck by lightning. It's still got some hot coals. We can have a fire, Lizzy." Ralph and Lizzy held hands and danced around in a circle yelling and laughing. Ralph used the old holey bucket to haul coals from the burning tree and had a cooking fire going within the hour.

Lizzy called the boys, "Come and watch so you will know how to ring a chicken's neck. I'm gonna do it just like Momma always done. Lizzy grasped the head of the fowl and using all her strength slung the chicken in a circle motion. Nothing happened so she tried again without success. Ralph walked over and took the chicken from her. He employed considerably more centrifugal force in his wind up, and the flopping body went flying to the ground. Peter and James both looked away. It was a sobering moment for the youngsters.

Lizzy continued her tutorial. "We can either skin the chicken or pluck it. Plucking is more work, but it preserves the fatty skin, and we dare not waste any of this chicken. I say pluck! Ya wanna help?"

The boys clapped, and Peter said "Yes, I helped Momma one time; I like pluckin' feathers."

Lizzy set the dish pan of water over the fire to heat. She cut open the belly and removed the innards. She saved the liver and heart to cook in the stew pot. She appointed James to bury the rest of the offal away from camp.

Lizzy said, "Dunking the chicken in boiling water makes the feathers come out easier." When the chicken was all plucked and washed, she cut eight strips of meat to roast on sticks. The rest of the chicken she cut into sections leaving the bones and placed them into the dish pan of clean boiling water. Soon the strips of meat were making sizzling sounds and dripping fat onto the flames, sending up a scrumptious aroma. Lizzy waited long enough for the meat to be well cooked and then said, "Here, Peter don't burn your mouth, blow on it, we get two strips each to eat right now while the rest of the chicken stews."

During the time Lizzy was preparing the chicken, Ralph found two small potatoes and an onion in the garden patch. Once the stew was cooking Lizzy took James and made a quick trip to the spring to gather some of the edible greenery like dandelion and watercress. Mamma always said the herbs would add flavor and nutrition to soups. Lizzy had collected greens with her before. Lizzy washed and chopped the vegetables for the soup and added them to the pot at the very last. When the chicken soup was judged done enough, the four half-starved youngsters sat upon flat rocks facing the fire. Lizzy dipped the stew and poured it into gourd bowls. The gourds were the closest thing to dishes they had. They were discovered hanging from a tree to cure. The four children were a sight blowing on the steaming gourds. Lizzy cooled Peter's soup before handing it to him.

The four Smithson children were ravenous. Peter led them in a very short prayer, "Dear God, sorry about killing the chicken, but you know how hongery we are. Thank you for sending us this good food. A man!"

It was a touching scene as all four children cooled the soup. The noise from blowing the food was nothing compared to the sounds of slurping and smacking. The sounds of eating included vocalizations like mummmm and ahhh. Toward the end of the meal, there was the sound of bone crunching. The bone marrow was especially satisfying. And of course, there was the finger licking, no doubt the loudest finger licking anybody ever heard.

The one and only cooking pot was the old dishpan from the fort. Lizzy kept reminding herself of her mother's wise saying, "Where there is a will there is a way." Lizzy and Ralph were proving to be quite resourceful at making do. There was enough of the soup for second helpings and not a drop went to waste. For a change the children went to bed with a full stomach. The thought, *Thank you Lord* kept repeating in Lizzy's mind! After the boys were in bed, Lizzy picked up the un-cracked bones to save for soup making later, just in case they could not catch another chicken.

The hammock was mostly a great idea. Peter and James could both sleep side by side. When Lizzy first lifted Peter and James up in the hammock, the rope stretched allowing the hammock to still touch the floor. Lizzy fixed the problem by shortening the rope. She gave them a hug and bid them "Goodnight and don't let the bed bugs bite." Ralph made his bed by placing three boards over some flat rocks to lift the platform off the dirt floor. Lizzy decided to guard the shed by placing her body in the doorway. She quickly sharpened a spear to hold for a weapon. She hardly slept at all.

That night, coyotes were attracted to the smell of the roasted chicken. When they came too close for comfort, Lizzy threw rocks at them. She awoke feeling stiff and exhausted. The pik pedik pik pikkk of scissor-tailed flycatchers had interrupted her intermittent catnaps.

Today, she planned to finish the grave. It was important to add more rock to the grave. They would hold a funeral service as soon as they had a cross ready. After a sparse breakfast of plums and pecans, they all four worked at stacking rocks on the grave. Ralph built up the diversion dam and lined it with flat stones in anticipation of more rain. Lizzy told Ralph, "I want to build some kind of door for that shed, strong enough to keep animals out. The coyotes come up purty close last night. It was scary. Something else to do today, we gotta fix us a bed. Next chore after that, we got to make some yucca soap for bathing. We need to gather some of them vines down by the bog for rope to tie the sticks together. We need enough vine to tie a cross for the grave and to make the shed door."

Ralph responded with, "Hey, good idea. Com'on James, let's go cut the vines. Bring the knife." As the two boys walked away, Ralph looked back and said, "Yeh, I know, watch out for rattlers and poison ivy. We promise." Lizzy smiled and began building the sleeping platform by finding the best sandstone slabs to stack under the boards. The platform was wide enough for both Ralph and Lizzy to stretch out flat. She finished by padding the surface with juniper branches.

Sure enough, the bed was a big improvement. Lizzy took a few steps back, placed her hands on her hips and thought, *a job well done.* Then Lizzy started gathering sticks to be bound together for the gate. It needed to be light weight but still strong. Then she noticed the fire and said, "Ops, Peter, hey Peter, put some wood on the fire. Remember, okay, good boy."

While the children sat down to eat some pecans, Lizzy said, "How about we make a cross for Momma and Papa's grave?

Ralph spoke up, "Here is a strand of vine."

James cleared his throat and said, "I can help with the cross."

Ralph said, "I'll be right back," He took the knife with him. In a few minutes he returned with two sticks the right size for the cross. By that time Lizzy had a pile of finger size sticks about five feet long to make a gate. "Peter, remember the fire, it's your job."

Planning the funeral had Lizzy in an emotional state, and with tears welling up in her eyes, she called the boys together and said, "I think we should wait until tomorrow to have the funeral, Ida and Jonas Smithson will get the proper Christian burial service they deserve. We can feel good about doing our duty for them. I'm thinking we will feel better afterwards but, in any case, it is the fitting thing to do." Lizzy complemented the boys on their crude cross. She hoped that the funeral would help them to cope with their stark reality, but she knew full well that eventually the four of them would suffer a delayed reaction. She was certain that trauma of this magnitude never stays buried in the subconscious forever.

Lizzy couldn't elude her thoughts on what the future held for them. Would they be able to survive? If they did, would they ever be normal and lead happy lives? The east-west dirt road that led to Gainesville was a quarter of a mile away. The turnoff to the Smithson homestead had a primitive entry way built of Century Plant poles. The property was open range and, therefore, unfenced. Lizzy woke during the night with an idea, and as soon as the boys were awake, she asked them to help make a sign to hang at the entry gate that said, "Need Help." First off, the following morning they finished the sign and posted it after praying that it would bring help. The isolated road hardly had any traffic, but just in case it would be worth the effort.

The following morning the four children walked to the grave and began piling on more rock. Ralph reinforced the diversion dam's mound with large slabs of sandstone. Lizzy noticed that something had been digging at the surface of the grave, and when the two younger boys were preoccupied, she used her foot to kick dirt into the hole. While Lizzy, James, and Peter worked to fortify the grave, Ralph was not yet satisfied with the diversion dam and continued adding stone. After an hour, they decided to go ahead with the funeral.

The children walked to the slough, undressed down to their undies and jumped into the pool. The spring water helped, but they needed soap to really get clean. After air-drying, they shook the dirt from their clothes and dressed. Back at the grave Lizzy looked at the expressions on the boys faces. Serious and sad aptly described her brothers, full of pain and grief. Lizzy wanted them to experience their grief, or it would cause problems in later life. Lizzy recalled hearing her parents discuss how damaging it can be. The loss the four children were feeling may have been healthy and necessary, but that didn't make it any easier. Lizzy opened the service with, "Amazing Grace, how sweet the sound. That saved a —wretch —like me. I was lost, but now I'm found—." Lizzy stopped singing and said, "I forgot the rest."

James said, "I 'member some of it. There's no less days to sing God's praise than when we first begun."

"Ralph, start the prayer."

Ralph asked, "What should I say?"

Peter spoke up and said, "I know, let me go first." Peter placed his hands together and bowed his head as he started, "Dear Hebenly Father, I need to speak to Momma and Poppa. We been missing you a lot. We might not can see you, but I'm purty sure you can see us. I been skeired without you here. We would be thankful if God would let you come back to life like happens in the Bible some of the time. We had a bad storm, hail was everwher' and lightnen' 'bout got us. I was the first one to see the rainbow, and I helped find a blanket and pan. I wish you could cook us some pancakes 'cause we ain't got much food except pecans and plums. I hope you both like it up in heaven. Tell Jesus we said hello. A-Man." Lizzy and Ralph grimaced to keep from smiling.

James placed his hands together below his chin, and started with, "God, I just want to thank you for what food we have got. Right now, we could use some more. Momma and Poppa, I hope you are not too sad; we are doing purty good, what with us bein' by ourselves. I wish you could come back, like in the Bible; I been prayin' for that. Well, I guess you already know that. If you cain't come back, please ask God to keep the Injuns away and help us figure out what to do. Amen."

Ralph started with, "Oh God, please help us out of this mess we're in. I also been thinkin' 'bout ask'n for a miracle like in Bible days. Thank you for givin' us such good parents. Please take good care of them and save room for us when we come up there. Amen." Lizzy's eyes filled with tears, and she moved close enough to the boys to wrap her arms about them.

She wiped her tears away with the back of her hand and bowed her head. "God, please help us know what to do. Please send someone to help us. Help me to be brave and keep away the coyotes and lions. And Lord, the Injuns, keep them away. Momma, and Poppa, we will always remember you and how you taught us right. God, please help us find enough food. Thank you, Jesus, for the blessings you gave us already. In Christ's name, amen." Lizzy and the boys didn't know the term 'closure,' but having the funeral behind them allowed them to experience finality and helped them concentrate their thoughts and efforts on survival.

Once when Lizzy had a quiet moment and was sitting by the cistern drinking from the bucket, she wondered what if—, they had all been taken prisoner by the Comanche. She knew things could be worse. Lizzy remembered hearing about a little girl named Cynthia Parker. The Nokoni had attacked the Parker family outpost and carried Cynthia and her little brother away.

Hard work, prayer, and overcoming the daily challenges one at a time got the kids the barest form of survival. Lizzy hardly ever rested. Her creativity grew keener and resulted in useful items made of clay and willow branches. She wove a drying rack for wild fruit and a clay smeared willow basket. The basket was waterproof after being cured in warm ashes. Conditions confronting the Smithson children would have doomed coddled and sheltered youngsters, but not these intelligent and strong children of the Texas prairie.

Since the garden vegetables were mostly gone, Lizzy decided to go after wild food. They gathered acorns, pecans, wild post oak grapes, and the fish in the slough. Lizzy remembered a time or two when her father harvested a few perch and catfish by seining with a net. The net had burned with the cabin, but maybe the hammock blanket or better yet the blanket from James and Pete's fort would catch some fish, despite some holes burned by flying coals. She punched a series of holes in each end of the blanket to thread long vertical sticks for handles. Then she and Ralph stripped to their underwear and walked into the chest deep water. They started at one end and moved the blanket slowly through the water. The pond bottom had a deep layer of mud. Suddenly, Lizzy stepped on something sharp that moved. She yelled, "Ouch!" She put her hand down to where she felt the pain. She lay back in the water and brought her foot to the surface, so Ralph could get a close look. Blood was oozing from a small puncture wound.

Ralph asked, "Does it hurt when I push on it?"

Lizzy answered, "No, not more. It's feeling better now, I'm okay, lets finish seining so we can get out of this water."

Ralph said, "I think you stepped on a mud cat. They got sharp fins with poison in the tips according to Poppa. It will only hurt a little while. I got one in my hand one time when me and Poppa was fishin'."

Ralph and Lizzy continued to drag the blanket through the water. After half an hour, Ralph said, "Let's see if we caught anything." When they raised the blanket to the surface, they had two hand size bluegills, and a larger catfish stuck in a hole of the blanket. When Ralph touched the catfish, it flopped loose and back into the water. Ralph and Lizzy just looked at each other and both said, "Opps," then Lizzy said, "We need to have a bag around our neck to put fish in."

James said, "I'll be right back." In a few minutes, a winded James came back with one of the bags that had held plumbs. Lizzy hung the drawstring over her head and started the seining all over again. This time they only caught perch, six medium-sized ones. Lizzy gathered the blanket by the sides while Ralph placed the flopping blue gills into the bag.

James and Peter were standing on the bank and watching with great interest. Peter asked to hold a fish, and Ralph pitched the smallest one toward his feet. The two younger boys stood bent over watching the flopping fish. It took a while before James found the courage to pick it up. He dropped it and then took hold of it a second time. James held it out for Peter to touch, and he stroked its back with one finger and then held his finger to his nose. "Yuk, it stinks and is slickery!" squealed Peter.

A mischievous James gave in to an ornery impulse and put the fish into Peter's trousers. It quickly became apparent that the wiggling fish terrified Peter. The undulating fish sent the child into a crazed fit as he screamed, "Lizzy, Lizzy!" His trousers were visibly moving, and Pete was running in a circle.

Ralph said, "Stay put Liz, I'll get him." He scrambled up the muddy bank and slipped back into the water twice before clearing the pond. James suddenly realized his prank was a terrible idea, and he had a guilty "cat ate the canary" expression on his face. Ralph managed to grab Peter's shirt and hold him suspended off the ground. The scared youngster was still moving his legs as though they were in contact with the ground. Ralph said, "Here Pete, hold on, I'll get rid of the fish." Ralph turned Peter upside down and shook the fish from his drawers. Pete was already tired of having so much bad luck, and the fish prank pushed him over the edge of despair. Ralph wrapped the youngster in his arms and said, "There Pete, tha fish is out, you're fine, look, that poor little fish must be scared of dark, stinky places." Ralph grinned at Peter and roughed his hair.

Peter wiped away his tears and looked up at Ralph and then Lizzy and lastly at James. "You're right Ralph, he was so scart he scart me. James, please never put things in my pants anymore."

James hugged Peter and said, "I'm sorry, I promise to never do it again. But you was purty funny jumping around like that." With that comment all four had a hearty laugh and put the incident behind them. Ralph suggested that they throw the little fish back in the water just to let him grow up more before someone ate him.

"Lizzy come on up here and take a break." After a short rest Lizzy and Ralph fished for another hour, catching another 12 perch, two mud cats, and a baby water moccasin. Ralph and Lizzy removed the spreader sticks and gathered the blanket at the top while they climbed up the bank with their catch.

First off Ralph crushed the snake's head with a large stone. "Liz, you think we can cook that snake? I heard of eatin' snake b'fore, ain't you?"

"I heard that some people eat rattlesnake, but I don't know about water moccasin. We can cook it if you want, and only take a little bit at first." Lizzy took the knife and gutted and scaled the fish. She left the preparation of the snake to Ralph. A small amount of edible meat could be picked off the fish heads, so Lizzy left the heads attached. Ralph had the perfect bed of coals ready for cooking by the time Lizzy finished preparing the fish.

James suddenly did a double take of Lizzy and said, "Liz, you are glowing, all sparkly like." Upon closer examination the amazed children realized that the glow was a coating of fish scales reflecting light the way sequins do. The scales had stuck to everything they fell upon due to the slime they were coated with. Lizzy said, "Ewu" and franticly brushed at them. She missed some in her hair and on her face, so Pete sat on her lap and picked them off one by one.

As soon as the fish began to sizzle upon a piece of tin salvaged from the cabin, the starving children began begging to start eating. Lizzy distracted them with a funny story about the time she swallowed a fish bone. The sound of her mother's voice played in her memory, "Fish needs to be cooked through and through in case it has some kind of parasite."

After devouring their catch an irresistible drowsiness came over the little family. James and Peter went to their hammock in the shed without an argument. Ralph built up the fire and offered to help with any cleanup. Lizzy told him there was nothing else to be done and that she would be along soon. Lizzy said, "I ate some of the snake, I kind of liked it, did you try it?"

"Yep, I finished it off, tasted good. Sure wish we had some salt." Lizzy was feeling more confident that they would be able to find enough food to stay alive at least for the near future. Before following the boys to bed a drowsy Lizzy took some time to relax by the fire and think about their situation. It felt so good to not be hungry. Mid-prayer, exhaustion took over, and Lizzy spent a couple of hours slumped upon a slab of rock only a few feet from the fire. The barking of coyote, and hoo-hoo of owls had become so commonplace to her subconscious mind her slumber was undisturbed by the normal night sounds.

After a few days of collecting acorns, they were ready to process them into flour. Because of the large amount of water needed Lizzy asked the boys to help her move the necessary items to the spring. Ralph and James had been craving acorn bread and gladly pitched in. Lizzy arranged a flat stone work bench in a shady spot next to the spring. With the dishpan of acorns boiling, Lizzy and the boys gathered their lunch. First, they scorched the spines from fresh new prickly pear pads and while they roasted, Lizzy crushed several ripe prickly pear apples. The third ingredient was smashed pecan-butter. The result was a sandwich of sorts. The children's natural sense of innovation had led to the palatable and nutritional recipe. She made enough for them to each have seconds and even thirds. Certainly, the sandwiches were an acquired taste, but hunger can be accommodating.

After lunch they drained the first water bath from the acorns and replaced it with fresh spring water to boil a second time. It was late afternoon when the acorns were ready to separate from their shells, and that could be done back at camp by the fire. The evening was spent shelling the acorn kernels and spreading them to dry. Once dry they were pounded and ground into powder between flat rocks.

The acorn powder came to almost three pounds. Lizzy estimated the volume that would measure three cups and saved the rest for later. She mixed up a stiff dough using pecan butter and a small amount water as the binding agent, pinched off small portions and patted them out by transferring them from hand to hand, tortilla style. The cakes were baked on an improvised griddle made from an iron lid from something burned in the cabin. Lizzy used a small amount of the powder to thicken some juice from wild grapes and prickly pear apples for pancake syrup. All four of the children stuffed their bellies full and went to bed happy.

Another rain storm came along, but Ralph had taken all possible precautions to keep the wood dry and to shelter the fire pit. The inverted watering trough from the pig pen was the perfect size to shelter the fire pit. He and James dug a channel around the fire to drain the water away.

The children had developed a routine, a very physically demanding normal. With each passing day gathering fire wood required longer treks from camp. The constant search for food was exhausting. Lizzy spent every waking hour splitting her time between the crucial tasks of survival. Ralph and James decided to upgrade their defense by whittling spears. The spear process prompted Ralph to attempt carving a bow and some arrows. The bow needed a lot of work before it became an effective weapon. Peter played nearby in a flat sandy spot where he out lined a make-believe fort with pebbles.

Lizzy was itching, and so were the boys. Perspiration caked with dust, lack of clean underwear, and daily contact with plants that had stickers and thorns that tore at their skin placed the children in danger. Since the second day Ralph and James had been digging up yucca root. Lizzy racked her mind to remember how the Apache lady made the soap. Lizzy asked the boys, "Yawl remember that Apache lady that showed Momma how to make yucca soap?"

Ralph said, "Not much but I will help all I can." The boys brought the pile of yucca roots to Lizzy and asked, "Liz, okay, what's next?"

Lizzy started by saying, "First we soak the roots in water for a few minutes and peel away the rough skin of the roots and rinse them off. Then we chop them into thin slices. After that we pound the slices into a pulp on a flat rock and let it dry. Best I remember, we scoop up the dried pulp and grind it between two flat rocks into a powder, should work. I know, sounds like a lot of work. If we all work together, we'll be finished faster than we think." Pete spoke up and said, "Hey, I want to help because I want to eat some of it."

Lizzy laughed and said, "We will eat the acorn flour and take a bath with the yucca root powder." Lizzy said, "You boys are awful smart for little boys, I mean big boys."

The yucca powder was less than pure with some chips of rock and a few dead bugs. Lizzy decided it would still get them clean. She asked, "Everbody ready to get a good bath? The children had stopped wearing their socks because they were full of holes. "Give me one of your socks and that will be your scrub cloth. Hold it open while I dump in a little yucca powder. We tie a knot where there ain't no holes. Remember, a little goes a long way. Be sparing with it. Because making yucca soap was so much work Lizzy decided to keep half of the yucca powder for washing the clothes and some just for washing faces and hands.

All four children were excited about the prospect of taking a real bath. Lizzy had the boys fall in line behind her and marched all the way to the little slough singing;

Three blind mice. Three blind mice.
See how they run. See how they run.
They all ran after the farmer's wife,
Who cut off their tails with a carving knife,
Did you ever see such a sight in your life,
As three blind mice. [2]

No doubt, the slough water turned brown from all the dirt they washed off. Lizzy demonstrated how to get the sock wet and massage it until a foamy lather covered the sock. Lizzy said, "This is the way to wash your hair." She rubbed the foamy sock all over her head, rinsed and repeated a couple of times. I figure we need to soap our head at least three times to get it really clean. Ralph followed her instruction and yelled, "Liz, it's sure enough working, just look at the bubbles, and it is taking off the dirt slick as a whistle." The boys scrubbed each other's backs.

They were splashing and yelling to stop the tickling, and jumping around in the water like little frogs. By this point they were forgetting to watch for Indians and were making too much noise, but they were children, and the Lord was on watch at this point. They didn't recall baths being this much fun. James speculated that maybe it was the yucca that got them giddy. Their joy of the moment brought a smile to Lizzy's face. She took her personal modesty seriously and constructed herself a skirt of grass and a garland of wide leaves to hang around her neck. Her effort to hide her nakedness worked well enough. She told the boys to keep looking the other way while she put on her "fig leaf" clothing.

In the meantime, the boys were left to their own devices to cover their nakedness. Ralph and James put their heads together and came up with the idea to tie a vine around their waist and then hang grass and small branches from the line. That would have worked well on a less windy day. Finally, Ralph attached a second vine from the front to the rear between his legs and wove grass underneath both vines. The result was better coverage, but the vine that went between his legs was scratchy. It made him walk bow legged. Then Ralph helped James first, to make his own grass loin cloth, much like his own. Peter got an abbreviated version of the loin cloth. The process was taking too long for Pete, and he was happy to go with just the vine around his waist with some grass hanging in the front. He figured modesty was for bigger kids.

While Lizzy prepared to do laundry, she was thinking about how awful her mouth and teeth felt. She rinsed her sock in the spring water and scrubbed her teeth with it and rinsed out her mouth. Then she thought of using a tiny stick to clean around her gum line and found just the right size yucca needle tip. Some of the juice from the yucca spear leaked into her mouth, and she thought it had a refreshing taste. She had just discovered another use for yucca. Lizzy shared her discovery with the boys. She cautioned them to be sure to rinse the sock first.

Having tangled hair caused Lizzy a lot of grief. She got the idea to squeeze yucca juice over her wet hair and use her fingers to comb through the snarls. What could she use for a comb that would do a better job than her fingers? Her eye fell on a catfish backbone that lay beside the spring. She picked up the backbone and washed it in the spring. She began running it through the yucca coated strands of hair, and it worked better than her fingers alone. Lizzy called Peter to come and stand in front of her. She cut off a yucca spear, removed the gel and rubbed it into Peter's wet hair. Lizzy said, "Now that we are all clean let's comb the tangles from our hair. How about using this fish's backbone like a comb? Be still, Pete." Lizzy broke open another yucca spear and removed the gel with her thumb. Lizzy finished up Pete's hair and then worked more on her own hair before beginning on the laundry.

The boys continued to have water fights and romped and yelled, seemingly without a care in the world. Lizzy considered it a sign they were feeling good and healing from their tragedy. Washing the clothes presented a challenge. The cloth was tattered and close to thread bare. She sprinkled some of the coarsely ground yucca powder onto each wet garment and rubbed it against a flattened rock working up a soapy lather. The stone that she chose for laundering the clothing lay next to the spring.

Lizzy's modesty covering was adequate, but she insisted that the boys not look at her. James said, "This makes me think of when Adam and Eve made clothes out of fig leaves, but God didn't like the leaf clothes and made better clothes out of animal skins. God said, no more running around naked since you ate the apple." Ralph spoke up and said I was thinkin' bout Adam and Eve too. Lizzy said, "me too."

Peter said, "Yea, I 'member that story, it was tha snake that got them to go against God." Lizzy carried the clothes back to the camp wet and hung them over bushes and tree limbs. It was a warm and sunny day, and the thread bear, tattered garments dried within a couple of hours. Pete wanted to hang his own clothes and dropped his shirt in the sand. He started to cry, but Ralph told him the sand would fall off as soon as the shirt was dry. Pete was okay with that and finished hanging his socks and trousers.

With the clothes drying Lizzy asked the boys to help gather firewood. It would be getting dark soon. An enthusiastic Peter tripped and fell, landing with one hand on a prickly pear. His palm was full of the painful spines and the surrounding countryside heard his pain. At first Lizzy held him close and tried to let him settle down.

"No Lizzy, I need Momma to be here, she knows how to take them stickers out. Stop, don't touch it, it hurts too much. Oh, it hurts!" It was a while before Lizzy could begin removing the spines. She used the knife blade to scrape away the spines. It was troubling when the poor child continued crying for what seemed the longest time. Lizzy sensed that Peter was not successfully adjusting to the loss of his parents.

He was just too young to deal with so much sorrow. Lizzy said a quick prayer asking for help in keeping Peter from overmuch grieving. The answer to Lizzy's prayer came about almost immediately. Looking back Lizzy thought, God sure works in mysterious ways.

That night the children feasted on the fish they seined from the slough. Their desert was a tart paste made from roasted fruit of the prickly pear plant. The fruit satisfied a craving for something sweet. The following day James found a nest of chicken eggs, and Lizzy boiled in the dishpan. They made a much-needed protein rich meal. Each day the priority was to find their next meal. Lizzy had been tracking the pig but so far failed to get close enough to capture it. She told the boys, "Pigs are smarter than they look."

The pig proved to be so elusive they were forced to focus on easier-to-get food like pecans, acorns, prickly pear fruit, plums, and grapes. James located a large previously overlooked garlic pod in the garden, and Lizzy told him to leave it until they were ready to use it. The boys surprised Lizzy with half a dozen bull frogs. Ralph's hand-made spear was like the one Jonas had demonstrated, hardening the tip in the fire. Lizzy fried the frog legs in pecan oil and according to Peter they were scrumptuss.

One evening just after sundown, Ralph climbed the tree where the remaining chickens were known to roost. With a hen in hand the limb suddenly snapped off send him hurtling to the ground. Luckily, he landed on a perfectly placed cushion a bush. The bush cushioned his impact, and he escaped with a few minor scratches. Lizzy cleaned and applied aloe gel to Ralph's injuries while complementing him on the tenacity it took to hang on to the chicken while plunging toward the ground. Ralph rung the hen's neck like an expert and handed it over to Lizzy to butcher, pluck, and cook. The nicely plump hen was consumed over a two-day period. They were getting better at finding food and cooking it too.

Autumn was upon them, and that meant winter weather was on the way. Lizzy began planning how to survive the cold. She organized her thoughts and set priorities. Lizzy brought Ralph into her private conversation. Ralph, "I reckon you know cold weather is on the way. There are some things we must do now if we are going to survive."

Ralph responded, "I been thinkin' 'bout that too. I'll help you do what you want me to. What should we do first?"

Lizzy said, "I guess clothing comes first and shoes. Next, we have to fix a fireplace inside our shed. That is going to be a big job. After that we must make warm bedding. I think I can make us all a two-sided garment stuffed with grass and leaves. I need to teach myself to weave fabric from yucca fiber using a stick loom."

Ralph thought for a minute before speaking, "I'm gonna git to work on the fireplace right now. Cutting a vent in the roof that will suck out the smoke won't be easy. You and me should be able to figure out something that will work." He started to say something, and Lizzy chimed in and they spoke the same words in unison, "Where there is a will—." They laughed and both said, "I sure miss Momma."

Then Lizzy brought up making shoes. "Does anybody have any ideas?"

James said, "Rabbit hides with the fur inside would be warm. We have lots of rabbits around."

Ralph suggested, "What we need is thicker leather like cow or pig skin, but rabbit is better than none. Or, we could get clay from the spring and mold it into a shoe and then dry it by the fire. If we did like the Egyptians and put straw in the mud, it would hold together better. Then we could stuff cattail fluff inside for warmth? Think it would work?"

Lizzy responded, "Brilliant idea, clay shoes, yes I like the idea!"

All four children began gathering yucca plant fiber, harvested and flattened cattail stems, and pods, and grass for weaving. Lizzy had taught herself to weave willow baskets and waterproof them with fire hardened clay. "Weaving fabric isn't that different."

James announced, "I been making sharp spears out of sticks to spear food like rabbits and frogs and fish. I been running a lot and I'm gittin' faster." He turned to leave, but Lizzy called him back. She had a frown on her face and hesitated to say what was on her mind. "James, before you go you need to know a mountain lion has been hanging around down by the slough. For now, I want you to stay close to camp and keep watch. Don't go down there alone and keep a spear with you. We cain't be too careful." Ralph went into the shed and began stacking rocks in a corner. Later he would cement them with clay.

The two older boys were working hard and doing a good job. They helped Lizzy gather food, yucca roots for soap, acorns for flour, and fiber for weaving into fabric. Staying so busy helped the days to pass quickly.

Lizzy was concerned about Peter. After a few weeks the child wasn't his usual funny and playful self. He was too quick to cry and wasn't eating well. At night while the four of them sat by the fire, Lizzy would cuddle her little brother in her arms and sing familiar songs to him. Time would tell if it helped him to feel more secure, it certainly didn't hurt.

When the children went to the slough, they collected every mature cattail they saw. The down would make stuffing for garments and coverings.

Lizzy and Ralph tried to work on the rock fireplace a few hours every day. The two of them managed to salvage a ten-foot span of stove pipe from the burned cabin. Lizzy said, "I figure that stove pipe will leak smoke. How you think we can seal it?"

Ralph replied, "I always try to think about what Poppa would do, and I'm guessin' clay from the spring."

Just the thought of snow and ice made Lizzy shiver. She brought up the subject of trapping rabbits. Ralph said, "I heard of trappin' rabbits with a dead fall. It's where a stick holds a big heavy rock up and it falls on the animal when it tries to take some food. I will try to build some of those traps. They discussed if they should try to walk into town. According to his tally of charcoal marks, it had been almost six weeks since the attack.

And the ever-present fear of the puma kept Lizzy on edge. The lion mostly came around after sundown. Lizzy had seen its tracks at the slough and other places too near for comfort. At every opportunity, she strengthened the gate to the shed, but she wasn't confident it would keep out a lion much less a bunch of Indians. The boys stocked the shed with the spears they had been making. She hoped the lion was finding enough food.

Ralph admitted that he too was afraid of the lion and suggested, "It would be a good idea to keep a fire burning directly in front of the shed after dark. Lizzy agreed to take turns building up the fire."

"Good idea, Ralph. Now let's go back and get some rest." The following day Ralph built a fire pit in front of the shed. James and Peter were curious about the reason, and Ralph told them it would be getting cold before long.

A few nights later their fear about the lion was realized. They were all four asleep when a terrible commotion startled them awake. It started with the pig making a pulsating, high pitched squealing noise. Crashing brush, stamping hoofs, and the most hideous hissing and growling shattered the air at close range. Lizzy assumed it was the lion attacking the surviving pig. She reached for her spear and peered through the slots of the shed's stick door. It was a moonless night, and the security fire had burned down to a few glowing coals. Lizzy tried to comfort James and Peter who were whimpering with fright. Lizzy said, "Don't be scared, it sounds like something is after the pig." The boys, plastered against the shed's back wall, all had a white-knuckle grasp on a spear. Ralph said, "If it eats the pig, it will leave us alone, besides we have these sharp spears." The pig had stopped squealing, but they could hear a scraping sound, likely from the lion pulling the pig back to its lair.

A big-eyed Ralph asked Lizzy to go out with him to build up the fire, so she could keep watch while he piled on the wood. It took every ounce of bravery those two youngsters had to leave the relative safety of the shed. The chore was completed quickly, and Lizzy took extra efforts to fortify the gate with some of the spears. Safely back in the shed they continued to stand along the back wall holding the sharpened sticks at the ready. After an hour of silence, Lizzy told the two younger boys to go back to sleep on the hammock. Soon afterwards Lizzy and Ralph lay on their bed and dozed until daylight.

The following day something happened that shook Lizzy to her core. Peter went missing!

CHEATIEBO, THE FOLKLORIST SERIES

3

VOICES CRYING
IN THE WILDERNESS

GLENDA SIMPSON

Chapter 1

...continued from the end of Book 2

THE SMITHSON CHILDREN

All three of the older children assumed he was with someone else. Lizzy quickly sent Ralph toward the road and James to the west where their fort was located. Lizzy headed south toward the slough. "Take a spear with you and watch out for snakes." The three of them were calling out to Peter, and the boys were whistling. Before a half mile had been covered, Lizzy heard Peter crying. When she reached him, he was trying to pull a fawn away from its mortally wounded mother. "Peter, what are you doing?"

"Liz, I saw the mother and baby walking and I followed. The mother is hurt, and she layed down on the ground. I toll the baby to come with me 'cause the momma cain't take care of her. I toll her she could come and live with us." Lizzy saw an arrow sticking in the doe's belly, and she panicked. Peter continued his chatter, "I saw the baby eating some grass so that means she is old enough to keep alive, ya think? How about we keep her for a pet, please, please!"

The sight of the arrow set Lizzy's heart to racing. She Immediately bent down and put her hand over Peter's mouth, "Quiet, Injuns might be back." She surveyed her surroundings but heard nothing more that the song of a meadowlark and buzzing insects. The blood on the deer's body had turned black and was dry.

Lizzy was about to tell Peter that they could not keep the fawn, but then she reconsidered. Lizzy decided the fawn would distract him from reality. It would be fun for all of them. She reasoned that the fawn would die if left to fend for itself, so there was no harm in trying to save it. Since the doe was still alive, Lizzy decided that the animal was edible and could provide them with a lot of meat. Okay, Peter you can keep your promise, here I'll carry her for you, and Lizzy hoisted the fawn under one arm. Lizzy yelled, "Ralph, James, I found Pete!" Both boys ran to meet Lizzy. Ralph took Peter and spun him around and hugged him. Lizzy sent James ahead with Peter so that she could talk to Ralph about butchering the injured doe.

"Ralph, the mother deer is almost dead. It has an Indian arrow in its belly. I didn't hear or see any sign of the Indians but seeing that arrow sure put the fear in me. We have to start being more careful. Do you think we can butcher the doe? Maybe we could slice off some roasts and cut some of it into strips for smoking?"

Ralph scratched his head and thought for a few seconds. Then he said, "We need to figure a way to sharpen the knife, but sure, let's give it a try. We sure need the food."

Ralph sent Lizzy back to camp and he walked back to where the doe lay. Ralph had been along on deer hunts and helped with dressing out the meat. Poppa had insisted that he learn how to field dress game. He was ready to give it his best effort.

Working with the dull, tip-less knife was a huge handicap. Ralph remembered watching both parents use a whet stone and looked around for a big rock that might sharpen the edge. He tried a couple of different rock types without much success. Lizzy was thinking about the dull blade too and it occurred to her that the whet stone might be in the ashes of the burned cabin and be in a useable state.

She knew such items were kept in a bottom drawer in the kitchen. Lizzy waded into the ruins of the cabin with trepidation. She used the shovel to scrape aside the thick layer of caked ashes. She found what was left of the wooden cupboard. It was blackened, but when she pulled on a drawer, some of the contents were not burned. She removed a stack of scorched cotton napkins, tablecloths, and cup towels. Underneath the charred material Lizzy found even more than she had hoped. Her eyes grew big and she yelled "Ralph" but then remembered that he had gone back to butcher the doe.

Lizzy chided herself for not looking through the ashes of the cabin sooner? At the bottom of the drawer hidden under the linen were several knives, a meat cleaver, a small meat saw, and yes, the whet stone. The layer of cotton material had insulated the tools from the extreme heat of the fire. In another drawer Lizzy found a cast iron skillet with a lid and a long-handled ladle. Some of the cloths on the bottom were useable too. What a find! She was so excited that she ran to tell Ralph the good news.

Ralph used his leather belt to hang the deer by its hind feet and hacked and sawed at the throat until the jugular was opened. He was thinking, how would Poppa do this? Getting the best of the meat cut into small portions for roasting on a spit and cut into strips for drying was going to be ——. That is when he heard Lizzy yelling and ran to meet her.

As Lizzy ran toward Ralph she was thinking, Momma always said, where there's a will there's a way. Lizzy hugged Ralph and said, "We can do this! I found the whet stone and some other stuff in the ruins of the cabin. Come see what I found." Walking back to the burned-out cabin Lizzy said to Ralph, "I'm thinkin' we need to cut up the deer away from our camp because the smell will attract animals that we don't want comin' too close." Ralph nodded his agreement. Lizzy and Ralph were able to carry the charred drawer with the scavenged items to the firelight. The sun had set and it was going to be a moonless night.

A jubilant Ralph looked through the find and yelled, "This is great Liz!" James and Peter walked over to see what the commotion was all about. James was carrying the fawn under one arm and Peter was holding on to an improvised grapevine tether. When James heard the good news he said, "I think we are going to make it, hey, when will the venison be ready to eat?"

Peter got a puzzled look and puckered up to cry. "No, no, we are not going to eat my baby, I will never let——."

Lizzy bent down and placed her hand over Pete's mouth and said, "We would never eat your fawn, but what if we eat some meat from the mother, she is hurt and going to die anyway, right? Are you okay with eating the doe? We really need more meat."

Peter sniffed and wiped his nose on his sleeve and nodded his agreement, with some hesitation. "I reckon the baby won't know what we're eating. I always liked ven-sin and I'm very hungry."

Lizzy and Ralph sat down by the fire and worked on sharpening a couple of the knives and the cleaver. With the sharp or at least sharper knives ready, they quickly made a span of rope by braiding three strands of knotted cloth from a towel. Ralph got the idea to make a torch by tying a towel smeared with mashed pecan oil to a long stick. It would light the way to where the deer was hanging. Ralph took along a clay pot of coals to start a fire. He grabbed two of the sharpened spears as an afterthought.

Ralph looked into James' eyes and spoke in a serious tone, "While me and Liz are gone keep Pete safe, keep the fire built up and crack some pecans for your supper. We'll get the meat ready to cook and hurry back fast as we can. Stay right here, real close to the fire." For a moment James looked a little scared but then snapped to attention, nodded and said, "Yes sir!" as he clicked his heels together and saluted the way he did when they played soldiers. Ralph saluted back and said, "At-ease Corporal Smithson."

Lizzy suggested, "Tear several strips of cloth from one of these towels and tie them together to make a leash and offer a drink of water to — hey, Pete what is her name?"

Pete turned his head to the side and said, "I been thinking about that, how about Moses, you know like the one in the Bible? Moses was saved by a woman, and I saved this Moses. I think Moses can be for a girl or boy."

Lizzy said, "Moses it is! Welcome to our family Moses. You sure have pretty eyes."

Lizzy built a fire while Ralph hoisted the doe still higher off the ground. The doe was well bled and ready to be dressed out and skinned. Ralph dug a deep hole to catch the entrails so that they could be quickly covered over. Penetrating the belly hide took all of the thrust Ralph could muster, even with the sharpened cleaver. Ralph asked, "Do we have any of the yucca powder left, Liz? This is going to get messy."

"No more than a handful, so we need to be digging up yucca roots ever chance we get. Second time around making yucca powder should go faster." The deer had begun to bloat and sprayed liquid when the hide was punctured. The stench was overpowering. "Whew, I'm gonna be sick" Ralph said as he turned away and retched. The fumes from the gut sack burned their eyes and induced gagging. They moved back and held their noses while the place aired out a little.

Ralph remembered a trick his Poppa used to mask bad smells. He made a paste of smashed cedar berries and rubbed it under his nose. There were lots of berries in the tree where the doe hung, and the paste really did help. Lizzy decided to do the same. Ralph said, "Stand back while I bury that pile of guts." As he worked Ralph confided, "When I went to cut her jugular, she looked right at me with a terrible fright in her eyes, and she tried to stand. I 'member Poppa saying doin' hard stuff makes men out of boys."

About the time they had finished removing the hide from the carcass, Ralph thought he heard something in the bushes. Ralph stopped and whispered, "Liz, there is something over behind those bushes. They listened for a moment and heard a low growling noise followed by rustling brush. The firelight was reflected in several sets of eyes peering from the darkness. The sight of orange eyes scared them, but they stayed in control of their faculties, and each picked up a knife and spear. As the creatures crept nearer, they recognized them as a pack of 5 or 6 coyotes. Ralph whispered, "The fire is keeping them back but not for long. Let's try to scare them away. First, I'm going to move the deer carcass higher into the tree out of their reach, and then we will run toward them yelling and throwing rocks."

The tactic worked and the pack tucked tails and ran over a ridge. Ralph decided that he and Lizzy should climb the biggest tree and let the coyotes dig up the buried entrails. Ralph threw the hide over his shoulder and started climbing a tree. "Come on up Liz."

Lizzy said, "Ralph, what if James and Peter decide to come see what we are doing, they could walk right up on the pack and might be attacked."

Ralph said, "You're right, we have to back away and hope the coyotes can't jump high enough to reach the meat. Remember, Poppa said to never turn our back or run from animals, we got to face them as we walk backwards and yell at them if they follow." True to form, they slowly retreated from the frightening scene. It was rough returning to the camp without a torch, and they both tripped and stumbled, bloodying their knees and palms. The sound of the coyotes fighting over the gut pile was both reassuring and nauseating.

Upon arrival back at camp Lizzy was relieved to see Peter and James playing with Moses. Lizzy started to pile on firewood and lots of it. It occurred to her that the lion might catch the scent of the deer and come into camp. She figured the coyotes would be gone by morning, and she and Ralph could finish their preparation of the deer carcass. James had both Pete and Moses on his lap. He was singing one of his original songs. James loved to make up songs, and he was surprisingly good at it.

Lizzy said, "James, why don't you and Pete make a bed for Moses inside with us. Pad it with juniper branches and dried grass." The boys jumped up and soon had a bed ready.

Lizzy and Ralph discussed building a drying rack for the meat as they lay in the little shed, trying to settle their minds enough to grow drowsy. They had their spears at their side just in case. Ralph mused, "I had my mouth all set to eat some of the venison tonight." He looked over at Lizzy, and she was watching James and Peter. They were both sound asleep.

Ralph continued, "I helped Poppa with smoking meat a few times. We can increase the smoke coming off the fire with some fresh cut mesquite branches. Poppa said smoke preserves the meat and flavors it too."

At first light Lizzy and Ralph rose without waking the two younger boys. Ralph experimented with a pile of sticks for the best model for the drying racks while Lizzy served up a meager meal. Lizzy told Ralph to stay at camp, and she would sneak down to see if the deer was still in the tree. She arrived just in time to catch a vulture tearing off a chunk of meat. She yelled and threw rocks until it took flight. She made a mental note to discard the meat around the missing chunk. She shouted, "you Buzzards have to be the nastiest creatures on earth." The coyotes were gone, and the pit that held the guts was emptied. Lizzy lowered the carcass onto the skin fur side down and pulled it back to camp. The process of cutting the meat into sections took a full day and left Ralph and Lizzy exhausted. They both conceded it would have been impossible without the meat saw and cleaver.

Lizzy felt a strange sensation when she considered the timing of finding the implements in the burned house and would believe until her dying day it was more than happenstance. She suggested quoting the 23rd Psalm once James and Pete were awake. With each advancing day the Bible passage, especially the ending, "For thou art with me" seemed to provide greater comfort and apply to their situation. Lizzy and Ralph were both determined to eat some of the meat before the day was over.

By sundown there were 20 thinly sliced kabobs of meat suspended over a bed of coals. The larger pieces of meat were suspended about three feet above the main fire on Ralph's rack. Keeping the fire going with the right amount of heat was the current priority. That meant they needed lots of wood both dry and green. Ralph and James stepped up to the task and worked with a maturity beyond their age. The Smithson boys were no weaklings. They didn't quit until they had enough wood piled up to feed the fire for a couple of days. Lizzy bragged on them and helped them wash the filth from their faces and hands. Gathering fire wood was another chore made easier by the tools Lizzy found in the burned house.

Darkness settled over the prairie, and the Smithson children were all four staring at the kabobs. The smoke from dripping fat smelled heavenly. By then all four were weak with hunger.

When Lizzy declared the meat done enough, she asked Pete to say a prayer. With an air of importance, the little rascal said, "Hebenly God, We ain't got no miracles from you yet but finding the deer was purty clost. I hope it tastes as good as it smells. We hope Moses don't figure out what we're eating. I'm too hungry to talk any more so A Man!"

Lizzy and Ralph were forced to look away to hide their amused expressions. Then Ralph said, "Good prayer Pete. Couldn't have said it better myself. James said, "This is cooked just right Lizzy, but it needs salt." The kabobs were devoured quickly directly off the sticks. Lizzy faulted herself for not making more.

Over the next three days, the children took turns tending the fire and guarding the racks of venison. After finding the arrows in the doe and the aggressive coyote encounter, she insisted they stay together and carry spears. Other than hearing the yelping of the coyotes, the nights had been without incident. After a breakfast of nuts and roasted prickly pear pads, all four children stayed together as they gathered firewood, and food for Moses. Lizzy was on edge.

What Moses really needed was her mother's milk. The fawn had developed a case of scours or as Pete put it, "Die-reya." Lizzy recalled a trick her mother had used for the condition and dug up some clay from near the spring and mixed it with water. It took Ralph, James and Lizzy all three to get the liquefied clay down Moses' throat, but it seemed to help. From somewhere in the recesses of her brain, Lizzy remembered her mother feeding rescued baby animals raw eggs. Lizzy told the boys to look for a hens' nest. There should be about four to five hens still alive and living close by. The boys spent hours searching. Lizzy cautioned them, "When you find a nest be careful not to disturb it and leave a couple of eggs there so thar she will continue using the nest." They finally found a nest in some dense brush, and James got all scratched up from the stickers and thorns. When Lizzy showed concern over his injuries, he retorted, "It's times like this when we got to be brave, just give me some of that aloe-vera gel to rub on. That's good stuff! At least I found these eggs."

--End of Excerpt--

www.ingramcontent.com/pod-product-compliance
Lightning Source LLC
Chambersburg PA
CBHW071838020726
47502CB00004B/1423